Wisdom
Lives Here

Wisdom
Lives Here

Katherine Butler

BOOK BOOK²

BOOK BOOK SQUARED
P.O. Box 60144
Colorado Springs, Colorado 80960

Published in the United States of America by Book Book Squared
Book Book Squared is an imprint of Rhyolite Press LLC
P.O. Box 60144
Colorado Springs, Colorado 80960

Butler, Katherine

Wisdom Lives Here / Katherine Butler

First edition - February 15, 2024

ISBN 978-1-943829-51-4

Book design/layout by Donald Kallaus
Cover art from original oil painting by Arabella Rhoden

"The meaning of life is to find your gift.
The purpose of life is to give it away."

— Pablo Picasso

Chapter One

Miles melted away as my heart started to harden. Was I running from or to? I have prayed ceaselessly since starting this journey. I have wrestled with God, pleaded with God, surrendered to God. Giving in to trust and faith, a belief that You do have a life of goodness and grace planned for me. I wasn't going to do this, God, give in to the fear of the unknown, but the closer I got to Haywood, Montana, the more my heart pounded. Never in my wildest dreams did I think I would pack all my belongings and set out to a land as foreign to me as if I had flown to the moon. Then I finally saw the splendor of snow-topped mountains as white as billowing clouds in a deep blue sky, crystal-clear lakes, and fields of rainbow-colored wildflowers, all so pastoral, all so peaceful, all so majestic. I had to pull over to view this grandeur or risk driving off the road! Fall came early in this part of the country with the golden and scarlet leaves breathtakingly displaying themselves against a blanket of greenery. God, you must have taken out your palette and streaked the sky with reds, oranges, pinks, and purples. So vast that sky, so unmatched through any painter's eye. *Only You, God… You brought me here.*

My journey began months ago when I made the life changing decision to move across the country where I knew no one and start a life completely surrendered to God. Or, so I thought. My own doubts continued to creep in as I realized the breadth and depth of this move. Could I really leave the security of a high paying job, all I had ever known living in the south, and friends I had made over the years? My prayers turned into questions and that was not surrender. So, as a birthday present to myself on August 31, I set a date to pack up and drive out of town.

Everything fell into place, my resignation at work was accepted, the quaint house I had researched and found in the tiny Western town of Haywood, Montana, was bought and paid for, the movers were set to pack up all my belongings and deliver them in two weeks, and my car search was under way. No more excuses, no putting off this plan. God, Bug, and I were moving out West to implement the pipe dream I had envisioned ever since Grams died.

I didn't need a 4X4 in Atlanta, but heading west and planning my new life out there made me reassess my mode of transportation. Who knew there were so many Sport Utility Vehicles? It was kind of fun researching just the right kind of car I would need in rural Montana. I was so used to my little Acura that looking for an SUV seemed like looking for a boat. After much reading, test driving and comparing, I decided to go with a Subaru Forester Touring, Jasper Green with Saddle Brown interior, color was important! Deciding between AWD and 4X4, I thought I would be fine with AWD since I didn't plan to drive in remote areas out West, but I did plan to drive in the snow. Surely Haywood was not too remote.

Leaving Atlanta in early September assured me of fairly good travel weather. The upper 90° heat, predicted for the day of my departure from the only home I had ever known, was just what I needed to get the heck out of Dodge and start my journey. I longed for a high of 75° and low of 40° that surely my destination would afford me. We'll see. Bug and I headed north on I-75 with the CD blaring Judy Garland's "Trolley Song" followed by "As Long as He Needs

Me." I was a sucker for the old-time songs that moved you. New artists were so hard to understand at times. And I needed a big distraction to keep my eyes clear and my heart upbeat, but tears started puddling in my eyes just when I thought I had this under control. My stoic exterior, always on top of everything, not needing any help, Miss Independence, cracked and the part of me I never let anyone see quivered and questioned again. *Okay, God, I'm surrendering. I do trust You. Please don't leave me! This move is actually happening, but it is also very intimidating to be so alone in this venture, except for You and Bug.*

Bug was short for Ladybug, my Boykin Spaniel, better known in the Carolinas as the Little Brown Dog. Small, yet mighty, this little one could melt you with her amber eyes, or at least she melted me, and instantly befriended you! She was a bundle of chocolate brown fur from curly top head and floppy ears to her little stubby tail, a tail that wagged from morning till night at the slightest chance of attention, swimming, or retrieving. Bug woke up as if every morning was Christmas, so excited to see me and start our day. Wise beyond her two years, she was my constant companion.

Bug came from a small town in South Carolina where the breeder of Boykin Spaniels carefully screened new owners and let the pups pick their new forever home. I wanted a female and she was the only female in a litter of three other males. Her brothers were boisterous and full of energy, but it was the spunky little female that wrapped her wiggly body around my heart. "She's a pistol," the breeder said, and she was right. She was a curious pup who found her love for water the day I met her. Lake Murray backed up to the kennel property and all the new families brought their 8-week-old Boykins to the water for their first swim. Bug was born to splash! She swam like a seasoned water dog on day one. She still looks for any chance to walk through a puddle or jump in a pond.

This was my first time traveling any distance with a dog. I had a new appreciation for rest stops. We stopped at everyone along the way, both of us needing to stretch and walk around a bit. Bug loved to run off leash, but luckily, she was content to sniff her way around each stop tethered to me. I packed some food for our first day of travel. We hadn't been on the road that long before the Jasper Rest Area in Tennessee brought us to lunchtime. Sitting on a picnic bench under a shade tree, looking at a serene lake, I was reminded of the special beauty of the South. So many shades of green in the trees, a view of our own Smoky Mountains with the blue haze that makes our Eastern slopes special in their own way. We didn't have the towering Rocky Mountains of the West, but I loved our worn-down aged display of Appalachia. *God, you are here in this setting. You are with me always. Please reassure me that I am doing the right thing. Please make this road trip a chance for me to detox from stress and open myself to a new beginning.*

While anxious to get to Montana, I was going at my own cautious pace, stopping when I needed a break and when I tired. Back on the road I was beginning to settle into a routine for our trip. The ticking of tires on the hot pavement was like a metronome keeping me focused on the road ahead. The sound lulled me into a soliloquy only Bug could hear, and she definitely wouldn't be judgmental. So many thoughts about my past, my health, my family I missed so much. I reminded myself not to be emotional at this point but rational.

I have to drive safely. Drive for a few hours, make a stop, check the map and start again. Think about the plan when I get to Haywood. Get settled in our new home, find the grocery store and coffee shop, meet the neighbors and then get acquainted with Haywood House. So much to think about and do when I get there. No time for second guessing or panicked emotions. It's all going to work out as planned.

Our first overnight was Paducah, Kentucky. This might be our shortest day of driving. The most notable change I observed, so far, was the traffic. Nothing was as crazy busy as Atlanta, thank goodness. I didn't miss the exhaust fumes, cacophony of horns blowing, disgruntled faces of drivers passing by that greeted me every morning and evening. Even navigating through Nashville on I-24 was a breeze compared to I-85 through the largest city in the South.

I decided to drive through Chick-fil-A for dinner so as not to leave Bug alone in the hotel room. This might be my last Chick-fil-A sandwich from the South. It tasted as scrumptious as always. A Chick-fil-A sandwich and sweet tea brought me the comfort I needed to stay positive and even excited about this adventure.

Because it stayed light fairly late into the evening right now, I took Bug for one last walk around the hotel before we both crashed for the night. I was exhausted and yet keyed up, realizing I had let my mind wander as to all I had in front of me. One day, one night at a time.

I wondered about Haywood. The website had pictures of a quaint Western town, old but not rundown. Not very big, just a little over 9,000 people. An assisted-living home was shown which was important for my plan. The house I bought looked almost too good to be true. Just the right size, two bedrooms, a bath, living room, kitchen, and big front porch. That was what sold me. I had always wanted a front porch with a swing and a couple of rocking chairs to sink into with my best friend beside me whiling away the evening, sipping wine, listening to birds, talking to God about this and that, about life, about dreams. The picture of the front of the house was so inviting; someone must have just moved out. It was just a few blocks from downtown, so Bug and I could walk most places. That was important too. I was so tired of driving in a big city, the noise, the stress, the impersonal feel to each day. Haywood sounded perfect! Soon sleep came to me with the promise of a sanctuary in God's country just days away.

We were up at dawn the second day of our journey ready to drive closer to my dream. I decided to take the secondary road 51 up to Centralia, Vandalia, Pana, and around Decatur. This was Illinois farm country with open land, the remnants of a crops harvested, and small towns. Since there weren't any rest stops along the way, I found a nice park in Pana to stop and let Bug stretch and sniff for a while. I wondered if Haywood was like Pana? The houses were old but well kept, the trees were big and shady. I was falling in love with small towns.

We pushed on towards Dubuque, Iowa, the next planned overnight. As we drove though Galena, Illinois, though, I decided this was our stop for the night. Another charming town with interesting shops along Main Street. I took a chance on the Cloran Mansion Bed and Breakfast having a room since they were pet friendly. I splurged for our one stay not at La Quinta! The room was gorgeous and spacious and Paul, the owner, went out of his way to make me feel so welcomed. The grounds were beautiful and perfect for Bug and me to wander in the evening and then sit in the gazebo for quiet time with the twinkling lights casting a magical spell and the smell of gardenias permeating the night air. While it certainly looked like a get-away for couples, I felt quite included with Bug as my significant other. My shoulders were beginning to relax, my jaw unclenched, excitement started to build as I found myself almost halfway to my new home. More prayer time with God tonight and such the perfect place, too. I also felt a closeness to Grams as if she was approving of my plan to make a difference in Haywood. I thought I would be more anxious and scared the further away from Atlanta I moved and the closer to Haywood I came. But right now, I think I was just emptying out my former life to allow the newness of my future to settle into my soul. *Stay close to me, God.*

Big mistake—a huge delicious calorie packed breakfast with French toast to die for, followed by hours of driving through gently rolling hills and flat plains, the landscape of Iowa. Bug and I stopped many times, got out to walk and breathed the new clean air, to keep from falling asleep. While I had made small talk with the people at places we had stayed each night, I had not really spoken to anyone at length for three days now. I was starting to get nervous and unsure about this move, again. I was certainly not a Chatty Kathy or so gregarious that this silent time was unusual; however, it was making me feel so alone. Nobody knew me here in Galena or where I was going. Would the people in Haywood even care that I had moved across the country to make a mark in their town? Would they even want me to be there? God, this was a huge mistake. I'd been so caught up in the excitement of the move I hadn't considered the down side—loneliness, being an outsider, not welcomed, not even noticed, and maybe not even a job. Should I turn around and go back? It was not too late, was it? I could start anew back in Georgia. At least I was familiar with the land, the people, their accent. I could drink sweet tea, eat my grits every morning, call out Hey, y'all! How did Montana people greet each other? What did they eat and drink if not grits and sweet tea? The tears started to come, and I couldn't hold them back.

I pulled into a small gas station just inside the city limits of Fort Dodge to collect myself, get gas, and a cup of coffee to keep me alert. No more pity party as I wiped away the trails of worry and doubt. I was paying for my coffee when the woman at the cash register said, "You're not from around here are you."

"You're right, how do you know?" I asked.

"Well, I've lived here all my life and pretty much worked at this filling station since I was old enough to draw a paycheck, and I've gotten to know most everyone around here, but I've never seen you before and I have a great memory for faces. Where are you going?"

"I'm going to a small town southwest of Billings, Montana, called Haywood. Are you familiar with that area at all?"

"I've never been to Haywood, but what I have heard about Montana is, it's God's country. Wide open spaces, mountains, friendly folks. I think you're going to like it there. Are you going for a vacation?"

"No, I'm moving there, sight unseen. Do you think I'm crazy?"

"Lady, I think you only go around once in this life, and if Haywood is calling you, you better go. I gotta call like that one time and passed it up. Here I still am in the town I was born in. I wish you good luck and Godspeed. Think of Marge when you get there. Maybe a little bit of me can join you on your adventure if only in your thoughts." And with that bit of encouragement from a total stranger, I felt God nodding at me to keep going. I was heading in the right direction.

We stopped in Murdo, South Dakota, for the night at Range Country Lodging—another pet-friendly hotel with a bit of local flare. There was even a mock chuck wagon where down-home breakfast was served. I was starting to get my Western legs! Cozy, warm and friendly, another small town was helping me get acclimated to my destination. The evening here was cool. I could feel the first inkling of a new weather pattern in the northern Midwest. Finally, a break from hot muggy nights to cool refreshing ones.

Bug and I walked for an hour or so thinking, praying, hoping for a peace to come over me. I was just enough on edge to fight God's call to surrender. How does one totally surrender to God's calling? That had been my question for the past two years. I thought I had that figured out when I decided to make a clean break from Atlanta. I researched all parts of the country looking for the right climate. I did love fall in the South and the beautiful changing leaves, but I was so tired of the heat and humidity. I wanted cooler days and snow. I wanted a more open space with an abundance of nature and less concrete and bricks, a small town with character and independent coffee houses, restaurants, and stores, not Starbucks, McDonalds and Lowe's. A place with a small assisted-living facility which was home to local residents. That was where I could pour out my desire to make everyone's life matter. I missed that with Grams. I was young and naïve about life, but something tugged at me when I would visit Grams. She had lost the gleam in her eyes. At that time, I was ready to get on with my own dreams, college, and a career and missed the fact she still had a life not being fulfilled anymore. Haywood, Montana, jumped out at me as I was searching the internet: small town, beautiful setting, assisted-living facility, and snow! My heart lurched every time I looked at photos of the town and the surrounding area. When I found the house for sale, I knew I had to go there. And here I was a day's drive away from my new life and scared to death.

I passed on the chuck-wagon-style breakfast to get on the road early. A granola bar and a mug of coffee would do me for a while. It was not long before we were driving through the north edge of the Badlands. Nothing but red craggy rock for miles. No vegetation, no water, no life of any kind. Very aptly named. How could anyone travel through this terrain hundreds of years ago? Surely this was not what would be greeting me in Montana. It had its own beauty, but this was not an area of abundant life and not the welcoming sight I was planning on seeing. I was relieved when we passed through Rapid City, South Dakota, and saw more inviting landscape. I marveled at the change in scenery out here. I sensed that this really was God's country. It was natural, open, and expansive with trees, grasses, mountains, and lakes. Man's desire to build bigger, better, modern, and new had not touched this beauty. I was almost there.

Twenty-seven endless driving hours, four days and three nights on the road, and over 2,000 backbreaking miles taking me away from all I had known to the unknown- from Atlanta, Georgia, to Haywood, Montana. Miles of second guessing myself, miles of holding back tears and sobs. I had become an emotional mess these past two years. *Oh, God, what have I done?* A tightness creeped into my chest, wrapping its tentacles around my heart. The stress returned I so hoped I had put behind me. I left what little security I did have to come to this wild land, a place of strangers. Talk about a fish out of water! I had only known the South, specifically Georgia. It was so different here. Georgia had its own beauty but it was hard to compare to the vastness, to the rawness of Montana. This vastness and openness welcomed by some, felt like emptiness to me. I'd been a city girl for nearly 40 years. How could I begin to live in a wilderness? What if the people in this tiny town didn't want a newcomer? Were they set in their ways? Would they think of me as a flash-in-the-pan kind of girl? Here today, gone tomorrow. I had dreamed of this moment for so long, imagined how I would feel when I drove into this town of Haywood, but now, what if I had made a mistake? What if I was more alone out here than I ever was in Atlanta? *Then what, God?*

We were here, though, and there was no turning back. I made up my mind to see this through. My friend always said, "Build a bridge and get over it." Well, it was time to build our bridge.

"Come on girl! Let's go find our new home." Ladybug stretched, looked at me with those amber eyes so piercing, as if to say "Really?" and laid back down. She'd believe me when the car was actually parked for more than an 8-hour over-night.

Haywood, Montana—the website said it was a "cozy niche in a vast beautiful land," just what I was looking for to start my new life, cozy and beautiful. I could just picture my new home, welcoming me like a long-lost friend with open arms and genuine warmth. As we pulled up to the address listed, I began to doubt cozy and replaced it with dilapidated. Thick untended vines in front of the porch entwined between the railings as if holding the place captive and together! They had been left to grow untamed indicating a home no longer cared for or loved. The porch itself, while I don't think it's a danger to walk on, had collected leaves and dirt in the corners making it look unkempt and no longer an inviting place to rock and while away an evening sipping wine or hot chocolate like I had envisioned. The windows were incapable of letting much sunshine in because of years of grime and streaks of dust like desert roads. One window was cracked and I could feel my fortitude cracking too. The picture I had seen must have been an earlier version of what now stood before me. I loved quaint, but really?

I let Bug out of the car and she immediately began to check out our new place as if she knew we had finally arrived. Nose to the ground and running all over, she must have realized this was a place for many adventures. She was all I needed and yet I wanted so desperately to fit in here, find friends. The sob that had been so close to erupting these past few weeks escaped, and the flow of tears began. This was supposed to be such an exciting time; why was I bawling like a baby? The worry, the anxiety, the unknown toppled over me like a strong wind whipping trees. The reality of this decision I made to start over in a new place, to change my life and turn it over to God, was finally happening. *God, please give me the strength and the faith to believe I'm doing the right thing.* I so desperately wanted this to work. Slowly the tears ebbed and I could look around with a clear vision. A good cry must be what I needed because I was determined to face this wild decision to go it alone.

My first impression of our new home was not the feeling of a long-lost friend welcoming us, so I began walking around the yard hoping for something redeeming to latch onto. The late afternoon chill in the air reminded me I was not in warm Georgia anymore. I pulled my sweater tighter around me and made a note to purchase warmer clothes soon. *God, someone long ago must have loved this place.* There was evidence of gardens in the front of the house long left unattended. Old hydrangea bushes and some type of holly bush lined the front of the porch. The blooms were withered but the plants looked hardy enough. Maybe I could bring them back to life. The huge tree in the backyard had a frayed rope-swing slowly stirring in the breeze. I could just imagine a home filled with laughing children running out to swing high. Didn't think I'd do that now! More forgotten gardens filled a portion of the backyard. Who lived here? Who loved flowers and children? Could I make this a loving home again? More questions than answers at this point.

The key the real estate lady sent me fit the front door lock and, as I turned it and pushed open the door, what greeted me upon entering was cobwebs, dust, dirty windows, and a few pieces of broken-down furniture filling the living room. I entered the kitchen and realized this house would need a lot of work to turn it back into a home. A big window over the sink may have once looked out on a passel of children running helter-skelter in the backyard, tile flooring that, when scrubbed clean, could be just the look I wanted, a black and white checked pattern, and decent but not updated appliances. *God, please don't let me give up on this place.* I need this challenge to make this house my home. Help me bring love and vitality back into it and please give me the strength and stamina for it too.

I was drawn away from my daydreaming at the sound of heavy footsteps on the porch and Bug's low growl. While she was my protector, I still grabbed for an iron skillet sitting on the stove just in case. I didn't know what to expect here. Did people just appear on your doorstep uninvited? Was I so naïve to think a young woman alone in a town of strangers was going to be welcomed with open arms? "Hello, is someone there?" I tentatively called out.

"More likely, what are you doing inside this house?" a gruff voice answered.

Standing on the porch was a huge man with scuffed cowboy boots, a heavy jacket worn and torn in multiple places, and a cowboy hat which had seen many a long day out in the wilderness. A face lined with a lifetime of hard work out in the elements and kind eyes, stared down at me. Straight out of a John Wayne movie! I called Bug to me, but for some reason she went right up to this stranger and started wagging her stubby tail, apparently looking for attention. I trusted her instincts so I gingerly put down the skillet, tentatively inched to the doorway, and bravely offered my hand. "Hi, I'm Claire James, the new owner of this house and this is Ladybug."

"It's about time we got some young blood in this town. My name is Sam—I live next door. Don't play loud music. And I hope you aren't allergic to dust, cause we've got a lot of it." And with that welcome, he was gone.

Chapter Two

Oh Lordy, I was feeling the effects of the long drive, aching back, stiff legs, tight and sore shoulders. My body didn't loosen up much after moving furniture around last night, either. I think this house might just be perfect for me, though. A nice size living room off to the right of the front door with a beautiful stone fireplace and wooden mantle. The warm honey nut brown wood flooring looked in surprisingly good shape. I loved the country style kitchen, with room for a small breakfast table, opening to the dining room. Plus, that big window over the sink looking out into the back yard. Having two nice size bedrooms with a bath in between was just perfect for me. The wide front porch was a bonus; I could envision myself there during early mornings and quiet evenings. I could wave to my neighbors passing by, or maybe share a cup of coffee or glass of wine with them. I'd hang a porch swing and while away the hours reading or knitting. Yes, there was work to be done here. It would be a labor of love to make it a beautiful home again. Back in Atlanta I had only known apartment living. My apartment had been very nice with upscale décor, white walls, gray furniture, but very icy appearing. Not this warm lived-in home that begged for color, big comfy stuffed chairs, hand-made afghans, a fire in the fireplace, and friends sitting around sipping wine and sharing hopes and dreams and everyday thoughts.

I had to get both Bug and myself out of this house, though, and into this gorgeous morning that had awakened me with a warm sun and chilly breeze. So, first on the agenda, was a walk to town. Bug and I had slept fitfully, what little sleep we had. With trepidation we listened to the creaks and groans of an old house. Uneasiness kept us company in the early hours of the morning. Finally settling down or maybe just falling asleep from exhaustion, I turned the night over to God and got a few hours of sleep. Not wanting to get back into the car for another day of driving, a brisk walk was something we both needed. "Come on Bug, let's go exploring."

I checked out the map the real estate agent sent me and set off in the direction of town, just four blocks away. I chose this town because of its size and quaintness. I wanted small and old, a town where people knew each other, waved to each other, and appreciated the beauty of history. Buildings and homes were taken care of and not torn down for something new and sleek and shiny. I had had enough of that in big city Atlanta. In Haywood, I wanted to hear birds singing instead of horns honking, see people walking instead of cars whizzing by everywhere. So far so good.

A coffee shop was first on my list of stops. The first wake-up cup at home was long gone. Sip & Savor—the wooden sign with gorgeous wildflowers painted on it beckoned me. Bells tinkled as I opened the maize-colored door, hoping Bug would be welcomed. The smell of rich fresh-roasted coffee and cinnamon greeted me as did a young woman with streaks of blue in her shoulder length blond hair, large hoop earrings, and a brightly colored peasant dress. She was just the opposite from me in looks. Her tall willowy body was in sharp contrast to my short 5' 3" frame. There were no, nor ever had been, any artificial streaks of color in my chin length curly brown hair, just a thick, shiny, auburn color with maybe sun streaks in the summer. Willowy was not an adjective to describe me, but I was slender, somewhat petite thanks to all the running I used to do. I'd been called "cute" but never drop dead gorgeous and my green eyes with gold specks were about the only feature that had ever gotten a positive compliment. "Hi, you must be the new lady in town. My name is Jasmine, welcome."

My first impression of Jasmine was she was an old soul. She had the look of a 60s hippy in a young body. Frank Sinatra music was playing in the background, blue gingham curtains hung at the windows, freshly cut flowers sat in mason jars on every table with colorful but mismatched chairs completing the look. Bug was not the only dog in the place, but you had the feeling this homey niche always stayed immaculate. Lord, this will be my home away from home!

"I know Haywood is not big, but how did you know I'm the new lady in town?"

"Sam is my first customer of the day, every day. In fact, he helps me open up and put the chairs in place. In return he gets the first cup of coffee and first cinnamon roll of the day. He said his neighbor finally moved in and kept him awake half the night moving furniture around."

"Oh dear, I'm so sorry if I kept him up. My furniture was delivered late yesterday afternoon and put in designated rooms. I just had to work on organizing a bit because tired as I was, I was too keyed up to sleep.

"Oh my gosh, I know what you mean. I'm not crazy organized or anything, but I can't live in chaos. My house is my sanctuary and if I can't find peace and comfort there, I'm a basket case!"

I knew right then Jasmine and I had a connection. I so needed a friend, even if she appeared to be ten years my junior. I hoped we would have a chance to get to know one another over cups of delicious coffee and homemade cinnamon rolls. Might have to limit the cinnamon rolls, though. They looked like they could add pounds just by smelling them.

Since the restaurant was not very busy, Jasmine sat down after she brought my coffee and a treat for Bug. "What brings you to our tiny out-of-the-way town? I understand you bought the old Collins place."

"It was time to make a big change. Atlanta was home for all my adult life. I was crazy busy and thought that's what I wanted. But one day I woke up, realized how lonely I was, how out of touch I was with God, and knew I had to leave or live that shallow life forever. After lots of praying and studying places in the Northwest, I kind of picked Montana and hoped for a little quiet town with a home for sale. That's the short of it and here I am! Now I need advice on where to get paint, because my whole house needs a fresh look."

"Tabs Hardware Store is your best bet in town. Otherwise, you have to drive 20 miles to the nearest Walmart. You can pretty much find anything you need in Tabs. It's 2 blocks down the street. Ladybug is welcome there, too. She's pretty much welcome anywhere in town. We love our pups. Next time you come, I'll have Scooter here. He's my border collie. He and Ladybug can get to know each other. He was feeling droopy so I took him over to Jack, so he could check him out. Jack is our vet in town. You'll want to get Ladybug over to see him soon." Just then the bells rang at the front door. "Gotta get back to work. See you again soon. Don't be a stranger."

Chapter Three

This house was going to have color! No more white trim with pale gray walls, the minimalist look I had back in Atlanta. I wanted bright, warm, cozy and welcoming colors. Kitchen first. At Tabs, I picked out a warm, soft yellow paint for the walls with white trim. What a great way to be greeted in the morning over a cup of coffee. I loved to cook, so fixing up this room was an easy first choice. I could just picture crisp white eyelet curtains at the window, and my colorful Fiesta-ware adorning the table. The wonderful smell of homemade bread and robust coffee would soon follow. Time to get busy. Having no time restraints or commitments yet, I jumped right in and started to work turning the dull kitchen walls into a refreshing place, taking only a short break in the afternoon for a bite of lunch. I was loving this color and might extend it to the dining room.

Later that day I could see the fruits of my labor. The color was luscious, even the splatters on my T-shirt were happy looking. I was not a very neat painter, but I really wanted to make this house my own. What better way than to do all the painting and fixing up in each room myself. The cabinets and drawers needed new knobs and, of course, the windows needed major washing inside and out. Already I was beginning to feel excitement and adventure creeping back into my life. All I had to do was get that last corner. I thought I could reach it without moving the ladder, but just as I stretched for the final stroke, I could feel the ladder tipping. "Oh, no, no, no..." The ladder scooted out from under me and I could feel myself falling. A feeling of shear panic enveloped me as I instantly realized how alone I was. My heart was in my throat as I tried to grab something, anything to break my fall. I saw the paint bucket tip and I gave a futile attempt to hold onto it, to no avail. Hitting the edge of the counter with my forehead was the last thing I remembered until I heard Bug barking. I didn't want to move since my head was pounding and blood was very evident on my yellow splattered, not so happy T-shirt now. My right arm was trapped under me with a shooting pain letting me know I was still alive. I had a death grip on the paint brush that had left a yellow brick road trail down the cabinet and counter, showing my descent, ending in a mess on my black and white tile floor. Woozy, but aware enough to know I needed help; I told Bug to go get Sam. Now my dog was very smart and I knew she understood what I said, but it could be that Sam came over at that moment to get her to stop barking.

"Criminee! What have you gone and done to yourself girl?" Sam grabbed a towel and held it against my bleeding head. What a mess he saw when he came into the kitchen. Blood everywhere mixed with my most luscious yellow paint all over the counter and floor!

"Oh Sam, I can't believe what I've done. Let me just clean this up quickly."

"That's the last thing you're going to do right now, girl. You're going to need stitches for that cut." Before I knew it, he was helping me out the door and into his truck and we were heading to the emergency room. I was still feeling dizzy and having trouble stopping the bleeding, so no complaints from me at the moment. I leaned my head back and closed my eyes, holding my arm close to me and hoping it was not broken. My heart started beating fast and tears collected behind my eyelids threatening to become a waterfall. Bug was on my lap comforting me, aware of the anxiety I was feeling. Once we arrived at the hospital, though, I refused to get out of the truck.

"I am fine. I don't have my purse with my insurance cards to show the receptionist. No one will treat me until I do, so let's just go home, and I'll put ice on my head, please!" My heart was beating out of my chest. This was so reminiscent of the last time I was in the emergency room in Atlanta. Fear gripped me causing me to feel faint. Sam obviously was used to making decisions and totally ignored my plan.

"You can walk in there, or I can carry you. Those are your choices. Let's go." I could see he was a man of few words, so arguing was not an option, but no way was I going to let him carry me inside! I got out of his truck, wobbled a bit until he came around and held on to my left arm and in we went, Bug too.

"Hey Sam. Who have you got there?" A man sitting with two sheepdogs got up to help me to a chair. Under his cowboy hat I looked into the bluest eyes I had ever seen. Yes, I was very woozy, but there was a kindness in those eyes that calmed me. This man immediately took Bug from me, and she went willingly. What was it with these men in Haywood that Bug instantly appeared to like? After that brief encounter with the dog man, I was whisked away by a matronly nurse to be examined. Sam stayed in the waiting room with Bug.

"I can't stay here over night! Bug has never been away from me! She has no place to go. Please, just let me go home. I'll be alright, I promise I'll take it easy," I pleaded with the doctor. The ER doctor was young and very efficient. Apparently, a concussion and ten stitches warranted an overnight hospital stay in this town. Luckily, the x-ray did not show a broken bone in my arm, so it was just in a sling for comfort. At that moment Sam and the blue-eyed stranger came into the room. "Bug is staying with me, and Jack can check on her, if need be," announced Sam. "You're not going to cause me to stay awake another night checking on you to make sure you haven't gone into a coma or something. No, we've got this taken care of. We watch over our people in Haywood, so you might as well get used to it."

"What Sam is saying with his gruff tone is Bug will be fine, you will be carefully watched over and that mess in the kitchen Sam described to me will not be left for you to deal with when you get home, so do as Doc orders and we'll see you tomorrow," said Jack. A kindness I had not been around in a while put me at ease as he gently squeezed my hand. And with that they walked out of the room with Bug in tow.

The tears started flowing before I could say another word. I couldn't have gotten off to a worse start in this new town. My next-door neighbor was totally put out with me and some stranger, all be it with gorgeous eyes, thought he had to clean up my mess! I wanted so badly for everything to go smoothly and to be able to do it all by myself. That was what I did, take care of everything all by myself. Now, I had to rely on my not so friendly neighbor and some guy I didn't know from Adam to take care of the most precious thing in my life, Bug. *Oh God, what have I gotten myself into?* Why can't anything be easy and go as I planned, and how am I going to fix up my house when I can't lift or move anything, and the paint is still sitting out, and I want to finish the baseboards, and, oh God, I can't do it alone! Heart wrenching sobs I couldn't control made me feel as deserted as I had ever been, until I heard a quiet voice, "Claire, I know coffee might not be on the doctor's orders today, but cinnamon rolls should be okay." Jasmine had slipped in, sat down beside me and made me realize; I was not alone.

Chapter Four

"How did you know?" I squeaked out between hiccups and sobs. "Well, this is a small town, and when Sam came by with Ladybug, I knew something was up. He said you'd probably need a cinnamon roll and a lady friend at the hospital and left. You know Sam doesn't mince words, so Jack filled me in on your fall, concussion, and stitches. Wow, girl you know how to make Jack's head turn and that's not easy to do."

"Who is Jack?"

"Only the most eligible bachelor in the county, and the nicest man you'll ever meet. Remember, I told you Jack is our veterinarian and overall handyman. You need anything done around your house, call Jack. And it won't hurt to get Ladybug on file at his animal hospital. He'll take such good care of her she might want to stay with him. No, seriously, he loves animals and they love him and because of that and all the help he offers to the town, there is no room in his life for a woman. Such a shame, but we all love Jack."

"That explains why Bug went with Sam and Jack so readily, like I wasn't even there. Really though, I'm glad she is going to be so well watched over since I am stuck here over night. Oh Jasmine, I think there might be an overturned bucket of paint in my kitchen!" And then the tears started flowing again.

"Not to worry. I'll run by your house and check. Looks like you need to take advantage of this night to rest. No more tears! We've got things under control. I've done my share of messing up a paint job, so I know how to fix it." Jasmine slowly got up as my eyes closed and left that scrumptious smelling pastry to lull me to sleep.

I vaguely remember being checked on through the night. Dreams of splashed paint and golden eyes looking helplessly at me made my night restless. Bug knew something was wrong, but I was powerless to do anything about it. Having gone with Sam. We both had to learn to trust.

By morning I was given enough of a clean bill of health to be discharged. However, no climbing ladders, no painting, no lifting more than a gallon of milk, and no running (that won't be a problem) until the next check up in a week. How was I going to get my house in order and get on with my life? *God, you are making me be patient and listen for Your still small voice, aren't You.* I guess old habits die hard. I am so used to going full speed ahead with an agenda, but I promised myself that things would change. *That is quite a wake-up call God!*

"Come on girl, let's get you home. Someone has been missing you," a gruff voice came through the door. And at that moment Bug came flying in the room, jumped on the bed and proceeded to wag her tail off whimpering and checking me out all over. It was all going to be alright. My best bud and I were heading home.

Sam pulled up to my house and helped me out of his huge pickup truck. Bug didn't seem to have any trouble getting out and hopped to the ground as if she was born to be a hunting dog scampering in and out of trucks. I had to admit I was moving slowly because I was not looking forward to the mess that would greet me as we walked in the house.

Pushing open the front door, I gasped at the sight of my totally transformed place. Oh my gosh! Was this really my house? The furniture in the living room had been moved making it cozy and welcoming around the fireplace. My big overstuffed chair, complete with a knitted afghan over it, sat beside Grams' antique end table with my favorite Tiffany lamp on top. Fresh cut flowers filled her favorite vase completing a homey look. How did someone know? Then the kitchen—what happened to the spilled paint and the unfinished walls and trim? The walls were all painted that liquid sunshine color and the trim was finished in a clean white. Best of all there was no spilled paint covering the floor! The countertops were cleaned off and my coffee pot and pottery mugs were sitting out waiting to be used. A cannister with suspicious smelling cinnamon rolls sat beside it.

"How did this happen? Sam, who did this?" Tears started flowing again. My goodness, I was a mess wearing my emotions on my sleeve.

"Let's just say it was a joint effort and kind of fun, but I'm beat and you have to go sit down for the rest of the day. I'll check on you tonight. Food is in the fridge. Hey Bug, come tell me goodbye." And with that Sam scratched Bug's ears and left for home.

Slowly I walked through my kitchen into the living room, my head aching and my heart swelling. My house was turning into a home because of the love of almost strangers. I sat down in my chair and felt it hug me like an old friend, as Bug hopped up and curled beside me. "We're going to be alright, girl. We picked a place full of love and kindness where people watch out for one another. We have to do our part when I get better. Then we'll have to start on our plan." With that thought, I fell asleep wrapped in the security that maybe, just maybe, we could find a family here.

I'm not sure how long I slept, but my growling stomach and stiff body made me realize I had been in this chair quite a while. Slowly unfolding and stretching arms and legs helped waken me to the sound of someone in my kitchen. "I can't fix any fancy kind of food, but I'm a hell of an egg cooker. Just stay where you are, and I'll bring you some supper. That dog of yours needs to eat too. Where do you keep her food?" That gruff voice only belonged to one person I knew, my all of a sudden endearing next-door neighbor.

"It's in the plastic container on the back porch." Bug heard the rattling of food in her bowl and abandoned me for her next favorite thing, food.

Sam sauntered into the living room with a tray full of the most delicious smelling food I had ever been around. On the plate was a mound of scrambled eggs mixed with fried potatoes, green chilies, sautéed onions, cheese, and a big dollop of salsa. Steam rose from the concoction. A big glass of milk accompanied this feast. "Oh my, Sam. What have you gone and done? I don't remember the last time anyone made supper for me." I tried to hold in a sob.

"Oh now, if you're going to cry about it, I'll eat it myself."

"Not so fast. It's just the medicine making me weepy." And I dove into the most scrumptious meal I'd had in a long time.

"Just a word of advice. If you don't want bears visiting you in the night, I'd move the dog food into the house. Just saying." Sam suddenly disappeared again, but now I knew he was as close as a whisper or a dog bark if I needed him.

In Atlanta, I barely knew my neighbors. The city hustled and bustled day and night, and I was right there with it clambering to get ahead, working insane hours, never slowing down or stopping to check on anyone, let alone the person next door.

Work was another place to stick my head in the sand. Oh, I thought I was a considerate co-worker, bringing in fruit trays, making exotic coffee with to-die-for creamer, poking my head in various offices to make sure everyone was alright. That was me, considerate Claire. First in in the morning, last to leave, begging off the invitation for after work drinks. I couldn't let anyone get close, I couldn't open up that chapter of my life, so I stayed ridiculously busy and aloof. How many years did that go on? I thought I had everything under control, but God's plan did not coincide with mine. I could have chosen to ignore that still small voice, and I did for quite a while, but when He came knocking on my door in the form of a heart attack, it was time to switch plans!

A heart attack at 38. I was diagnosed with SCAD, spontaneous coronary artery dissection. How could that happen? I ate sensibly, ran five miles a day, every day, only had the one glass of red wine limit per night, but stress was the kicker. I couldn't slow down, couldn't relax, couldn't go to church because then I would have to think and remember, so I ran myself into the ground. That was two years, seven months, and three days ago.

Chapter Five

Ihad no idea I could pass a week of rest just knitting, reading, and
sleeping. I also gave up on the idea of painting the whole house
myself. Another trip to Tab's to pick out paint, but this time I'd have
to hire someone to do the grit work. One good thing about that was
I never had been much of a painter. The house will surely look a
whole lot better with a professional touch. My new mantra was to
follow doctor's orders, live in the moment, and let God lead the way.
That was the hard one. I loved God unconditionally and knew his
plan was the best plan, the only plan. But it was so hard letting go,
giving up control. That was why I was here in Haywood, Montana.
How different it was from Atlanta, Georgia, and the fast pace life
style I was caught up in for so many years.

My week's confinement was over, now off to the doctor's office
to get the okay to resume normal activities, so that I could thank
my guardian angels. All week long, gratitude ideas for my three
new friends had been rolling around in my brain. I finally came
up with homemade bread. It couldn't quite compete with Jasmine's
cinnamon rolls, but it was the next best thing. Searching through
all my cookbooks, I found the recipe that would bring accolades to
my baking skills. God, I'm not trying to bring attention to myself,
but I cannot do things half way. After many failed attempts, this

loaf gave off the melt in your mouth aroma, the perfect rise, and the golden crust signifying success. I couldn't wait to take it over to Sam. I wrapped the loaf up in a muslin napkin, hurried across the yard with Ladybug at my side, and knocked on his door. "It's about time you brought that bread over. I've been smelling it for days and except for the one loaf that burned I was ready to try anything."

"Oh Sam, I wanted it to be perfect so I could thank you from the bottom of my heart for taking care of me. I just…"

"Now listen, that's what we do here. I've told you before, we watch out for each other. And remember, no more ladders in the kitchen." And with that, he took the loaf of bread, reached down, scratched Bug behind her ears and started to close the door, but not before I gave him a quick hug and a peck on the cheek.

The next two loaves were going to Jasmine and Jack. Delivering to Jasmine was easy; she was always at the Sip & Savor. When I walked in the café, sights and smells immediately brought a warmth and a feeling of home. Cinnamon and coffee were real smells. No lighting a scented candle here. I knew she had this gift for baking, a Midas touch for everything edible, but sometimes even the best baker needed to be treated. She was excited with the loaf of bread I brought and had plans already to slather it in apple butter. Jasmine was like an open book. What you saw was what you got and that was a compassionate, giving woman. I filled her in on my week of being house-bound and thanked her profusely again for cleaning up my mess in the kitchen. After a hug and a big thanks, we promised to get together soon. I wish Jasmine and I could have a close friendship, if only I could let go and trust.

Next was a walk down an old historic street outside of downtown Haywood to the Haywood Animal Hospital. I was very nervous about this particular thank you, as I hadn't heard or talked to Jack since first meeting him at the hospital the night he helped clean up my kitchen. Oh, my goodness! I couldn't believe this was the animal hospital. The sign in front confirmed it, but it looked like an old mission style, two-story mansion with a creamy white stucco exterior and a red terra cotta tile roof. It had to be at least 100 years old. Walking in the front door, I was awed by the beautiful historic entrance with what looked like original tile flooring, the kind that was hexagon tiles in a soft green shade. Around the high ceiling was gorgeous wide molding. The ceiling actually looked rounded! The room to the right had beautiful black and white tile flooring with old fashion heat registers under all the tall windows. A few people, with various size dogs, a cat, and what looked like a lamb, were waiting in that area which must be the lobby. I tentatively approached the woman behind the desk and asked to speak to Jack Thompson for just a minute.

"You must be the new gal in town. Hey, pretty golden eyes, what's your name? Is she here for a check-up or a problem? You don't need an appointment, just be willing to wait a few minutes. Jack will be happy to see her. He went on and on about how friendly and well-mannered she was when he met her last week. We love all our animals here, but she's kind of special. Oh, don't mind me, I kind of run off at the mouth a bit. My name's June. I've been working here since Jack opened this animal hospital. What did you say your name was?"

Wow, I thought, that was a lot of energy for a woman who looked to be my grandma! "My name is Claire James and this is Ladybug. I hadn't planned on a check-up for Bug today. I just wanted to come by and thank Jack for his help last week."

"You are totally welcome. I was glad to help and loved getting to know this little brown dog." Bug was immediately by his side, looking up with those honey dripping eyes, as Jack stepped into the waiting room.

I was usually never at a loss for words. Working in corporate America, you get used to meeting new people, impressive people, but at this moment I couldn't say anything intelligent, just "Oh, you know Boykins are also called "little brown dogs?"

Jack kneeled down to tussle Bug's ears, "No, I didn't. She's just a cute little brown dog is all."

Time to cut this awkward moment in the bud. "Well, I just wanted to thank you for your help cleaning up my kitchen last week and give you a little token of my appreciation." I handed him the loaf of bread and then said, "I can't believe this is an animal hospital. It's so beautiful. I would have thought someone lived here."

Jack chuckled, "Someone does, me. I live upstairs and run my business down here. It's very convenient to live where I work. Of course, I'm not here too often since most of my patients are on ranches, but I do see the town pets. I bought this house five years ago and turned the downstairs rooms into a lobby and exam rooms, except for the kitchen. That's in the back of the house, and there is a back staircase that takes me to my living quarters. Pretty good setup for a bachelor."

I felt my face turning a bright red as I stuttered, "I… I… didn't mean to bother you, thanks again for all you did last week. We'll be back with an appointment for Bug."

"I hope so." Jack said with a small grin.

Reluctantly Bug followed me out the door towards home. The song, "Should I Stay or Should I Go," started ringing in my head. What was going on here! I was acting like a school girl and yet I think I wanted to spend more time getting to know Jack the vet.

Chapter Six

My first order of business in Haywood was delayed because of my untimely fall, but now it was time. I needed to find a church. I knew I could be close to God anywhere, and, goodness knows, I could talk to him anywhere, anytime, but there was something about a physical church, being part of a family of believers that was comforting and complete. I looked up the Methodist church in town and found it not far from the animal hospital. Grams was Methodist and this seemed like a good place to start my search. As soon as I entered the sanctuary, a peace settled over me. That was a good sign. I looked around and saw Jasmine sitting close to the front. I walked to her pew, and she scooted over for me to slide in next to her.

She whispered, "I was going to give you another week to recoup before I invited you to Trinity, but I'm so glad you're here today. I think you'll find a home here."

I smiled and squeezed her hand. Listening to the organ prelude, I looked around and saw people nodding and smiling back at me. God, I want this to be right, and I think it is. Pastor Michael began preaching after a beautiful anthem by the choir. The warmth of his tone, the compassion of his message, and the closeness I felt to God, helped me decide. I really thought I had found a church home.

After the service many people came up and introduced themselves to me, such an inviting welcome. Jasmine introduced me to Pastor Michael. He chuckled and revealed that somehow the word had spread about my dramatic arrival to Haywood. He assured me next time he would be at the hospital checking on me. Next time?

Manny was set to transform my house into a warm inviting sanctuary. I met him at Tab's and he gave me lots of helpful hints on picking out paint for the rest of my house. Multiple cans had been placed in every room and my dream of a vivid display of color was happening. Terra cotta would be the welcoming color in my living room. A warm deep tone to set off my artwork. It also complimented the brown woodwork in the living room, mantle, and flooring. Next would be a soft tan in the dining room and hallway, another earthy color to be the background for the beauty of the pictures I chose for that room. He convinced me this would be a compatible color for the living room and that the kitchen could stand alone with the subtle wake-up yellow. In the bathroom, a light sage green and a delicate Williamsburg blue for the bedrooms would help give a peaceful night's sleep. All that to go with white for all the trim. Who knew there could be a gazillion colors of white? Manny had free reign in the house during the day as I planned to be at Sip & Savor for breakfast and lunch, and at Haywood House to start implementing my plan.

Haywood House. I pulled up the website to learn more about the only assisted-living facility in Haywood. The building looked to be about 20 years old. A beautiful red brick single- story structure with white shutters at each window and an inviting portico with white columns surrounded by potted plants. Four rocking chairs with floral padded seats spoke of home. The pictures posted showed smiling people engaged in a variety of activities: bingo, singing, ice cream socials, arts and crafts, and meals. It warmed my heart to see these people looking happy. I wish Grams could have been in a place like this. While she never lost her positive outlook, I wish she could have been engaged with friends the way these people seemingly were.

Well, time to put my plan in motion. I would first have to visit alone, without Bug. If my idea was accepted, then I'd bring her to meet everyone. That dog had such a sense of love, compassion, understanding, and patience about her. All the needs of older people who had been left behind in life. Or maybe not left behind, but like toys, put on a shelf to be thought about, but not played with. Are the people at Haywood House in need of extra love and purpose? *God, You have led me here, please help me be the blessing I want to be.*

Walking through front doors, I immediately felt a difference from where Grams lived out her last days. First, the inviting smell of cinnamon and cleanliness was present. Was Jasmine here with rolls? Then looking around, I saw flowers, comfy furniture, and people dressed in regular clothes, not hospital uniforms. I went up to the desk and spoke to a smiling woman engaged in a conversation with a lady in a wheelchair.

"Hi, my name is Claire James and I have an appointment with Mrs. Blanton. I'm a little early, so I can just sit out here and wait for her."

"You'll do no such thing! Come join us for coffee by the fire and tell us all about yourself," said the lady in the wheelchair taking charge. She was dressed in a flannel plaid shirt, jeans, and cowboy boots. She looked ready to jump on a horse and ride the range, but I realized she was not getting up and walking to the fireplace as she rolled her wheelchair over to a group of ladies. Lots of talking was going on, so unlike Grams' place. Maybe my plan wasn't needed here. Just as I sat down and was ready to share with these ladies, Mrs. Blanton walked up, introduced herself, and said we could meet in her office down the hall.

"I'll come see you all after my meeting," I said to the ladies. I really did want to spend time with them.

Mrs. Blanton looked over the résumé I had sent her and commented on how much corporate experience I had, including a lot of high recommendations on work ethic and dedication. She paused at that point and looked at me directly and said, "How are you going to make a difference here? We don't need to become a corporate place with lots of schedules and outward good looks. These people have lived in Haywood all their lives, they just need a comfortable place to rest and know they are well cared for by staff. It seems to be working very nicely for us. You can see the smiles on people's faces and the nice surroundings. What more do we need?"

"Mrs. Blanton, my first impression of Haywood House is very positive. I immediately felt a different presence than the place where my Grams lived out her last days. I don't have a lot of experience working in an assisted-living facility, but my heart is pulled to people who have lived rich full lives and now have to rely on others to take care of them. I want them to know they still have a lot of wisdom to share and are a vital part of the community. I want them to feel they still have a purpose. I have a plan to bring that part of their lives to everyday living at Haywood House. I know I am a newcomer here. What do I know about your community? But I'm willing to learn and I'm a hard worker.

"There is one part I left out of my proposal. I want to bring my dog, Ladybug, to interact with the residents. She has a very special personality around vulnerable people. She senses sadness, loneliness, and need. Bug will befriend anyone who needs a friend. Can I please bring her here and see if she is a good fit with everyone?"

"I can only pay minimum wage and part time, no benefits. You can try bringing your dog, but if any of our people object, you'll have to leave her at home. After you have had a chance to look around and meet the staff, you can make plans to come back tomorrow and start implementing your plan. I warn you though, people are set in their ways and may not take to an outsider changing things. We'll give it a month."

"Thank you so much, Mrs. Blanton. You'll not be disappointed and the people at Haywood House will truly be enriched. I can't wait to start!"

I walked around the facility noting the private rooms were open and looked neat. The dining room was starting to fill with people ready for lunch, so I decided not to bother anyone today. The sitting area I saw when I first came in was empty except for one lady I hadn't seen when I first arrived. She was by herself, sitting by the fire, gazing out the window. She looked pensive. What was weighing her down? I would make it my priority to meet this woman tomorrow. *God, you have already placed a special person on my heart.* Bug will love her. I hope she loves dogs.

Chapter Seven

Wow, the weather could change in a heartbeat here. Yesterday was a beautiful fall day, the leaves were a bounty of color, gently falling to the ground. Fall had always been my favorite time of year. It was only the end of September and today I felt like winter had arrived. The temperature had dropped into the 30's and snow was starting to fall. Bug and I had planned on walking to Haywood House, but we didn't need to track in snow on the first day of my job. Maybe we could go on a nice walk this afternoon. I loved the quiet of a snowy day.

Last night I was up into the wee hours of the night working on my plan. While the residents at Haywood House looked happy and well taken care of, I felt like something was missing. People, no matter what age or stage of life, need to be needed and wanted to give back. *God, help me listen closely to their stories today. Give me the ability to understand what made their life vital when they were independent. Guide me to a place where I can stir the longing to live with purpose. Oh Lord, be with me the whole time because I am scared to death I'll mess up!*

The fire was blazing and lots of people were sitting in the common room visiting with one another when we arrived. Ladybug was looking her best after having a bath and a long brushing last night. I brought her into the room and she immediately sought out the lady sitting off by herself I had seen yesterday. She went up and sat in front of her and looked longingly at her with those melt me amber eyes. The lady seemed startled at first, with the unsolicited attention brought to her. Everyone else had gotten quiet and was watching the two of them. Slowly the lady reached down and offered her hand to Bug. Bug sniffed it and gently placed her paw in the lady's lap. A smile ever so small appeared on her face and tears gathered in eyes. She was remembering another time. A time when life had meaning, fullness, love, and purpose. We are in the right place to do good, God. Thank you for leading me here.

I spent the morning getting to know those gathered by the fire. We shared stories over coffee, and eventually, Bug came over to greet each person there. She was a hit, and now I didn't have to worry about bringing her to work. I was getting an idea of what their lives were like in the past. Mrs. Darby loved to garden and had the most beautiful field of wildflowers back in the day. She knew the names of native flowers and lit up while talking about them. Agnes, who only goes by her first name, was quite a knitter. She owned a yarn shop at one time on Main Street. The afghan on her lap was one of many she knitted over the years. Ms. Sally was a kindergarten teacher for 50 years at the elementary school. What a wealth of knowledge and wisdom! You could tell teaching was a calling for her as she reminisced about the children. Mr. Evans was a cattle rancher, and now his grandson runs his ranch. Mrs. Sharp was the town librarian and touched every single book in that library. These people were vital to this town. Yes, they were being taking care of, but not cared about.

This week I gathered information about everyone and just generally let them get to know me, me with my heart shield in place. Let's become friends but at a safe distance. I was good at that. Bug had already gone back to lay at that lady's feet. I needed to meet her.

"Hi, I'm Claire and this is Ladybug. I see she has already taken to you. I hope you don't mind. She has a way of finding the people she wants to be with, and I have no say in the matter."

"I miss my dog. She was sold to a family that moved away. That's the story of my life. One disappointment after another. You better take her away now because I'm sure she won't be back, and I don't want to get attached." And with that she turned and wheeled away. There was a sad story in this woman's life. Could I help her find a little joy? I was no stranger to sadness and life's rocky roads so, just maybe, we could connect. Bug certainly had!

There was such an eerie light at night when snow was falling. Almost like angels were lighting the sky. The quietness was deafening. I loved this peace.

"In the quiet, of this moment
In the quiet of this space
Be with us, Lord."

God, you have made a perfect moment, sitting on my front porch, wrapped in the coziest of blankets, and drinking hot cocoa with whipped cream, Bug curled up beside me, and watching the snow fall, I am falling in love with Haywood, Montana.

I have met the most amazing people. They have lived such full lives, using their talents and gifts from God. They have helped make Haywood the town it is today, but they have stopped living, stopped contributing, and stopped having a purpose. Oh, they seem to be happy. They are certainly well taken care of and live in a very nice place. But the light in their eyes is dim, not sparkling. I want to restore that sparkle, tap into their wisdom, give them a purpose. *Help me, God*, because I know I can't do it alone. I sure will try, though. You know me. I need to pace myself, feel my way in this new town, but I am nothing if I'm not full speed ahead! I'm running with this idea.

Who is the lady that Bug has befriended? What is her story? The emptiness in her voice when she told me to take Bug away tore at my heart. Surely the final chapter of her life did not end like this. And the snow fell.

Chapter Eight

The first week at Haywood House had flown by. I knew I was part-time, but I couldn't help coming here every day to talk to people and start implementing my plan. I had spent hours at Sip & Savor scribbling notes about everyone's special gifts and nibbling on a cinnamon roll or two. Jasmine had been a fountain of information, sharing what she remembered and had heard about most everyone at the home. More hours spent late into the night thinking and planning. One night, Sam came over about midnight to ask if I was having trouble with my electricity. He thought maybe it wasn't turning off properly. He said most normal people go to bed by 10:00pm. All I could say was, "That's true about normal people."

By the end of the week, I was ready to try out my first idea. Mrs. Darby had talked about her green thumb and love of wildflowers. With my help finding natural plants and grasses, Mrs. Darby was going to turn Haywood House into a *Southern Living* photo op! I had her make a list of plants along with pictures, so that I found just the right ones. Then she would create her magic throughout Haywood House by designing wreaths, centerpieces, and decorative vases with the beauty of Montana everywhere.

Mrs. Darby was excited and with that enthusiasm recruited a few of her friends to help. They made two wreaths that would have sold for big bucks at Williams Sonoma. A gorgeous bow adorned the autumn-colored wildflowers and grasses that took me several trips to various meadows to find. They decided their placement on the front doors would offer a warm welcome. There was a fun buzz of activity taking place. I saw the first sparkle! I couldn't wait to see what Mrs. Darby designed for the vases on the mantle. She and her friends were going back and forth about how tall the arrangements should be. I stayed out of that discussion.

The library idea was next. Haywood House had books, donated by the townspeople, stacked on shelves in the sitting room collecting dust. There was no order to them and not a great variety. Most were contemporary paperbacks and political spy novels. Jasmine agreed to put up a sign at the coffee house with a basket below asking for donations of classics or old bestsellers in excellent condition. We had about forty in the basket after the first week. I approached Mrs. Sharp about help with organizing a few donated books with possibly a checkout system and she took it from there. She had the housekeeper take all the books off the shelves and dust them. Next came piles of books in alphabetical order by author's last name. Then she had to sort them by genres. She mentioned she used to have hundreds of pocket holders and check out cards at the library, but now books were all checked out with a scanner and a bar code. A wisp of nostalgia crossed her face and I knew what I could do.

"Mrs. Sharp, I know where I can get some of those pockets and cards if you would like to use that as your check out system." Thank goodness for Amazon! Oh my, a sparkle was in her eyes with that revelation, and she totally agreed that was what the Haywood House library needed. I was in the second week of my month trial period, and I felt so charged. I was making a difference. Life was coming back to the people at Haywood House. Only good could come from all of this. And then, the beginning of the third week, I was called into Mrs. Blanton's office.

I was so sure that she was going to praise me up and down, maybe give me a raise, or ask that I join the staff permanently that I could barely hold back a smile. I wanted to jump right in and tell her the rest of my ideas; however, the look on her face caused me to rethink the reason for this meeting. Something wasn't right.

"Ms. James, please have a seat. I'd like you to tell me how you think your little project is going," she said without a hint of gladness in her voice.

"Oh, Mrs. Blanton, I think everything is off to a wonderful start! Mrs. Darby is so excited about fixing the flower arrangements, and Mrs. Sharp is busy as can be with the library, and my other ideas are ready to be shared. I just feel like there is so much life to their days now. Not that there wasn't before. Oh dear, I don't mean to make it sound like this wasn't a good place before I came I…"

"Ms. James, let me comment on your first two weeks here. You have certainly given Mrs. Darby and Mrs. Sharp some new things to focus on, however, we have 25 residents here at Haywood House. The favoritism you have shown to these two people is causing strife among the others. Also, there is too much activity for these ladies. They need to have a slower pace, time during their day to rest. At this rate they will wear themselves out and possibly get sick. We can't have that, Ms. James. Now you have two more weeks before your trial period comes to an end. I suggest you reevaluate your plans, slow down, and be content with introducing another bingo game for all to participate or some new jigsaw puzzles, something calming and open to all, equally. Do you understand what is needed here?"

Tears were forming faster than I could handle them. No, this couldn't be right. I saw sparkles in their eyes. I was on the right track. I knew I was. I thanked Mrs. Blanton for her input into my first two weeks and left in such a hurry I forgot Bug. Outside I broke down in sobs wondering how I could have missed the negatives of my plan. I would never want to leave anyone out causing them to feel rejected or ignored. *God, how did this happen?* I had to get home before anyone saw me in this state. Just as I headed down the walk, I heard my name called out from the doorway. I turned and saw Mrs. Darby there with Bug.

"Looks like you forgot someone! Oh, dear me, Claire, I'll bet you don't have a hankie. Well, here is mine, it's not been used. What has you in such a state?"

I couldn't let her know about my dressing down. I had to handle this on my own. "I'm okay, Mrs. Darby. Seems like I caught a cold or something and thought I'd better leave quickly and not spread my germs. So sorry to have made you come out in the cold. I'll be fine in a day or two. I probably should stay home tomorrow, so please tell everyone I'll be back soon." I had to leave quickly before I really started bawling. Heart shield went up, let no one in, handle this yourself.

Once at home I collapsed into my big comfortable chair and held Bug tightly. She knew I needed her right now. *God, I have You and Bug, and that's all I need.* Where did I go wrong? Should I just slink out of town and go back to Atlanta and get lost in the busyness and blandness of each day, where people leave each other alone and don't try to meddle in each other's lives? How could I have been so blind as to not see people hurting? I don't want to give up, but I have to do something differently. God, please help me. I know you have plans for me. Plans to prosper. Not in a material way, but in a way to bring meaning to these lives. I can't give up, but I can't give in either. I'm such a bull in a china shop kind of girl. Rushing in full head of steam and leaving a mess in my wake. I promised to listen to You God, to surrender to You, to lean on You. Show me the way, I'll listen and follow.

Hours later, still curled up in my chair, lots of tissue all around and a darkness creeping in, I heard a knock on my door. Sam opened the door slowly and Bug jumped down to greet him. "I was worried something was wrong. I saw you come home early and then no lights turned on. I just want to make sure you're alright."

I uncurled from my chair and walked over to Sam and laid my head on his shoulder. His arms encircled me in a protective hug, and I felt my heart shield start to crack. During the hours lost in prayer and time with God, I realized my way was not the only way. I couldn't do everything by myself. I didn't want to be alone in my safe little world. I needed to start letting people in and risk a bit of hurt to gain a lot of love and friendship. I asked him to stay so I could share my mess with him.

Sam went to the kitchen to start a fresh pot of coffee then said, "You know, it's up to you, but another friend is hurting for you too, Jasmine. She came by and said she heard you had a bad cold, though she suspected something else going on from what Mrs. Darby said. I'd like to call her over here if that's alright."

I slowly nodded my head. *Can I do this, God? Can I let them in?* I didn't have a choice if I was going to heal from the past and move on to the kind of life I had only envisioned in dreams.

Jasmine arrived and we sat around, warmed by the flames of a crackling fire and the heartfelt company of those who cared. I began telling them about my disastrous meeting with Mrs. Blanton and how I was so positive my plan would improve the lives of the residents. Then words just started spilling out of me, and I was reliving the moment I was alone without my Grams, who raised me. I was only 19 years old and on my own. My heart shield went up because that was the only way I could cope with being so alone. Grams was the world to me and the only person I could turn to for help, comfort, and love. When Grams died, she left everything she had to me, and it was enough to get me through college. Without her or anyone else in my life, I was able to throw myself into my studies. And I continued to use that same crazy way of life when I landed a lucrative job in Atlanta. What I didn't know was the heart issue that took my mom early in my life, was also the problem I had when I turned 38. Twenty odd years later, much had improved in the area of women's cardiac conditions. I was saved, my mom was not. That part of my life I was not yet willing to share with Jasmine and Sam. Safe to say I had an awakening that brought me to Haywood.

Jasmine came over to me, looked me in the eye and said that family does not have to be blood related. A chosen family could often be the best kind. She needed a sister, and so did I. We hugged each other with joyful tears falling and Sam, not wanting to be left out, patted both our shoulders. "Time to resolve this Haywood House problem", he said.

Into the wee hours of the night, we hashed over new ideas. The weight of the world was now shared with my friends. I didn't have to do this all by myself. By the time Jasmine needed to start on her cinnamon rolls at the coffee house, I had a passel of notes, new ideas, and a wonderful outlook for next week. I also had two very special people in my corner. Two people I could rely on and lean on and begin to share life's trials and triumphs. I also had two very sleepy new friends, so off we all went to the Sip & Savor to greet the day, make rolls and coffee, and put down the chairs.

Chapter Nine

I used the weekend to plan, relax, explore the town, and get some much-needed exercise and fresh air. Bug was all for that. Back in Atlanta, we would go on 3-4 mile walks every day. She needed the exercise and I needed walking for my rehab since I wasn't running any more. I bundled up on Sunday after church on another chilly but sunny day. I was getting used to the colder temperature and being wise about what to wear. A picnic lunch of cheese and crackers, apple slices and sweet ice tea, you can't take the southern out of a Georgia girl, was all I needed, with a couple of treats for Bug. We drove to the park for some time with nature and with God. Haywood had a beautiful state park close by with trails, picnic tables, and trickling brooks. It was easy to lose track of time in such a beautiful setting.

Walking the trails gave me time to think about all that had happened the last few days. I prayed for guidance, discernment, direction, and peace. I thanked God for the new relationships I was establishing and the connection I was feeling with Haywood. After this time with God, I could now lay my head in His lap and leave all my concerns with Him.

Before I knew it, dusk was settling in with a gorgeous sky of purple and pink hues showcasing the vastness of this country. As I peeked through rich evergreens, I witnessed God closing the door on this day. Bug and I still had a bit of a hike out of the park, though, so we best start heading back in the right direction.

We were hustling along the trail when I heard a soft rustling sound behind us. Bug immediately started her low growl. I knew when Bug was in protective mode. She just didn't growl without a serious reason. I reached down and grabbed ahold of her collar. Something wasn't right. Something was there. I froze in place, trying to get Bug to sit still and be quiet. My heart started beating like a drum in my chest. No, I didn't need to have that problem now. I knew stress could bring on another episode for my heart. Oh, please, just be a feeling of panic, not another heart attack. Think, Claire, what are the safety precautions to take if wild animals are nearby? Or what if it's a person stalking me? Forget that thought. This was not Atlanta. We were in small town Haywood, Montana. How did I get myself into this predicament? And Bug. I couldn't let anything happen to Bug! I knew she would do anything to protect me but that little brown dog was no match for a dangerous wild animal. My eyes were darting all around. I didn't see anything but I did hear the rustling again behind me off to my right. Slowly I attached Bug's leash to her collar. I couldn't have her chasing a mountain lion or bear. Then I saw what appeared to be a young tawny colored cat staring at me from the trail. It was in a crouched position as if ready to lunge at us. How did it slip up on us? Did it think Bug was some sort of prey? I thought mountain lions were afraid of people. *Oh, dear God, please help me!* I think I'm supposed to make a lot of noise and appear aggressive.

"Go away! Don't you dare come near me!" I yelled and waved my arms in the air, stomping my feet. Bug was trying to get loose, pulling on the leash, barking, and growling.

"No, Bug, no! Stop! You can't chase that animal!" I screamed. She pulled so hard that I tripped trying to hold her and went down. A sharp pain in my leg caused me to cry in agony. That must have instigated a surprise reaction by the mountain lion, and it disappeared into the brush. Still holding onto the leash to stop Bug's chase, I was shaking like a leaf as I assessed the damage to my leg. Blood was gushing out of a hole in my jeans. I looked to see a jagged rock sticking up out of the ground that must have slashed into my leg.

The pain was excruciating, so I tried not to move. Taking deep breaths, I started to calm down and realized I had to get some help. I was fairly confident the animal would not come back, but I didn't want to take that chance. I took the scarf from around my neck and tied it around the cut on my leg. My heart had slowed to a dull thump, and I felt no piercing pain in my chest so I was certain the only concern I had at the moment was my leg. Now, to hobble to the car. I barely stepped with my injured leg, but the pain was still intense. I didn't do well with pain or blood! My blood pressure must have dropped into my boots because I was feeling light headed. I wanted to sit down again, but knew I needed to get back to the car. The bleeding had slowed but had soaked through the scarf. I found a good size stick along the trail to use as a crutch which helped ease the pressure on my leg. The car was farther away than I thought. Should I phone someone to come get me?

We slowly made our way to the car. I wanted so badly to just go home, but the bleeding had not completely stopped, and I didn't feel very well. I think my adrenaline had tanked and the sight of all that blood was not sitting too well with me. I started to feel clammy and hot at the same time. More deep breaths. Off to the ER again. I was so thankful for this small town because everything was close by and easily accessible, not like Atlanta which would have taken 10 times as long to get to an urgent care.

The car was creeping along because I was afraid to press down hard on the accelerator with my injured leg, wouldn't you know it was my right leg! I pulled over for a minute because I felt my blood pressure dropping again. *Please, God don't let me pass out.* More deep breaths. I closed my eyes and prayed for strength to make it to the ER. Maybe just a quick look by a nurse, clean up and a bandage and then I could go home and take care of it. I finally pulled up to the front, got out and gingerly dragged my leg into the waiting room, Bug in tow. No, no, no. Not again. There sat Jack talking to some people. Did he hang out regularly in the ER? He immediately looked up and rushed over to me for which I was thankful, because about that time, I must have fainted. I thought I heard him say, "We have to stop meeting like this."

When I came to, the doctor was in the middle of cleaning me up and putting in 15 stitches. He then wrote a prescription for antibiotics and sent me home with instructions to keep my leg elevated for the night. He seemed to know I wouldn't follow a 24-hour instruction. "Just elevate it whenever possible for the next couple of days," he said. "Sorry about your jeans, I had to cut them to get to your wound."

"Don't worry. I appreciate you fixing me up right away. Usually I'm more surefooted than that, but Bug was determined to chase away the danger and she is amazingly strong. I wasn't about to let go of her leash." A memory flashed before my eyes about a time I was water skiing, fell, and did not let go of the rope. Not a good outcome that time either!

Jack was still in the waiting room with Bug when I limped out. "Let me have your keys, I'll drive you home. Haywood doesn't need to worry about you being on the road tonight with a gimpy leg on the gas pedal."

His arm securely tucked under mine, I felt the urge to give in and let him take care of me. I leaned into him ever so slightly, as we walked to the door. I wanted to protest, but he was right and I was still a bit shaky. I think the enormity of what just happened had taken a toll on me. "How will you get back here to get your car?"

"Not to worry, Sam will drive me."

Oh great, now Sam would know and have to check on me again. But then I remembered last Friday night and realized that's what friends do. I had to be okay with this. "Thank you," I said and meant it.

I offered to have him come in for a cup of coffee, but he seemed to pick up on the weariness in my voice and said he would hold me to it another time. After settling me in with a fire in the fireplace, Bug fed and content to lay down beside me, and my leg propped up on the ottoman, Jack started to leave. "I'll have Sam come check on you in a while. Follow doctor's orders with your leg elevated, and if you see any redness, swelling, or run a fever, march yourself back to the ER. Well, maybe not march, but get it looked at for sure. Doc Evans is very thorough, and I don't expect any complications. And just a word of caution, don't walk alone at dusk in the park. It's very rare for a mountain lion to attack a person, they are generally afraid of people, but one might go after Bug if it feels threatened. I'm going to hold you to that cup of coffee one of these days. Take care, bye, Bug."

An hour later Sam walked through the door carrying a plate of something that smelled delicious. "Girl, I have to say, I haven't had this much activity in years. You're either keeping me young or causing me to go completely gray. I stopped by the café and stew was the dish of the day. Thought you could use some meat on your bones, and I knew you weren't supposed to get up and fix anything. Got myself some, too, but I'm going to eat it at home and let you rest. You be sure and follow up on that coffee with Jack. He needs the company. Bye, Bug." Sam left the stew on the table, scratched Bug's ears, and was gone. I had to say I sure was glad Bug was a big hit with these tough Montana men.

A full stomach, warm and cozy in my chair by the fire, Bug

beside me, I reflected on the day. I felt such a connection with God on my walk. He was with me the whole time. Even when I felt panic on the trail, I also felt protected, not just by Bug, but more than that. God was with me no matter what life threw in my way, a heart attack, a dressing down from my boss, even a wild animal. He had placed special people to take care of me and comfort me and walk with me on this journey of life. I wasn't sure where we were going, but I was all in with Him and my new friends.

Chapter Ten

There was no way I could stay away from work today, even though my leg was very sore. I'd have to cut my time short and prop it up this afternoon. As I walked through the door at Haywood House Monday morning, I was bombarded with questions and comments: How are you feeling? We missed you Friday. Are you over your cold? Why are you limping? Come let me show you what I did with the library over the weekend. Look at the vases I put on the mantle yesterday. I truly felt missed. I answered one question at a time, giving a very brief account of my injury and confessing that I didn't have a cold, just was a bit emotional on Thursday. It felt so good to be back with these people. I felt a warmth as if Grams was here or watching over me. Now, for the hard part, admitting I started off on the wrong foot. As I explained, but not putting Mrs. Blanton in a bad light, I saw questions on some faces.

"Claire, I've not felt this energized in years," said Mrs. Darby.

"Me neither," piped up Mrs. Sharp.

"We've been so happy to help with the flower arranging. I remember the garden I had at my old house. I never had a green thumb, but I always liked fresh flowers in the house. Jane and I love being a part of Doris's decorating. Plus, she needs help." said a lady I hadn't met yet.

Jane agreed, "Mrs. Darby is an excellent decorator." Maybe I hadn't left everyone else out. Some people liked to be in charge and others wanted to help in a supportive capacity. I was pretty good at finding the leaders. I had to make sure the supporters felt included. "That is so wonderful, Miss Jane, and I'm sorry, what is your name?" I asked the lady who willingly helped Mrs. Darby and Jane.

"Belva. Belva Collins."

"Wait, did you own the house on Maple Street? The one with the rope swing in the backyard?"

"I sure did! Brought up 3 rough and tumble boys in that house. Never really had the time to put into my gardens, but I planted flowers just the same. My house was the gathering place for all the boys on the block. My land, how many peanut butter and jelly sandwiches I made and chocolate chip cookies! I was famous for my cookies, or those boys just knew I was a soft touch. Haywood was the best place to raise a family back then. Kids everywhere and all the parents watched out for them. Didn't matter if one was your own or not. They were all cared for or reprimanded if necessary. Good days, those were good days."

"Mrs. Collins, I'm living in your house now. I knew that a lot of love lived in that house before me. I'm so glad to find out it was you. We'll have to talk more, and I'll tell you what I have done since I've moved in this fall." I felt a closeness to Mrs. Collins in the intimacy of sharing the same home, a home filled with happiness, some sadness, secrets, and dreams. I couldn't wait to get to know her better and maybe bring her out to the house.

"Now, for my idea, and I want all of you to tell me your honest opinion. I know you gather together to watch TV shows and the occasional movie, but how about a regular movie night, every Friday night with movies you love from your era, such as *Oklahoma, My Fair Lady, Casablanca*, to give you some examples."

"You can get those movies? I thought we could only watch what was coming on TV each week. I think that would be wonderful. Will you take requests?" asked Mrs. Miller.

"I absolutely will. How about if I put out a suggestion sheet and you all write down movies you'd like to see. I can't guarantee I can get every one of them, but I'll try."

"And let's have popcorn! And lemonade. Or cookies and hot cocoa. When can we start?" The buzz was building and the sparkle in their eyes was spreading! Well, Mrs. Blanton, it's not bingo, but I think I was starting to reach everyone. I would take your constructive criticism and make this a warm wonderful place.

"I sure could use an artist's touch with the posters I'd like to display, letting you all know what's coming. Anyone willing to help me?'

"Geraldine is a fantastic artist. She used to win all the blue ribbons at 4H and the State Fair. I know it's been a while, but you haven't lost your touch, have you Geraldine?" All eyes turned to the lady sitting with Bug at her feet. A delicate hand slowly petted the little brown dog, the dog that rarely leaves her side when we come here. Geraldine had not spoken to me since the first week when I introduced myself to her. I thought I'd give her some time to warm up to me like she had to Bug. Maybe this will be the icebreaker I needed to get to know her.

"I might be able to give you some advice on posters. I haven't painted in years though, so just advice," she directed her eyes back down at Bug and said no more.

When she saw my paltry attempt at painting, I was counting on her to do more than give advice. I needed to get some art supplies and poster paper. I was so excited I could hardly contain myself! The mood here was one of anticipation with a spark of joy. God, joy comes from Your love, a love of contentment. The love You have for others and wanting them to live life fully, no matter the circumstances. Haywood House was not where these people planned to live their twilight years. I got that. No one ever thinks they would have to rely on others to do the basic things they had done all their adult life. No one wanted to give up their home and have to live dependent on strangers to take care of them. I wanted these precious people to know how valued and valuable they were. That their talents, intellect, compassion, and wisdom were still a part of them and worth sharing with others. Life goes by in the twinkling of an eye. Hopes and dreams might have been realized or not, but life was not over because of a change of address. And so, I wanted to reach into Geraldine and find the artist, the woman with a troubled past, who loved dogs. I wanted her to know she had not been forgotten. That none of them had been forgotten.

It was time to go, I needed to put my leg up for a while. It was starting to throb a little. I called to Bug, and as she got up, Geraldine leaned down and gave her a kiss on her head. It was uncanny the connection Bug had made with her already. I told Geraldine we'd be back again soon with art supplies. She said one word, "Watercolors."

Bug and I headed home with all sorts of ideas spinning in my head again. I knew I needed to slow down, but time was not a luxury with this plan. I would think everything through and run it by Jasmine. After lunch and a power nap, my leg was feeling better. I called Jasmine to see if she was up for a road trip. I needed to find watercolors in a bigger town than Haywood. Also, I needed a Best Buy to purchase movies. She was all in and since the Sip & Savor closed at 2:00pm, we had the rest of the day to go shopping and treat ourselves to dinner.

When I told Sam I was going to Laurel with Jasmine, he wanted me to leave Bug with him. I knew she would be happy and taken care of while I was gone, so much better than her being alone at home. Jasmine offered to drive which was fine with me since my leg was still a bit achy. I told Jasmine all that transpired this morning and about movie night.

As I'm telling her about Geraldine, she recalled the circumstances that made her have to go to Haywood House. "Geraldine was indeed quite an artist. She sold many of her watercolors when she was younger and supported her family that way, as her husband died very young and left her with two children to raise. Her daughter, Cassie, left Haywood after high school and rarely came back. She was quite beautiful and hoped for a career in Hollywood. She never made it big, but stayed out there the rest of her life. Geraldine's son, Ben, stayed around here, dabbling in the rodeo circuit, and then working on different ranches. I think they had a good relationship, mother and son, until he fell for a girl who didn't get along with Geraldine. They had a child that was the apple of Geraldine's eye. She doted on that boy. He seemed to inherit her gift for beauty and color and they spent a lot of time together. A few years ago, Ben died in a ranch accident loading a steer onto a truck. It was so tragic and devastated Geraldine. His wife packed up and left with the grandson, and taking her beloved dog, Jingles. All the life seemed to be sucked out of her. She apparently doesn't hear from her daughter or her daughter-in-law. So sad."

"That is not going to be how she spends the rest of her life. No one should just be put in a place, then abandoned. Bug chose to bond with her. I feel as if she is a deeply caring person and I'm determined to make her life worth living again. First, I think we have to help her find the passion she had for painting."

We pulled up to a Hobby Lobby in Laurel and went straight to the art section, gathering supplies we needed for a watercolor artist. Then off to Best Buy for some old classic movies. I couldn't resist going to a Western clothing store and buying new jeans, a pair of boots, and a warm jacket. Jasmine was just the stylist I needed. In her artsy way, we found the right outfits for me to stay warm but also fashionable. Apparently, Ariat boots were the ones to buy, so I extravagantly bought some hiking boots and stylish ones. Wool socks were a must which I could attest to after my unfortunate hike on Sunday. I hadn't had this much fun in a very long time. Before we knew it, our stomachs were growling. The Jackson Grille was famous for grilled hamburgers and skinny fries. We both caved in on chocolate milkshakes, too. Although, a glass of wine would have been tempting.

Time to head home. I believe I might have overdone my activities because my leg started to throb again, but I couldn't remember when I had talked and shared and laughed so much. Jasmine was a wonderful listener, the kind of person you felt you had known all your life. I was usually the one doing the listening, so I wouldn't have to talk. I'd navigated my relationships for so long this way that I forgot how comforting it was to share with a listener. She was so down to earth, such a people person, that I found myself opening up to her and wanting her opinions. We clicked on so many levels and so many interests. She loved to knit. Of course, baking kept her very busy at the coffee shop. She also had a deep-seated compassion for vulnerable people. Often Jasmine could be found taking an I.O.U. for coffee or cinnamon rolls from someone a little strapped for cash. An I.O.U. she never called back. Lowering my heart guard with her and Sam had been easier than I thought it would be. But one person I couldn't let in was Jack.

Chapter Eleven

This week continued to be busy setting the movie schedule, finding more dried flowers for the wreaths to decorate the doors inside Haywood House with the glory of fall, and getting people to help Mrs. Sharp put card pockets in all the books. She wanted to run her library like she did in years gone by with a card checkout. I loved it. And so did the residents. It was what they knew and remembered. Their world needed to be validated not antiquated. Thank goodness again for Amazon and being able to send off for items like library cards and pockets, old movies, and a movie house popcorn popper.

The most rewarding part of the week came when Geraldine uncovered the beautiful poster of a scene from the movie *Oklahoma* to display for our first movie night. The talent she must have had earlier in her life burst forth in a timeless depiction of life on the plains. The poster was a collage of colors with an old red barn set against a gorgeous blue, purple, and pink sky with waves of golden wheat in the forefront. Oh my, that talent could not go to waste! I was almost speechless when I saw it, but I was able to tell her she would be my forever go to girl for any advertising. I loved listening to the other ladies going on about how beautiful the poster was. One of the ladies told her she would help her in any way just to be a part of such artistic talent. I heard Geraldine say she could help her decide on a scene for the *My Fair Lady* movie. Was this her first interaction in months?

God, these were such small changes in the big picture of life and yet, upon these, relationships were being built and nurtured. Everyone had a deep desire to be needed, wanted, valued, appreciated, missed, and loved. What was life without these things? I think it was most evident when people were at a point when they had to depend on others. Were they needed, valued, or even missed? Were they put on a shelf and taken down for a quick visit? Put back up there till the next visit? Or maybe there were no visits in which case they stayed on the shelf, forgotten. Did I do this to Grams? Did she feel forgotten except when I breezed in and out so wrapped up in school and my part-time job? I was so young then. I do remember our talks and walks out in the garden at her assisted-living facility. She would start to open up to me more when we were outside. She always loved gardens. Why didn't I see that then? Why didn't I help her nurture that love again? Why was I so self-absorbed? Well, these ladies were all my Grams, and I was determined not to ignore them or miss out on any of the invaluable wisdom they may share. Most people must live a lifetime of experiences in order to be wise, to have an understanding, to bestow knowledge that would help others grow in truth and grace. They would not be forgotten.

One person had me a bit baffled, Mr. Gaston. He was often in the living room during the morning, but off to himself reading. Whenever I went over to say good morning, he was very polite, stood and greeted me, and told me to have a fine day, then proceeded to sit down and go back to reading his book. Once or twice when Geraldine had not been in the main room, Bug would go over and sit regally beside Mr. Gaston as if she knew something special about this man. He'd pet her, say something quietly, and then go back to reading. I hoped he'd be willing to join in with some of our activities.

He seemed lonely.

My mind was reeling with so much anticipation over what we'd get into next that I was surprised to see Jack coming in the door greeting people as he entered. I heard a lot of chatter going on and people seemingly anxious to get his attention. Of course, Bug secured his attention first. She went running over to him as if she hadn't seen him in forever. She was like that. She had an uncanny way of making close friends instantly and not forgetting. Her tail wagged as if it would fall off, her eyes glistened, and it really looked as if she was smiling. Jack was one of those friends who gleaned the special welcome.

"Where have you been, Jack Thompson," drilled Mrs. Darby. "And don't tell me those animals are keeping you busy. They can't all be sick all the time."

"Well, actually you are right. I'm having a nice reprieve right now from all those sick animals, and I came looking for a certain Ms. James, because she owes me a cup of coffee. I understand you all are keeping her pretty busy these days. Who's going to show me around so I can see what you have been up to around here?" That got everyone busy talking at once showing Jack the flowers, the library, and talking about the movies coming up soon. Then he spotted the poster. He went up to it, not saying a word. Tears seemed to gather in his eyes. What was that all about? Then he went over to Geraldine, took hold of her hands, squeezed them and whispered, "The beauty you bring is not lost. Thank you." Geraldine seemed touched by his attention and held her arms up for an awkward, long needed hug. Jack promised to be back soon, but now must whisk me away for that cup of coffee before his afternoon break filled with an animal emergency.

I was surprised when we pulled up to Jasmine's as I thought she usually closed at 2:00pm. Apparently, she opened up for special people. Not only was a fresh pot of coffee awaiting us but a new bakery item, apple pie. Oh my, I could just die and go to heaven right now. The smell of cinnamon mixed with apples and a homemade crust was a perfect afternoon treat. As we settled in after some small talk, my curiosity got the best of me and I had to ask about the exchange with Geraldine. "I sensed a deep connection between the two of you. Do you mind my asking about how you know each other?"

"I grew up with Geraldine's kids. We lived close to each other and spent all our time nursing hurt animals back to health, riding horses, and generally living the good life in the great outdoors. Cassie, her daughter, was wild and beautiful. I have to admit, I had a crush on her from the time I was in first grade. I think she viewed me as another brother at the time, but I was content with that just so I could be with her. Ben and I were thick as thieves. I had an older and younger sister so hanging out with Ben, made him like the brother I never had. Geraldine raised those kids pretty much by herself. She was a gifted artist and supported the family that way. I loved going into her studio. It was like an art gallery in New York City. She was a prolific painter and would become obsessed with her work. There were many times Cassie and Ben would eat supper with my family because Geraldine would be lost in her passion. Mom and Dad never minded, knowing how their mom couldn't break away from the drive she had to create, my folk's kind of took them under their wing.

"Cassie's demons haunted her through high school. Like I said, she was beautiful and that beauty cost her a lot. She fell in with a rough crowd in Laurel and started ignoring Ben and me. We wanted to continue the life we had when we were younger, but she wanted more glamor. She took off the day after graduating from high school for California convinced that she would make it big in modeling or acting. It broke Geraldine's heart to see her go, but I think what broke her heart even more was knowing she hadn't been there for Cassie, hadn't been the mother Cassie needed. Cassie was a young girl when she lost her father. Her mother was given a beautiful gift, and could not turn away from it to be the mother her two children needed so desperately. Obsession is a cruel curse. It cost Geraldine a close relationship with her daughter and ultimately her ability to continue using her gift.

"Ben and I drifted apart when I went off to school. Ben didn't have that drive to become a veterinarian like I did, but he did continue to work around animals. He stayed around here, living with his mom and working different cattle ranches. It was a satisfying arrangement until Ben fell in love with Angie. After a while they married and bought a house of their own. From the beginning, Angie and Geraldine rubbed each other the wrong way. I think Angie was jealous of her mother-in-law. Ben was still close to his mom and stayed in a protective role, but Angie wanted Ben all to herself. Things went along okay for a while. Then the baby was born. Something clicked with Geraldine, as if her mothering instincts finally came alive. She doted on that baby and he loved her back just as fiercely.

"As little Ben grew, it was clear he had his grandmother's artistic ability. They would spend hours together in her studio. She, teaching him all she could, and he, absorbing it like a sponge. Little Ben wanted a dog, but Angie did not want one in the house, so Geraldine bought a beautiful border collie for her grandson and kept the pup at her house. Little Ben and Chloe, the dog, grew up together. I had never seen Geraldine so happy. She blossomed during those years with her art as well as her heart. The one thorn she could never remove was Cassie choosing to leave Haywood and not coming back." Jack's phone vibrated and he had to take the call. I could tell he had an emergency that couldn't be ignored. A horse was caught in a wire fence and he had to go take care of it before the horse injured itself even more. I couldn't believe how quickly the time went.

"I am so sorry Claire. I've been going on all this time and haven't heard a word about you and what brought you to Haywood. Please give me another rain check soon."

"I will. I want to know how Geraldine could lose the very breath of her life and end up in Haywood House. She is so sad and so alone. You must get going though and free that horse. I'll hold you to that rain check." He gently caressed my cheek, rubbed Bug's ear, and was gone. I gazed out the window to see him again before he was out of sight. I gathered our cups and dishes and contemplated what just took place. I wanted to get to know Jack Thompson. If he wanted to know more about me, I'd have to let go and trust. *God, make me go slowly here.* I think he is a good man, but we've both lived our lives independently with no time for, or need of, another person. We had that in common, but could two independent people build a relationship of dependence on one another? Only time would tell.

Chapter Twelve

An idea to involve Ms. Sally and the elementary school had been bouncing around in my head. She had a deep understanding of children, and they had an overwhelming capacity for love and exuberance. We needed to bring some of that here. I asked Ms. Sally to meet me this morning. After chatting a bit, I asked her to share her greatest joys of teaching. Not surprising, the children were the first on her list.

"I miss them so much, their curiosity, spontaneity, fearlessness, joy. That was the beauty of teaching kindergarten. Oh yes, those darlings were full of energy and the last couple of years I taught were quite wearing; however, 5-year-olds haven't developed prejudices or attitudes. They genuinely love school and usually their teacher. The world opens up to so many of them at that time in their young lives. We would have wonder time every day. I wonder what… and someone would share something they wanted to learn that day. School is different now with planned lessons on computers and curriculums developed by people out of the classroom. I knew what my children needed and wanted to learn. Each year was a little different and I planned accordingly. I know the world is changing and children have to change, too. The freedom to be a child lasts such a short time. Let them be children," said Ms. Sally with the wistfulness of long ago thoughts.

Just as I thought, Ms. Sally had a lifetime of experience and wisdom in the classroom with the youngest learners. She taught in the years before technology became the focus in schools. The years when kids learned by hands-on activities centered around units they understood such as, fall, apples, pumpkins, Halloween, pilgrims, Thanksgiving, etc. What if she could share some of her knowledge with young educators and administrators at Haywood Elementary? Would they be willing to listen, try something new? Would she even want to meet with them? I had to take it slowly and not push my idea too much like I had been known to do.

"Ms. Sally, have you thought of sharing some of your teaching methods with young teachers today?"

"I would love to but they don't have time to listen to an old lady reminisce about the old days. I'm sure their days are full of teaching, planning, meetings, and so forth."

"What if the kindergarten teachers at the elementary school came here one afternoon to get a glimpse of teaching before computers. Would you be willing to explain to them how you taught your Halloween unit, since it's almost Halloween?" I asked with fingers crossed.

"Well, I could tell them about going to the pumpkin patch on old Charlie's farm, measuring pumpkins, counting seeds, and patterning. We had the best time decorating the room." A look of longing and love filled her eyes. She built her life around little ones and the wonder of opening up their world. While she didn't have the stamina for teaching any more, she did have all the wisdom and creativity to give to a new generation of educators. Would she be willing? It didn't take long to see that spark start to glimmer. "Well, maybe I could at least talk to some of them. If they want to... They probably don't have time for an old biddy woman, stuck in the past."

'We'll see about that. I'll do the contacting and set up a meeting day. Oh, Miss Sally, this is so exciting! I would love to see some of the past ideas intermingled with the new. You are just the person to sell them on the idea. I'll let you know what I find out. This is going to be great."

Chapter Thirteen

Haywood Elementary School had two kindergarten and two 1st grade classes. I thought it might be beneficial to offer to all four of the teachers a chance to meet with Ms. Sally. The principle agreed to gather them together after school to hear my proposal. I explained a little bit of Ms. Sally's background and her years of teaching. I knew she was the best one to sell them on an idea of bringing hands-on lessons to their charges. All agreed to meet the next afternoon at Haywood House.

Ms. Sally was excited but nervous. As soon as she started talking about her days in the classroom, though, it was like she was transported back in time to the passion that was her life for 50 years. She explained how teachers were in charge of their own lesson plans. Everything was handmade, not bought in a package at a school supply store. And if a field trip was needed to enhance the learning, it could be taken. Mostly the trips were within walking distance and parents were fine with letting their children go. Often parents joined them, too.

The time flew by and the teachers, though interested, had to leave. They thanked Ms. Sally and genuinely seemed to appreciate the wisdom she so vividly gave to them. One teacher hung back though. She was the youngest of the four and was very quiet during the hour, but seemed to hang on every word that Ms. Sally spoke. I remembered her from the introductions when the teachers first arrived, Sarah Jones. She had been teaching only two years and, like me, was a newcomer to Haywood.

"Ms. Sally, I would like to try some of the ways you taught the October lessons in the weeks remaining in this month. I don't know that I could schedule a field trip in this short amount of time, but maybe we could come up with an alternative. Would you mind if I came back tomorrow to talk with you some more?" asked Sarah.

Ms. Sally leaned in closely to Sarah, took her hands in hers and with glistening eyes said, "You truly have a calling to teach young eager minds. I would be honored to share the ways that worked so many years ago. Children haven't changed that much. The young ones still have wonder, boundless energy, and love. Let's foster that together."

Ms. Sally could no longer handle the rigors of the classroom, but she had the wisdom of 50 years to give to someone who could. I saw a budding relationship between Sarah and Ms. Sally becoming a meaningful connection for both of them.

Sarah did come back the next day with plans to meet every week after that. Ms. Sally was over the moon sharing her ideas, and Sarah was just the teacher to appreciate all of the ways Ms. Sally educated her children well beyond the basics back in her day. Technology in education was amazing in today's classrooms, but little children still needed to find the wonder in the real world.

Chapter Fourteen

Our first Friday movie night was here. I came early to set up the living room. I wanted a seat for everyone regardless if all would be coming or not. Jasmine came over after closing Sip & Savor to help. She was such a natural when it came to entertaining. She had the idea to have apple cider, popcorn, and oatmeal cookies, all displayed as if we were at a barn dance, much like in *Oklahoma*. She brought in a couple of bales of hay, some lanterns, and red and white checked table cloths. She put a punch bowl on the table with red solo cups for the cider, napkins, and her homemade cookies. We couldn't go wrong. I fired up the popcorn machine and filled cute red and white popcorn bags for everyone. The movie was set to start at 7:00pm. The smell of buttered popcorn, reminiscent of walking in the door of a movie theater, started bringing the first moviegoers. As the room began to fill up, I sensed an anticipation growing much like being in a theater on opening night of a new production. I wanted to introduce the movie and thank everyone for coming.

Just then there was a scuffle as Ms. Geraldine came in with her wheelchair. She bumped into Mr. Evans as he was getting his popcorn and the bag flew out of his hands, landed in her lap, and as she turned away, a chain reaction seemed to take place. I felt like

I was witnessing a disaster in slow motion! More bags of popcorn became upended, a cookie was dropped, and Mrs. Collins ended up on the floor. I rushed over to her in a panic, worried she was hurt with a broken hip, or worse. When I got to her side, she was laughing so hard she could barely speak. "Are you alright, Mrs. Collins? I am so sorry this happened; I should have thought to pass out the refreshments after everyone was seated. Oh, this is all my fault! I didn't consider the safest way to organize the night. Please tell me you're not hurt."

Through tears and laughter, she said she hadn't had this much excitement or attention since her boys played a trick on her Halloween night 1958! "I'm pretty padded back there and though I don't bounce up like I used to, it's pretty safe to say nothing is broken. Was I the preview before the movie? Everyone, I'm fine and now that the ice has been broken for our first movie night, let's help pick up the spilled popcorn and get this show started!" Jasmine and I gingerly picked up Mrs. Collins and friends started coming over to check on her. Others found a broom and started sweeping up popcorn and a comradery seemed to take place as people chipped in to help.

Ms. Geraldine wheeled over to me and apologized for starting the ruckus, but winked when she said she thought everyone would look forward to movie night from now on. "Who knows what the next preview feature might be!" I sensed a little tom foolery in her.

All in all, the night was a success. More popcorn was made, cookies, and drinks (next time with tops), were passed out and all was enjoyed. Many of the residents sang along with familiar tunes. When Gordon MacRae sang "Oh What a Beautiful Morning" you could almost hear all the ladies swoon. My favorite was the ending when the cast sang "Oklahoma" one last time. Rogers and Hammerstein musicals were the best. Everyone seemed to enjoy the movie and a burst of applause at the end indicated a good evening was had by all. After everyone mingled for a bit, they headed happily off to their rooms. Jasmine and I cleaned up. It was after 10:00pm when all of the chairs were put away and every kernel of popcorn picked up. I do believe Bug helped out there. I hugged Jasmine and thanked her for all she did. She said she hadn't had that much fun or drama in a very long time. Well, first movie night wouldn't be forgotten here at Haywood House. Even Mrs. Blanton seemed pleased over all. She shook my hand and thanked me for bringing some joy to everyone tonight. And, said she was especially glad Mrs. Collins didn't need a trip to the ER!

"Come on, Bug. Let's head home." We went out into the cold night air. I was so glad we walked here earlier. A walk home was just what I needed. The stars shone like glitter on a Christmas card and the moon was filling out it's orb ready to be full on Halloween. Could the night be more glorious? I'm learning, God, to live in the moment, seek the joy, and find gratitude in the simple things of life. Tonight could have been a disaster, but it wasn't. It was laughter, concern, friendship, and happiness. It was good.

"Mind if I walk you home?" Jack asked quietly slipping in beside me. I was so lost in my thoughts I never heard him approach.

"How did you know where to find me?"

"Jasmine filled me in on a bit of the excitement tonight and I thought you might want to share a little, too. Sounds like the first movie night was an overall success."

"Oh, Jack, it was, but for a moment I thought it was a complete failure. I have a lot to learn about planning and pacing for seniors. I don't want them to feel they are inept at taking care of themselves, and yet, I have to make it easy for them to participate as adults without accidents. I certainly don't want to be the cause of an injury or an embarrassment."

"You handled it perfectly because you showed genuine concern. You love these people, Claire, and they know it. The time you've spent with them, the interest you show in them, the way you tap into their passion and bring it back to life for them, they see all that. They love you for it, too. I think you have found a home here, and I for one am very glad. I was hoping I could talk you into the rain check coffee tonight or perhaps a glass of wine. I'm pretty good at building a fire."

"I have a better idea, a glass of wine and cozy quilts out on the porch to enjoy this beautiful night. Maybe Sam will join us!" I laughed knowing full well he would check on us and then leave us alone to enjoy the snippet of time we had together before the demands of Jack's chosen life's work would be calling him away.

Chapter Fifteen

Bug and I planned to hike the park trail again in the light of day this chilly, cloudy Sunday afternoon. I felt bundled appropriately for Montana weather. Lots of layering, long underwear, long sleeve turtleneck, weatherproof jacket with hood, a scarf, gloves, lined pants, and warm boots. I was probably over doing it, but it was cold today. I needed time to reflect on all that had happened in such a short time. My life in Atlanta was always crazy busy, but in the way of corporate America. Meetings were scheduled, phone conversations through lunch, many reports to be written and reviewed, and always a deadline looming. I ate, drank, and slept my job. Staying insanely busy was a way to keep from thinking of the past. I didn't want to think about how I was robbed of my childhood: growing up without a father, watching my friends' dads picking them up from school, playing with them on the playground, the laughter and the hugs, taking care of a sick mother who worked all the time when she wasn't in bed exhausted or ill, and no siblings to share the load.

Mom died when I was in high school, such a hard time for a young girl to lose her mother. All I knew was that her heart gave out. I think I became numb at that time to mask the hurt and grief I felt. How do you handle grief when you are 16 years old without parents, just my wonderful steady Grams? And then she was gone, too. I learned early in my life how hard it was to lose someone you love, so I vowed after Grams died, I would depend solely on myself, not get involved in any relationships, not risk my heart being broken again. No more parts to shatter.

Well, I wasn't a nun and did have some fun times with some really nice guys, but they tired of waiting for me to become more committed. I could walk away because it was so much easier than having someone else doing the leaving. So many years spent in the shell of a life never getting close to anyone. That's when I put up my heart shield.

God forced my hand when I had the heart attack. I was lucky to survive and realized in those moments in CCU, all by myself, no one to really care if I lived or died, but I cared. I wanted to live. I just didn't want to live the way I had been living the last 20 years. God and I had a heart-to-heart conversation during many prayers. Taking one day at a time, I started leaning on Him. Grams had always been close to God by praying daily, reading her Bible, and going to church. I loved her sense of calm, her trust, her faith, and her quoted Bible scripture. She would say to me, "Child, lean not on your own understanding, but trust in God… I know the plans I have for you… Come to me all you who are weary and heavy burdened, and I will give you rest…" Grams would always know the right verse for me, but I was stubborn or just immature and didn't think I needed that kind of advice. *God, thank goodness You give second, third and even twentieth chances to know You.*

I requested more time off after I was released from the hospital, though I could have returned fairly soon. I needed to reassess my life and lifestyle which clearly wasn't working for me. I was faithful with rehab, took walks that turned into daily prayer time, sometimes hours in length, and took the biggest risk of my life that turned into the biggest blessing. I adopted Bug. I needed a companion and something to focus on besides my health and work. Plus, I needed to love. As more and more of God's love flowed into me, more was expected of me: to share, to give, to care for, and to love back. I couldn't believe I took that risk, but it was one of the trusts I turned over to God. I thought learning to love a dog would be different enough from loving a person, that I could handle the chance I took with her. Little did I know that this little fur ball would become such an important part of my world. Her unconditional love for me had cracked the shield around my heart, and I couldn't imagine life without her.

And now I was beginning to let people into my heart. Jasmine, Sam, Jack, and the wonderful people at Haywood House were part of my life now, a wonderful part. I was not so naïve to think my heart wouldn't be broken again, but I was learning that the more I loved, the richer my life was. The more I gave to others, the more I received in return. How selfish of me to live in my own little world. Not anymore.

Time gets away from me so easily. I get caught up in conversations with You, God, and forget to be smart about my surroundings. I needed to head back as snow that started as a dusting began to fall harder now. It was so beautiful earlier and so gentle falling on the trees and bushes and trail. Now it was difficult to see the path I needed to take back to the parking lot where I left my car. Oh dear, who would have thought it could snow so hard and blow so hard to make visibility nil. I guess it could happen here. Why didn't I heed the winter warning? I heard about it on the radio coming to the park. Winter warnings in Atlanta often were disappointing. We always hoped for a beautiful snow that might halt everything for 24 hours but it rarely happened that way. So, with this being the first winter weather I'd experienced here, I had to admit, I didn't take it seriously. It was just cloudy earlier, then snow started falling sporadically, just enough to be beautiful. Now it was a threat!

Bug, we need to be smart about this. What was once sporadic

snowfall was coming down heavily and blanketing the trail. There was no way to tell the direction we needed to go, so we probably shouldn't walk any further. Was this what a blizzard was like? We needed shelter though. I'd read enough about blizzard problems to know heavy and drifting snow could disorient someone quickly. First, Bug, I'm tying you to me. We have to stick together. The last thing I need is to lose you. *God, please, please don't leave me, either!* This was so incredibly stupid of me to get myself in this mess! How long do blizzards last, will anyone come looking for me? I had to think about safety measures I'd read about: build a shelter, don't eat the snow, and hang a brightly colored scarf for someone to see. Will anyone know to come looking for me? Do I even want them out in this mess?

Back to being smart about this. Fortunately, a few weeks ago when I checked out survival kits on Amazon, on a whim I ordered one because it is easy to have Amazon bring necessities or frivolities to your door. When the kit came, I looked over the contents and then stuck it in my backpack. I remembered a gizmo to cut branches, a wire saw. I needed to cut some now and make a small lean-to, quickly. Luckily, there was a big rock we just passed to use as one protective side. I piled up the branches to break the blowing snow and tied my scarf to the tree branch nearby. It was slow going to dig out just enough space for Bug and me to crawl in and stay relatively dry. The two of us huddled together would help keep each other warm. Another tip I remembered from reading about blizzards was to keep moving your arms and legs, fingers and toes. I dressed warmly for the hike, but I had to keep Bug warm. Animals were pretty resilient in the outdoors, but Bug was an awfully spoiled indoor pet. I couldn't take a chance on her getting too cold. I searched my backpack for necessities. I had water, protein bars, a flashlight, and in the kit was an emergency blanket, yay! The blanket would keep in our body heat. The snow was still falling, but the wind seemed to have died down some. How long had we been out here? I know we started our hike after lunch. It was now 4:30. It would soon be getting dark, but I couldn't think about that now. Time to stand up and exercise. I peeked out of shelter and saw nothing but white. Snow was still falling, not at the rate it was earlier, but fairly heavy none the less. Maybe the brunt of the storm had passed. Could we find our way out of here before dark? My instinct told me to stay put, but I really didn't want to spend the night here. Bug and I settled back down staying dry and fairly warm.

My thoughts turned to Haywood House and the people who had adopted me into their family. I think being a loner and basically around adults most of my life made it easy for me to connect with older people. I didn't see them at the end of their life, more like they had earned the right to speak their mind, to offer wisdom to us who hadn't traveled that road all the way yet. Some people were open to their sage advice, others were too busy being busy to stop and listen or think or learn. One thing I had learned was that gifts were to be shared, not possessively kept. Perfection was not the goal. Sometimes I thought when you were younger, you felt the keen sense of competition. There was always someone who was brighter, better, or faster. How could you meet that high bar? But what had you gained by not trying? Someone had been deprived of your gift if you selfishly kept it for yourself. God gave you, and you alone, specific talents, gifts, and personality traits. Did He say "Claire, your life is going to be okay, adequate. I made you to get by and gave you mediocre abilities, so good luck." No! God made each of us to be His best and brightest child. What we did with what He gave us was our gift back to him. So many of us fail to give back to our Father. We sometimes hid behind the fact that it was hard to give our best. We didn't want to have to start over if we'd messed up. It was easier to quit and settle for just okay. *God, forgive me for the times I quit, for the times I didn't try, for the excuses I used to keep from being the person You made me to be. Forgive me for not sharing the love You put deep in my heart for You and those You have chosen to put in my life. I'm getting a bit sleepy now, God. I would just love to lay down feeling Your presence and drift away.* But I had Bug and I couldn't risk not keeping us safe. I had to get up and move around, modified jumping jacks and walking in place.

Bug started her low growl. Oh no, please, please, please not a wild animal! I couldn't defend ourselves trapped in this hole. I reached for my flashlight, the only weapon I had besides the pocket knife. Then Bug started yipping and pulling on her lease. I couldn't let you go, Bug. I'd never find you in this snow. No pulling! I turned on the flashlight and pointed it in the direction she was lunging. And then I heard a faint noise, a voice. Bug started barking wildly as if she knew the voice.

"We're here, over here!" I waved the flashlight wildly trying to gauge where the voice was coming from in the still falling snow. The stillness the white landscape had afforded us these last few hours, our sanctuary of silence, was broken with more yelling and lights making an array of glistening shimmers on the snow. As much as Bug wanted to going running towards our rescuers, I couldn't let her go. Finally, breaking through the white wall of snow that had held us captive in this wilderness were three people resembling sasquatches and angels both!

"Claire! Oh, Claire! Oh my God, thank goodness we have found you. Are you alright?" Jack's voice cut through the silence, and never had I heard a more welcomed sound. He wrapped his arms around me in a hug I could stay in forever. Tears started to flow and I started shaking uncontrollably as I realized how scared I had been as well as embarrassed and bone chilling cold. Bug was getting plenty of attention from Jasmine and appeared ready to head back down the trail. Jack's friend, Paul, started gathering the blanket, backpack, and food in the shelter. We needed to head back quickly before the darkness and cold complicate our return even more.

"How are we going to know which way to go?" I asked trying to regain my sense of calm.

"I left us markers along the trail, bright red pieces of cloth tied to tree branches. Your red scarf was perfect, Claire. It was the first thing we saw, before we heard Bug. What a happy sight and sound that was! It's supposed to snow all night and that would not have been good for you." said Jasmine.

Just then I heard two piercing gunshots. What in the world?

"I'm letting Sam know we have found you. The only way we could convince him to stay back at the parking lot was to tell him someone needed to be at your car in case you returned on your own, and that we would signal when we found you. This is kind of a freaky snowstorm. We don't usually get this much this early, but we respect mother nature and I imagine you will now too. Follow me and hold on to this rope. Jasmine is behind you and Paul will bring up the rear. We'll keep an eye out for the red cloths Jasmine hung. We're not too far away from the parking lot, but if we get turned around, we're in trouble. Can you walk alright?"

"I'm okay but I'm worried about Bug in this deep snow. It's so cold. I can't believe so much has fallen in such a short time."

"Bug is okay, but if she gets sluggish, I can carry her. Let's just keep moving. There's a red cloth up ahead. We're good. Jasmine tied off five of them. Is everyone doing alright?" Jack yelled behind him to Jasmine and Paul.

"We're good. Keep moving."

I followed slowly and deliberately in Jack's footsteps. He was taking on the brunt of the wind and snow. I wanted to break down and cry, but I must be strong and not cause any more problems than I already had. Will I ever be able to adapt to life out here when my first snowstorm was a major disaster? We passed another, then another red cloth. We were on the right path. I heard a horn honking in the distance.

"That's Sam guiding us in to where the truck is parked. We're almost there." Jack was now carrying Bug. If anything happened to her or any of these people because of my foolishness, I'd never forgive myself. We trudged to the place where Sam had his truck running with the lights on to guide us the rest of the way. He bounded out of the truck running to me and grabbed me in a fierce bearhug.

"I oughta tan your hide, you had us so scared," Sam's voice was quivering with emotion. Then he hugged me again without the rib-crunching force. I hugged him back and started to cry and apologized and shook all at the same time. "Come on, let's all get back home and get you some dry clothes, food, and a warm fire. Then you can tell us how in the world you thought it would be alright to go hiking in a winter storm. Girl, I swear."

Back at my house, Jack and Paul built a fire while Sam and Jasmine were concocting something in the kitchen. I was still shaking from the cold and the scare, so I put on some warm jogging pants, wool socks, and a sweatshirt. In by the fire and under an afghan with Bug snuggled up beside me, I began to feel the cold leave my body. Jasmine handed me a mug of hot cocoa. It felt good just holding it.

"I am so incredibly sorry for putting all of you in danger. I don't know what I would have done if anything happened to you while looking for me. It was foolish to go out today. I saw the snow warning, but never in my wildest dreams did I imagine something like this. It never snows like this in Atlanta."

"Claire, you're not in the sunny South any more. But I will admit this is definitely not normal for this time of year. Big snows like this bordering on a blizzard usually come in February or occasionally the early spring. I'm just so relieved that you were sensible enough to hole up and not try to find your way back to the car. That's a mistake some people make when caught outdoors like this. You get disoriented and almost walk in circles getting nowhere but extremely tired and cold. Keeping Bug with you was smart, too, because she could get lost easily, also. I checked her over when we got back and she is just fine, but animals can have negative effects from the cold, too. It's 15 degrees out there now, definitely frostbite weather. That blanket was a life saver for both of you." Jack was visibly shaken now that this whole ordeal was over, but thank goodness for a happy ending. I reached for his hand to reassure him we were okay. At that gesture Sam, Jasmine, and Paul headed for the kitchen to make some supper for everyone. I know it will include eggs and potatoes.

"Thank you, Jack. I had some time to think while we were waiting out the storm. I have met some amazing people in Haywood in such a short amount of time. And I truly feel like this can be home for me. I have a lot to learn about living in Montana; but I want to stay. Do you think I can make it here?"

"Absolutely, but we might have to have more discussions about safety. We'll turn you into a Western woman yet." He pulled me into his arms and I felt as if I had come home at last. No more walls, no more shields, no more dodging a relationship. I didn't know where this was going but I was not putting any blockades up on this journey.

The threesome came out with a meal worthy of a king. Who knew I had that much food to make such a delicious feast? We ate, talked a lot more, laughed a bunch, and I got a lot of pointers on being a Western woman in Montana. Now, will I remember all of it? I hope so. It was getting late, still snowing, but not windy like before. Sam decided the guys would all stay at his house for the night. Jasmine was staying with me. She and I had some ideas to kick around for the holidays and couldn't wait to start planning. In the morning, if the weather cleared, everyone could make their way home.

We said good night to the rescuers. Sam couldn't resist one more jab as he said, "Girl, I'm going to have to up my health insurance with you around. Just about had a heart attack, but all is well. Night, Bug." I kissed his cheek and watched to make sure they got across the yard safely, using the flashlight beam to guide them to Sam's front door.

I poured a glass of red wine for Jasmine and myself. Back in front of the fire, she told me how worried Jack was when he found out I was in the park when the storm hit. He organized all of them to go find me. They just about had to tie Sam to the truck to keep him from coming along on the trail. She said that Jack knew the park better than anyone since he grew up playing there as a boy. "He really cares, Claire."

"So do I. We'll take it slowly and see where all of this leads. It's nothing if not exciting. I sure have managed to stir up some adventure!

"Tell me about Sam. He seems like such a loner, but he also must have had quite a full life. He's so mysterious to me. Showing up when I need him, helping you out, being a friend to Jack. What's his story?"

"Sam has always lived in Montana. He grew up on his mom and dad's cattle ranch east of Haywood, and then took it over when they passed away. It was never a big operation, just family owned and operated pretty much. Sam had a couple of brothers who worked the ranch when they were younger, but both of them left Montana, one to join the service, army I think, the other went off to college in Colorado and stayed there. That was fine with Sam. He couldn't imagine any other life. Sam met Sandy in high school when she moved from California with her family. They fell in love instantly and married right after graduation. Sandy loved ranch life like Sam. I think they envisioned having lots of kids and just living the life of cattle ranchers for the rest of their days. Only they never had any children, not sure why. Sandy still found ways to be around kids. Every year they would host a mini rodeo, mainly for kids 5-12 years old from town. The older kids already were involved in 4H and teenage events. Families would come out to the ranch and bring covered dishes and desserts. Sandy and Sam would make up a huge pot of baked beans and always had never-ending trays of their famous hickory smoked barbeque. Sam swore his beans were just from an ordinary recipe but I know he had to have some secret ingredient for them to taste that good. All day the kids would try their hand at barrel racing, roping, and mutton busting."

"I've heard of barrel racing and different roping events, but what's mutton busting?"

"Mutton busting is riding sheep. The little ones would put on safety helmets, climb on a sheep, then they were all released at the same time. The kid who stayed on his or her sheep the longest was the big winner. Of course, they all got ribbons, but the winner also got his or her very own shiny belt buckle. Sandy made sure every child got a ribbon for each of the events entered. Many kids had their first taste of rodeo life at Sam and Sandy's.

"They also invited kids to the ranch at Christmas. Sandy loved Christmas. She always went a little overboard and Sam couldn't deny her anything. They decorated the house and trees with tiny white lights. Big red ribbons tied onto wreaths were hung at every window. It was so beautiful. Sam would take the kids on a sleigh ride around the ranch. The sleigh was pulled by a couple of their horses and big bells would jingle along the way. Many times, it would be snowing and it seemed like the perfect night when that happened. Sandy would be ready for them back at the house with hot cocoa and cut out cookies she had decorated. Christmas carols were always playing in the background. Each child received a red or green stocking filled with trinkets, candy, and a book. I wasn't into the rodeo scene, but I loved Christmas at Sam and Sandy's. I think the whole town has missed Christmas at their ranch, or at least the older folks and us grown up kids. I'll have to fill you in with how it all came to a stop at another time. I don't know about you. but my eyes are not wanting to stay open any longer after your adventure today."

"You are so right. I'm finally warm and exhausted. The guest room is ready for you. Help yourself to toiletries in the bathroom. There are extra toothbrushes and soap in the top left drawer and clean towels on the towel rack to the left of the sink. I'll let Bug out and we can call it a night. Thanks so much Jasmine for all you have done for me today. I guess I could have really gotten myself in a pickle if you hadn't come looking for me."

"I heard you mention after church you might go for a walk in the park, so when the weather turned, I called your house and didn't get an answer. I told Jack what I suspected, and he picked up me, Sam, and Paul. We found your car in the parking lot at the park and knew you were in trouble. We're all so thankful you used common sense out there. We could have had quite a different ending. Have a good night's sleep dear friend. More adventures to come, I'm sure." and Jasmine left with a wink.

Chapter Sixteen

Jasmine, Jack and Paul were all able to return to their homes on Monday. The snow had continued to fall, but the wind had died down, and since they were used to navigating winter weather, it was time for them to get back to their routines. Paul was a good friend of Jack and worked at the hospital as an ER doctor. I remembered seeing him there on my disastrous ladder debacle. He had a sweet family. His daughter was in Sarah's kindergarten class and his son was in fifth grade. I'd have to thank him again for his part in my rescue and let his family know how much I appreciated them sharing him yesterday. There were a lot of selfless people in Haywood.

I stayed snug in my house, thankful for plenty of firewood and food. I was still a Southern girl when it came to snow. If I had milk and bread, I was good for a week! Curling up in my big comfy chair in front of the fireplace, I picked up my knitting and thought back over the last 24 hours. Never in my life had I felt this type of friendship, this closeness. I knew my mother's love and Grams' love, but this was different. I could lean on these people, not because they were family, because they cared about me as a friend. *Thank you, God, for bringing me here.* It's still early, but I feel like I can put down roots here.

I wanted to know more about the people who have been put

in my path. Jasmine had a deep soul. She seemed to be a loner and yet a friend to everyone. She knew when someone was needy or hurting and was there to offer comfort. Then she'd be gone. She had appeared both times I had had disasters bringing cinnamon rolls or providing a shoulder to cry on. She'd been there when I needed a helper at Haywood House, also. Sam had mentioned other times Jasmine had been there for people who were down on their luck or a little out of sorts. She had the gift of compassion seasoned with empathy. What was her story?

I finished knitting her a scarf out of soft blues, purples, and pinks. I was so glad I brought my stash of yarn from Atlanta. There was a wonderful yarn shop there where I splurged on gorgeous wool yarn so soft to the touch. I didn't have anything in mind to make at the time, but You did, God. Now, I was making a scarf for Sam out of yarn that was a little thicker than what I used for Jasmine. The barn red and browns just seemed perfect for him. Warm wool scarves were essential in Montana. I planned to give these as Christmas presents. Now, I just had to come up with one for Jack.

There was a time when I thought being by myself on a weekend was melancholy. What woman at 38 would have no social life at all? I would mope around hoping the hours would pass until I could be busy again, lost in my work. Now, this alone time was reflective and comforting. I was spending more hours reading devotionals and the Bible, praying for wise counsel and coming up with new ideas for Haywood House. I was enjoying this peaceful time. I might need a bigger stash of yarn, though, if winters started this early in Montana!

Chapter Seventeen

The snow stopped Monday night, and after 20 inches had accumulated, it was officially declared a fall blizzard, the first of the season. Not sure I liked the term, first. How many more were to come? I was assured that this was highly unusual weather for the beginning of November. Snow yes, but blizzard conditions, no. People started back to work and their daily routine by Tuesday. I had lots of ideas to share at Haywood House and couldn't wait to get there. Bug and I waited for the roads to be passable about mid-morning. When we walked through the door, people immediately came up to us asking about the excitement of how we managed to become lost in the blizzard and had to be rescued. My how news travels! We gathered by the fireplace and I gave a short version of my exciting weekend. Mainly, though, I apologized for putting my friends in danger. I actually called them my friends. I told them I had a new respect for this beautiful part of the country and wouldn't be putting myself in that kind of situation again.

Now for scheduling the next movie night. I gave them three choices and it was decided that we would see *The King and I*. Geraldine agreed to make a poster. I was sure Yul Brynner and Deborah Kerr would look stunning! The date was set for a week from Friday. That would give Jasmine and me time to come up with refreshments and cups with lids. I was thinking tea and scones along with popcorn. Jasmine was the expert baker, though, so I would check with her first. I absolutely loved musicals and was so glad that was the type of movie everyone wanted to see, although we'll probably have some Westerns thrown in there after the holidays.

My next idea needed Mrs. Blanton's approval, so I asked to speak with her when she was free. While I was waiting for her, I wandered around the building and noticed different residents' rooms with doors opened, some with a few pictures and a homey feel. But some with just the basic bed, chair, and dresser, were not warm, inviting settings. Not much was needed to change the bare look, maybe pictures on the wall, a quilt or comforter on the bed, colorful pillows, a pretty lamp on the nightstand, and/or curtains at the window in addition to the blinds. I was making a note to ask about this, too. I understood the bare necessities if residents were here for just a short time; however, most of the people here had moved in indefinitely. I did have my sewing machine, hmm…

When Mrs. Blanton was free, we met in her office. We chatted about the weather and then I introduced my latest idea. I first asked about Thanksgiving dinner and how that day was planned. She said about half the residents go to family homes for the holiday and the others stayed here and had a traditional turkey and dressing meal for lunch. That was what I thought probably happened. Grams stayed at her assisted-living the year she was there for Thanksgiving. I was a freshman in college and had no place to take her, so we both ate there. I must say it wasn't very special and I think holidays should be. So, my proposal to Mrs. Blanton was that we plan a special Thanksgiving dinner complete with decorations and a beautifully set table or tables. Jasmine and I could plan it and do the cooking. Other people in the town could come if they might be alone on that day (I was specifically thinking of Jack and Sam). I was holding my breath waiting for her to say something.

"Would this meal be open for staff members to come as well?"

"Absolutely, and they would be considered guests, not workers for that part of the day. Do you think we could try this?" I asked with a tentativeness in my voice that exposed my fear that this was just a pipe dream.

Mrs. Blanton hesitated a bit then said, "I want to be part of the planning and, of course, I'll be there that day to make sure everything goes smoothly. That being said, I think you can try this experiment for a holiday celebration. Just remember, we put our residents first in all manner of health and safety."

Before I knew it, I had crossed the room and embraced her in a bear hug. "Oh, thank you so much Mrs. Blanton. This is going to be so wonderful and special. Jasmine and I will start on the plans and menu right away, then bring them by for you to approve. You won't regret this decision, I know it!"

"I hope not, Ms. James." As she showed me to the door, she happened to mention one of her favorite dishes for Thanksgiving. "Maybe cranberry apple crunch could be on the menu."

I gave her a thumbs up.

Chapter Eighteen

Jasmine and I made a date to meet at Sip & Savor around 4:00pm. She already had notebooks spread out, cookbooks opened, and a yellow legal pad of paper ready for our holiday agenda. On my way over there I kept thinking something was different about Mrs. Blanton's reaction to my idea. She seemed to like it well enough, but also seemed a bit sad or certainly not overly excited about it.

When I enter the coffee shop Jasmine had two mugs of steaming coffee ready for us and of course her famous cinnamon rolls. There was no resisting this girl's temptations.

Jasmine was a pro at organizing dinners like this. Four times a year she opened up her coffee shop for a town dinner inviting those who were a bit more needy, alone, or in some way cut off from family to enjoy a sit-down dinner with music and laughter. She did the cooking and serving. The people were encouraged to stay and visit for a few hours. The menus changed depending on the time of year. In the fall, she usually prepared a chicken and dumplings main course with squash casserole, baked apples, green beans, and pecan pie. In the winter it was always chili and cornbread, ambrosia salad, with pound cake for dessert. Spring brought meat loaf, mashed potatoes and gravy, corn, homemade bread, and cream pies. The summer was always hamburgers and hot dogs, slaw, baked beans, chips, and homemade ice cream. Other town members knew about Jasmine's heart for those who might be considered the fringe of society and willingly helped out monetarily. Jack and Sam always showed up to help and stayed for the clean-up and dishes. There were usually between 20 to 40 people at these special dinners and everyone left satisfied and feeling a bit more loved. I wanted to be part of this wonderful tradition and would gladly help Jasmine with the cooking.

Back to our meal planning for Thanksgiving. Fluffy mashed potatoes with turkey gravy, green beans, cranberry crunch (of course), sweet potato casserole with a brown sugar, butter, and pecan topping, squash casserole, turkey dressing, and pecan and pumpkin pies with homemade whipped cream would round out the menu. We'd of course have roasted turkey, probably two as we wanted to plan for half the residents, the staff, and some people from town. We were thinking along the lines of Jasmine's other dinners in number, but we also wanted to make it family oriented and intimate. Holidays were all about family, the more the merrier, and we didn't want anyone to feel left out. We were going to be busy cooks getting all this ready. Luckily, Jasmine had a nice size kitchen at Sip & Savor and all the cooking pots and pans needed.

Another important part of making this a special holiday dinner was the table decorations. We'd have white linen tablecloths, adorned with colorful fall napkins. Each table would have a fall centerpiece of seasonal foliage and a candle. Unfortunately, it would have to be a battery-operated candle for safety reasons, but they were pretty real looking now. I remembered having a chocolate turkey wrapped in colorful foil a few times at Thanksgiving. I loved that touch. I thought I'd look for chocolate fall leaves wrapped in foil to put around each centerpiece. I loved my chocolate!

Jasmine and I made plans to go shopping and then set a date to start our cooking and baking. Some of our dishes could be made ahead of time and frozen, leaving the week of Thanksgiving to the turkeys, potatoes, dressing, and gravy. I asked Mrs. Blanton to start a sign-up sheet so we would know how many people would be attending and how many place settings we would need.

Our movie nights had been fun getting everyone together, but this would be like family, albeit one big family. I felt overwhelmed with love for these people, but first things first. I needed to have everything ready for our *King and I* movie night. That included cups with tops on them.

Chapter Nineteen

I had so many ideas floating around in my head. How could I make a difference at Haywood House? God, You know my pace on all of this. I want it done yesterday! As I sat in my living room, the fire cast a warm glow and created a comforting, crackling sound while I cozied up in my chair with Bug beside me. I have such a closeness to You, God. I love this time of prayer and devotion that we have carved out in the evenings. I am now noticing at Haywood the gifts and talents I've been given are beginning to enrich their lives. I'm enjoying the ability to organize and set forth a plan.

I had the talent to sew, quilt, and knit. I think that was the direction I wanted to pursue next. I could make self-binding lap quilts for everyone. I had a lot of beautiful fabric I brought from Georgia. When Jasmine and I go shopping in Laurel, I'll buy some flannel fabric for the backing. What if I enlisted the help of some of the ladies at Haywood to design the quilts? I could have the fabric cut in 6-inch squares, and they could help me lay out the top piece in different designs. What fun that would be! I am racing ahead again, but I feel that these ideas are the nudges I have ignored in the past. Nudges to connect with people, to help people, to find my purpose, to validate the lives of the people at Haywood House. I could start cutting squares tonight and bring them to the ladies tomorrow. Usually I used 5-inch squares for my self-binding quilts, but these had to be put together quickly in order to get one for each person, and I think the 6-inch plan would be less stressful for them to design, too. Off to the kitchen to start a pot of coffee, get my material out and begin our next project. *I'm so glad I have You to share this with, God.*

By 2:00am my back, arm, and hand were sore from cutting, but I had a huge pile of beautiful 6-inch squares to take to the ladies. I wondered if they would be as excited as I was, or was this too much? Here I am like a bull in a china shop going full speed ahead. I couldn't wait to enlist their help to start putting these quilts together. Surely, they would remember when they had this drive and ability to create beautiful things. I just wanted to bring another spark to their lives. Time to call it a night and pray for an embracing of my newest idea.

I woke up to the sound of rain splattering against my window. It was cold and dreary, but not so cold as to be icy or dangerous, just miserable. I remembered Grams being depressed on days like this. She could never get warm and couldn't find an uplifting activity to cheer her. This was just the day to take my quilt squares, set up tables by the fireplace, and engage the ladies in a cheerful project.

I had another thought, since the ladies all love to see Jack whenever he can drop by, I wondered if he could bring some cookies by on his break and brighten their day. When I called his office, June said he was at the Reynold's ranch tending to a horse about to give birth. He shouldn't be long though as he had been there most of the night. "What can I help you with?"

"I hate to bother him after such a long night with no sleep. I thought he might want to take a break sometime this morning and bring some cookies to Haywood House for our quilting bee, but that can happen another day. Please don't bother him with this, June. There will be lots of other chances to pop in on the ladies."

"He may have caught a couple of hours sleep since all went well. I'll give him the message. He loves to run by and visit with everyone when he can. Don't be a stranger around here. We love seeing Bug. She's personality plus and so smart! Take care."

"Thanks so much, June. We'll be by before long."

Bug and I had to drive to Haywood House this morning because of the weather and all I had to carry. As I pulled out of the driveway, I saw Sam on his porch holding a big mug of coffee. I waved and he did, too. But was he looking a little sad and lonely on this dark, damp day? He would definitely be on the top of the Thanksgiving dinner list. I'd have to fill him in on our plans. I thought he needed to look forward to something.

As I popped in the door at Haywood House, I noticed a bit of a buzz in the air. Some of the ladies were gathered around the fireplace chatting away. A couple others were sitting with Geraldine as she painted the next poster for *The King and I* movie night. Mr. Evans was playing checkers with Mr. Abernathy. That was the first time I'd seen that happen. It warmed my heart to see these people engaging with one another. I just wished Mr. Gaston would join in with some of the residents, but I'd continue to give him space. Time to see if I had any takers to design some quilt tops. As I sauntered over to the fireplace, Bug took up her usual spot right next to Geraldine. Geraldine casually reached down to scratch Bug's ears and then gave her a hug. Such love shared between those two. I began pulling out the squares I cut last night and the ladies took notice and eased over to the table to see what I had.

"Has anyone ever quilted before?" I asked. Knowing full well they probably all had.

"Land, Girl, of course we have. We used to meet at the church every Wednesday afternoon to hand quilt whatever quilt was ready to put on the frame. We would spend hours quilting, talking, and catching up on all the gossip in town. Oh, those were good days," said Mrs. Darby with a faraway look in her eyes.

"Well, I don't have a quilt ready for hand quilting, but I do have a bunch of squares that need to be arranged in 5x5 row patterns. I want to make some self-binding lap quilts and I need help. Here's an example of what I'm talking about. This one was made with 5-inch squares, but it's the same idea." And I showed them a quilt I made back in Atlanta. "I thought if anyone wanted to join me, I'm going to lay out some tops in the dining room."

"I'll join you, and you know who else would be good at picking out the squares? Mr. Abernathy. He owned a dress shop in town and has such an eye for color and fashion. I'll go ask him to join us when he finishes his checkers game," Mrs. Darby said as she headed in the direction of the men playing checkers.

A few other inquisitive women came into the dining room to see what we were doing, and before long all the tables were covered with colorful designs. Mr. Abernathy was going around checking all the quilt tops for pleasing color and contrast. This was just what I had hoped would happen. By the time we had to clean up for lunch, we had 8 quilt tops ready for me to sew together. I also had been given tips on the best flannel colors and quality for the backing. Mr. Abernathy had some fabric stored from days when he helped design outfits for ladies. He was going to ask his daughter to bring some of the bolts over one day this week. Another twinkle in an eye!

I had a chance to swing by the animal hospital to make sure Jack hadn't purchased any cookies yet. We could do that next time. As I walked in the door with Bug, I just about collided with Jack.

"Hey, I was just leaving to pick up Sarah's delicious chocolate chip cookies at the diner for your sewing group. Sorry I'm running late. I sat down for a minute in my office and must have fallen asleep."

"I'm so glad you squeezed in some rest. I really didn't want you coming over once June told me about your long night. How is the foal?"

"The foal is fine and mother, too. It's a beautiful, coal-black, filly with a white marking down its nose. I love being a part of bringing new life into the world even though I was not really needed at all. The mother had everything under control. Tell me about your quilting bee."

"I had an idea to bring the ladies together again in another way. I felt many of them might have quilted in their younger days and I want to make lap quilts for everyone. So, I enlisted their help in designing the tops. We have 8 tops ready for me to sew and guess what? Mr. Abernathy jumped in and was a master at putting color and patterns together. He also is going to have his daughter bring over some fabric he used when he had his clothing store. I can't wait to see it."

"Mr. Abernathy was a genius when it came to fashion. We always wondered why he wanted to stay here in this little town of Haywood. People from all around, even as far as Billings, would come here to have him design and make clothes for special occasions. I think he just liked the small-town life," said Jack stifling a yawn.

That was my cue to head home and start sewing. "We'll do the cookie treat another day, if you don't mind. We'll be working on this project for a while, so I'll let you know the next day I recruit my sewing bees. Thanks so much for wanting to help. Come on, Bug, we've got a lot to keep us busy the next couple of days. Bye, Jack, take care of yourself, get some rest," I said as I touched his arm and smiled. He was a good man.

Chapter Twenty

All week the sewing machine had been whirring with breaks for me to cut more squares of fabric. I gasped when I saw the bolts of fabric Mr. Abernathy showed me on Thursday. The cotton material was exquisite. He had many Western themes, as well as, beautiful floral and solid pieces. I told him I couldn't possibly use his gorgeous fabric for the lap quilts, but he said he only wished he had thought of the idea and didn't want all this material to sit in storage and go to waste any longer. We would have the loveliest lap quilts around.

A knock on the door stirred up Bug and caught me off guard. Her deep bark could scare anyone away, but usually when the door was opened, she melted into a puddle waiting to be petted. Such a guard dog! Who could that be at this hour? Glancing at the clock, I saw it was after 11:00pm. Looking out the window, I saw Sam standing on the front porch. What was he doing up so late?

"Sam, what's wrong? Are you feeling okay?"

"I'm just fine except for a lack of sleep. Every night this week you have been up past midnight and it's time you get a decent night's sleep, so I can get a decent night's sleep, too." I saw through Sam's gruffness now and knew it was his way of worrying about me without getting mushy about it. I forgot when I got in my work zone that he watched over me like a mother hen and pretty much knew all my comings and goings. I didn't mind that at all. It was comforting to know someone cared that much.

"Oh Sam, I'm so sorry. I keep losing track of time. Come in for just a second and let me show you what I've been doing into the wee hours of the night. I have about half the blankets made for my friends at Haywood House. I want to have all of them ready for Christmas and once I get started on a project, I'm relentless about finishing it. What do you think? Will they like them?"

Sam stood there staring at a particular blanket with Mr. Abernathy's fabric. The squares had a beautiful deep red, vibrant blue and emerald green nature print with a shiny gold thread weaving through the design. It was one of my favorites. His eyes welled up and he coughed to hide his emotion. "Hank made a dress for my wife out of that material one year for one of our Christmas get-togethers. She looked beautiful in it." He cleared his throat and said, "Well, I just came over to tell you to get some sleep. Bye, Bug," and then he leaned down and scratched her ears, patted my shoulder and left.

"Bye, Sam. I'll turn the lights out soon. Thanks for coming by and checking on me. It means a lot."

Now I knew what I could make Sam for Christmas. I would do my best to make it worthy of his wife's memory.

Chapter Twenty One

It was movie night and everything was ready for *The King and I.* The living room was full and everyone sounded excited to see this classic film. Mrs. Blanton, Jasmine, and I discussed the refreshments ahead of time and decided to have small bags of popcorn and cups of soda with tops and straws during the show, and our scones after the show in the dining room. People could linger and visit, or take a treat back to their rooms if they were tired. Jasmine and I would pass out the popcorn and drinks after everyone was seated. No catastrophe this time! The lights went down and the movie began. The music was beautiful as were the costumes. I just felt transported in time to a magical place. I was so drawn into the story that I barely noticed someone slipping in beside me. It was Jack. He smiled and took my hand. His hand was warm and comforting. A feeling of joy rushed over me. *Thank you, God, for putting this man in my life for whatever reason and however long.* I will remember this moment.

Everyone appeared to be singing along with "Hello Young Lovers" but when "Shall We Dance" began, we were all leaning in feeling the magnetic pull between Deborah Kerr and Yul Brynner. Oh, what a romantic scene, I wasn't the only one sniffling at the end of the show. Mrs. Sharp, who loved the written word and anything classic, was having a hard time holding back her tears, too. Time to cheer everyone up with our official invitation to next week's Thanksgiving dinner.

"Ladies and Gentlemen, we would like to invite anyone who doesn't have family plans to join us for a Thanksgiving dinner next Thursday at 4:00pm in the dining room. Jasmine and I will be hosting this event with Jack's and Sam's assistance. This dinner is open to our Haywood House residents and staff. Bring your appetite and holiday cheer. We are so looking forward to being with all of you.

"Oh, and this Monday I will be back with more squares as we finish building the last of our lap quilts. Your help has been invaluable. What a great team we are! Let's go into the dining room and taste the scrumptious scones Jasmine made for our culture celebration of an English treat."

Jasmine had decorated the tables with baskets of different kinds of scones, blueberry, cinnamon, orange cranberry, and my favorite, chocolate chip. Since it was getting late, we encouraged those who wanted to, to take a scone back to their room for a later snack or for breakfast. Everyone seemed very agreeable to that plan. I had to remember most of the people here were ready for bed or in bed by 9:00pm and it was going on 10:00. Time got away from me. It was so sweet to see the ladies go by and hug Jasmine and thank her for thinking of them in such a special way. Jasmine was indeed a giving soul. She had made extra scones for the staff's breakfast tomorrow and fixed a bag for both Jack and Sam. We cleaned up the dining room, packed up the baskets for Jasmine, and walked out to our cars. Bug clearly wanted to go with Jack, so he told her to load up, and he'd meet me back at my house. Jasmine and I were gloating in the success of the evening, already looking forward to our Christmas movie line up in December. We made plans for next week to cook and bake everything for Thanksgiving.

When I arrived at my house, I saw Jack talking to Sam on his porch. Why was Sam still up? I walked over to see them. "Sam, Jasmine wanted me to give you some scones for a late-night snack. They're really yummy."

"I imagine so if Jasmine made them. Do me a favor and don't stay up till all hours tonight. I'll thank Jasmine in the morning." Sam turned to go, but not before I reached up and kissed him on the cheek.

"Lights out soon, Sam, I promise," I said with a chuckle.

Jack and I walked back to my porch. It was late and I knew we should call it a night, but I was not quite ready to do that. "How about a cup of hot cocoa or a glass of wine out here on the porch?" I asked hopefully.

Jack took my hands in his and the warmth of them spread a peace over me like a soft favorite blanket. I didn't want to move. I had hungered for such a touch but had never known it. It felt so right.

"Ms. James, I would love to spend more of the evening with you, but then we would have to suffer the wrath of Sam. Instead, would you do me the honor of accompanying me to dinner and dancing tomorrow night in Laurel?"

"Dr. Thompson, I would be honored to accompany you to Laurel tomorrow night. Dinner sounds wonderful, but dancing? I'm a little rusty."

"Not to worry. We'll start out with the slow ones," he said with a wink. Then, with a brush of his lips on my forehead, he turned and walked to his truck. "I'll pick you up at 6:30. Bye, Bug!"

I leaned against the door, taking in the feeling of excitement and anticipation. God, have You brought this man into my life to fulfill a longing for love and family? I was getting ahead of myself, but I missed family so much. It just felt so right when I was with him. Dinner and dancing? What in the world was I going to wear?

Chapter Twenty Two

All day Saturday I kept looking at the clock. Luckily, I had plenty to keep me busy. I finished 5 more blankets bringing the total to 21. Four more to go in order to have one for every resident, but I'd like to make one for Mrs. Blanton, too. And then there was Sam's special blanket. I thought I'd make his bigger. There was still time and plenty of fabric squares, thanks to Mr. Abernathy.

I couldn't resist calling Jasmine after the Sip & Savor closed at 2:00pm. When I told her about Jack asking me to dinner and dancing, she didn't seem surprised at all.

"Jasmine, what should I wear? Do you have any idea what restaurant we'll be going to? I'm so excited but terribly nervous. I was used to clubs in Atlanta, not dance halls in Laurel. Well, really, I wasn't that used to clubs. I went one time. It was a disaster and I know people don't wear the same outfits in Montana. Did I say I'm nervous?"

"Yes, twice, and I can hear it in your voice. Calm down and let me explain about dancing in Montana. First of all, you need to wear those fancy boots you bought when we went shopping a couple of weeks ago. Next, ladies wear jeans, a fancy shirt, and jacket or a dress. I would go with a dress. Now, I'm not talking about a little black evening dress, I'm talking about a fancy Western dress. I want you to come over to my house right now and go shopping in my closet. I have lots of dresses that will fit you since we're about the same size. You don't have time to go shopping in Laurel, come back home, and still be rested and ready for your special date. I'll meet you at my house in 20 minutes."

As I pulled up to Jasmine's house, I saw her personality everywhere. There was evidence of many small gardens that must be full of beautiful flowers in the spring and summer, a gorgeous wreath on the barn red door, and curtains at the windows, not modern shutters or blinds. Her house was small and welcoming. I'd been by her house before but never in it. Scooter greeted Bug and me at the door with one bark and a big wag of his tail. As Jasmine opened the door, I felt like I was walking into a *Southern Living* cabin. It was just beautiful and so Jasmine. Soft music was playing and cut flowers were everywhere. How could this talented, giving woman be alone? I wanted to know her story. As I gained her trust and friendship, I was hoping she would open up to me. I guess it was a two-way street, though. I needed to let her in to my life, too.

"Come on back to my bedroom. My house is small, but it suits me, and I have just what I need. And the one thing I really need is a large walk-in closet. I've loved dressing up since I was a little girl. Some things don't change. So, come pick out something that makes you feel special for this memorable night."

Jasmine's bedroom was totally feminine. White lace curtains at the windows, a soft pink hue to the walls, a comforter with delicate pink flowers, and lots of pillows on the bed. There was a nightstand on either side of the bed with delicate lamps and more fresh flowers. Covering the floor, a white shag carpet, so lush that you just want to take off your shoes and sink your toes into it. "Oh, Jasmine, your bedroom is absolutely gorgeous. Did you design it yourself?"

"I did. When you live by yourself, you get to make all the decorating decisions, and I love decorating. Again, I often draw upon my childhood. I have always loved pink and girly, so it was not hard to envision my bedroom when I bought this little house. This is where I pamper myself. But come on in my closet and let's get you something for your big date. After tonight, I can see us shopping again to build up your wardrobe."

One look in Jasmine's closet and I knew I'd find something that would be perfect for dinner and dancing with Jack. My goodness, it was like a dress shop in there!

"Jasmine, I know you like skirts and peasant dresses, but I had no idea there are so many kinds. And all in one place!"

"I told you I am a girly girl!'

After about 30 minutes of trying on different styles of dresses, we both agreed on one with a lacy bodice and a flowing navy and light blue skirt. I had a denim jacket that would go perfectly with this dress. Jasmine gave me a big hug and told me how happy she was that Jack and I were going out on a real date. She had been praying for this, for both Jack and me. "You are two of my favorite people and I want you to be happy together. Now go and finish getting ready. And tell me all about it after church tomorrow!"

I promised I would, and thanked her profusely. Then Bug and I hurried home to put a lot of finishing touches on this girl who hadn't been on a real date in years.

Jack arrived promptly at 6:30pm. I had to admit I was a little worried he would have a vet emergency and have to cancel, but here he was. I opened the door, and standing in front of me, was a man out to win my heart. He had a delicate bouquet of prairie smoke flowers. I knew what they were because of the wildflower lessons I'd gotten from Mrs. Darby. They were a smoky pink color and one of my favorites.

"Thank you so much, Jack. They're beautiful. Let me get a vase, I'll just be a minute." I felt as giddy as a school girl on a first date. Jack was so handsome in his navy jacket over a Western shirt and a string tie. *God, please be with us tonight and make it magical.*

The restaurant was very casual with a totally Montana décor. There was a bar with dark mahogany wood and mirrors behind a whole host of liquor bottles. Lots of people were already at the bar chatting and laughing. Then to the left, the band was setting up by the dance floor. Jack and I found a table off to the opposite side where it was a little quieter and the lighting was dimmer. He suggested a cowboy steak, baked potato, and salad with a beer for him and a glass of red wine for me.

After some easy conversation about antics at Haywood House, plus some of his recent vet adventures, he said it was time for me to share a little about what brought me to Haywood. I found myself opening up in a way I never had in the past. I told Jack about my childhood and the loss of my mother. How Grams took me in and raised me until she could no longer take care of herself, let alone me. I wanted to share everything with this kind man, but something brought me up short in telling him about my heart condition. Was I afraid of scaring him away? Luckily for me, at that time a favorite song was being played by the band, a *Honeysuckle Rose* song, and it was slow, too. He took my hand and we weaved our way to the dance floor. The singer's rendition of "Loving You is Easier" was hauntingly beautiful, and I couldn't help but put my head on Jack's shoulder and melt into the easy way we moved together. I didn't want this song to end. But end it did, and I looked into Jack's eyes and found comfort, safety, and kindness. That was enough for now.

The night was everything I had hoped for and yet over too soon. We danced to a few more Willie Nelson songs, and I even tried line dancing. That I would have to work on in the privacy of my living room. Jack was a good sport and very comfortable on the dance floor. He promised we would come back again and I said, "As long as we could dance away the calories in that huge steak."

Back home, Jack walked me to the door, and I let Bug out to

greet us. You would have thought we had been gone for a week, but that's how she was. Her little body wiggled all over the place and her tail was moving a mile a minute, so happy to be reunited again. Jack squatted down to scratch her ears and love on her a bit. Loving animals was second nature to him. After Bug settled down, Jack stood up, drew me close to him, and kissed me. So tender. He looked at me in a gentle way and said, "I think I have been waiting all this time for you." He brushed my lips again, squeezed my hand, and left.

I called Bug to the porch, waved goodbye, and slowly sank into the rocking chair. I was unsure just what he meant exactly, but I think it was a good thing. I hugged my knees to my chest, closed my eyes, and thanked God for the magic.

Chapter Twenty Three

I loved this little Methodist church in town. The congregation was not large but the people were some of the friendliest folks I had ever been around. The service was at 10:00am every Sunday morning and very traditional. To me that was what was so special about Trinity Methodist. I felt Grams close to me when I entered the sanctuary. She always took me to her church every Sunday. I remembered the hymns sung there. The same ones were sung here. I slid into the pew and sat next to Jasmine giving her a thumbs up about last night. She patted my knee and said, "Details, later." Pastor Michael had been at this church for 15 years. That's not very common, as Methodist ministers were usually moved around after about 6 years. Everyone here loved Michael. Both he and the congregation were happy he had stayed all these years. *God, You have brought me to a place where I can learn more about Your word, practice being a disciple for You, and share the kindness that seems to be evident with everyone in this small town.*

Pastor Michael's sermon was on gratitude, living a life that was rich in appreciation and thankfulness. Only then could we come to know what Jesus tried to teach us about grace. How we could truly offer compassion and kindness to others. He talked about Mother Teresa's favorite Bible verse, Matthew 25:40, "Truly I tell you, whatever you did for one of the least of these brothers and sisters of mine, you did for me." My thoughts strayed to our Thanksgiving dinner and I was overwhelmed with tears. You brought me here to really understand a servant's life. It is so much richer than my life back in Atlanta. Though materially I have less, in what counts, I have so much more.

Chapter Twenty Four

Jasmine and I had met at her place earlier in the week to put the finishing touches on our Thanksgiving menu. All we had to do today was heat up the casseroles and dressing, roast the turkey, make the mashed potatoes, and bake the pies. Whew! Now, as I awakened to Thanksgiving Day, I was greeted with a cold, dismal, icy morning. The best part of a day like this was the warmth we felt as we gathered together as a family. I could hardly wait to scramble out of bed, throw on my worn, but warm, bathrobe and feed Bug. Her quick trip outside brought in a rush of cold air and sleet clinging to her coat. She was still getting used to Montana weather!

I didn't have to be over at Haywood House until 11:00am, so I decided a fire in the fireplace would knock the chill out of the air and make it cozy inside. I started a big pot of coffee, heated up the cinnamon roll Jasmine sent home with me last night, and turned on my CD player with Dino softly playing my favorite hymns on the piano. Coffee was ready, so I took a big mug to my chair by the fireplace, snuggled in with a soft quilt pulled up around Bug and me, and thought about all that had brought me to this moment in my life. I used to feel pretty sorry for myself growing up with Mom so sick and dying at a young age, and Grams taking me in but also not in the best of health. For a long time, I decided to just rely on myself, because everyone I loved had left me. But You never left me, God, and because I learned to lean on You, and trust You, and follow You, I am here now. The peace and love I felt in this place were indescribable. Each day was a gift to be treasured and a chance to pay forward this incredible life I was now living. Oh, I missed Mom and Grams so much. I would love to share this life with them. I needed to honor their memory by each day being a blessing to others. They both sacrificed a lot for me, and through their example of living selflessly, they helped make me the strong independent woman I was today. They taught me to always turn to You, God. I strayed from that advice for a while when I was on my own in Atlanta, but now, I saw their wisdom. I had so much to be grateful for in this life I had in Haywood. I had come to know the most amazing people. They were just everyday people, but having a relationship with them, getting to know their likes and dislikes, their talents, their memories, their loves, their heartache, meant I had invested in them. I had come to love them. I thought putting a wall up between people and myself would protect me from the sadness of loss. I realized I was missing out on the greatest part of life, love. There would be more loss, but I now realized the joy of unconditional love. For that I had a lot to be thankful.

Chapter Twenty Five

Despite the dreariness outside, inside Haywood House, there was a buzz of festive activity. A blazing fire in the living room was keeping the damp out and lending a warm glow. The Thanksgiving Day Macy's Parade marched across the TV, and a good many people were gathered around enjoying the beautiful floats. Jasmine was in the kitchen making the pecan pies, and I was ready for my assignments.

As soon as the residents finished a light lunch in the dining room, I began turning the tables into a *Southern Living* display of autumn beauty. Jasmine had the touch when it came to decorating, but I was a fast learner and not too shabby when it came to fixing up a place. Each table was adorned with a white linen tablecloth, a centerpiece with lush fall foliage, an almost real looking fake candle (for safety reasons), chocolate leaves wrapped in shiny colorful foil scattered around the centerpiece, beautiful rust-colored napkins, and Haywood House's best dinnerware. We had selected some instrumental songs from the 40s and 50s to play softly in the background. Jasmine, Jack, and I would do all the serving as the staff members were our guests today. In all, we would have 24 people, including Sam and Mrs. Blanton eating with us. The smells from the kitchen were mouth-watering. The pies were baked and cooling and the casseroles and dressing were in the ovens. Jack brought the turkeys, and gravy from Jasmine's cafe when he came at 3:00pm. Everything was falling into place perfectly. I peeked out from the dining room to see Sam visiting with Geraldine and Mr. Abernathy. Knowing they both would give her attention, Bug found her place between Geraldine and Sam. My heart filled with so much love. Tears streamed down my face. Goodness, I'd never get a handle on these emotions! But it was all good.

At 4:00pm Jack invited everyone to come to the dining room. The murmurs, smiles, and sparkle in everyone's eyes made all our efforts to make this a special holiday for those who no longer had a chance to celebrate with family, worth it. We were family now. What a wonderous and big family we were, too. After the initial astonishment of the transformed dining room, everyone found a seat and began talking at once. We had divided the 24 guests into three tables of 8. They seemed to naturally find a place to feel comfortable. I just really believed these last couple of months of renewed activities, encouragement of talents, and chances to work together had brought everyone closer. Even the staff seemed comfortable with our new family. Jack drew everyone's attention after a few minutes of chit-chat.

"Ladies and Gentlemen, what a beautiful gathering we have today. There is so much for us to be grateful for on this Thanksgiving Day. I look around and see the faces of long-standing friends, people who have helped build this unique town, people with gifts and talents so readily shared. I am incredibly moved by the outpouring of love and acceptance you have shown to our newest member of Haywood. Without her vision and heart, we would not be celebrating like this today. She came here to make a difference in your lives, believing that your wisdom and your abilities still matter, even though you are no longer as independent as you once were. This isn't your home in the sense of where you raised your family, but it is now your home where you remain honored and respected for your place in Haywood. Let's now give a warm Haywood thank you to Claire James for today, for yesterday, and all the tomorrows."

A huge round of applause filled the room. I looked out at the faces of these dear people. People who had become so important to me in such a short time. The faces were lined and aged with a lifetime of trials and joys. They were once young and carefree, then dream-filled adults, responsible parents, and hardworking members of society. They put their future on hold for others they loved and yet they still found fulfillment. I wanted these years to also be memorable and happy in a different way from when they were independent, and yet, still meaningful. I didn't know why I bothered with make-up. Tears were flowing again and my heart was racing. I looked at Jack and there were tears in his eyes, too. This man was kindness through and through.

"I am so humbled by Jack's words about me. I came here a little naive in that I never had any formal background in working with an assisted-living facility. I just had a dream. You have welcomed me into your town and your lives and given me the kind of life I could only hope for. I love each and every one of you. Thank you from the bottom of my heart." Thank goodness Jasmine was there to hand me tissues!

"Now, we don't want to wait a minute longer for this feast that our own fabulous Jasmine has put together with Claire's help. Let's give Jasmine a round of applause." Jack led them in another hearty round which assured me they knew what a treat was in store for them.

Jack continued, "Let's bow our heads and give thanks. Dear Father, we come together humbly asking for your blessings on this Thanksgiving Day. We come as a family thanking you for bringing us together. Keep us close to You and to each other. We thank You for this bounty before us and for those who have prepared it. In

Your loving Son's name, Amen."

The dinner was superb. Many people had seconds even though we reminded them to save room for pie. We all took our time enjoying the feast and each other's company. I do believe Mrs. Blanton had the best time of all. She took it upon herself to circulate the room, talking to every resident and staff member. I noticed she spent a little extra time talking with Mr. Gaston. I was so happy to see he joined us today, although he didn't open up to anyone else, I was aware of. What was his story?

An ease seemed to permeate the room as if it was infused with a spirit of holiness and grace. A sanctuary where everyone felt included, welcomed, and worthy. While no one was in a rush to leave, after 2 hours of eating and visiting, people were ready for that holiday nap. Lingering long enough for hugs and promises of seeing each other tomorrow, they slowly started towards their rooms. I didn't want to spoil this comradery, so I just waved from the kitchen with plans to see them all soon.

Sam hung back with Jack, Jasmine, and me to help with the clean-up. We were bone-tired and a bit giddy after all was said and done. Someone mentioned Christmas dinner and got a rousing NOOOO from the others! We'd need to ponder that idea after some rest. With the dining room and kitchen cleaned and ready for breakfast in the morning, we decided to pack up some leftovers for the skeletal staff on Friday. Since it was still part of the holiday, only a few workers would be on duty. I definitely wanted to leave Mrs. Blanton some cranberry apple crunch, as she had a second helping at dinner. It really was her favorite. I couldn't wait to put my feet up, and Jasmine was right in there with me. It was decided, as soon as we were done, to meet at Sam's for an evening toddy and the last of the football games. A perfect end to a perfect day.

Chapter Twenty Six

Indulging herself in a much-needed vacation, Jasmine closed down the Sip & Savor for the rest of the weekend. We talked at Sam's about going shopping in Billings but not until Saturday. We both wanted Friday as a day of rest. I promised to do just that since I had a hard time keeping my eyes open during the second half of the football game. The long hours of working on the quilts, helping with the meal preparation, and making sure everything went off without a hitch for the Thanksgiving dinner were taking its toll. I was exhausted but so happy. Jack, ever the gentleman, saw Jasmine to her car and then walked me to my door. The temperature had dropped as the day drew to a close and now it was below freezing. A slight wind and delicate snowflakes filled the air. I shivered as we stood at my door, and Jack pulled me close to him as I laid my head on his shoulder. He held me tightly, so much so that the wind could not penetrate nor chill this moment. I felt safe in his arms as if a guardian angel had been sent to wipe away fears and doubts and to cloak me in a downy wrap. I didn't want to move. Soon Jack tipped my chin and gently kissed my lips. Don't leave yet I wanted to say, but words would break the spell. I touched his cheek and slowly pulled away. He opened the door and Bug and I slipped inside, and the spell was not broken.

Only my cold nose poked out of the warm comforter as I slowly awoke Friday morning. There was definitely a change in the weather. This must be Montana cold, as I felt it creeping in through the window sash. Snow had fallen through the night blanketing the yard where not a footstep or animal track could be seen. I was always amazed at the quietness snow brings. It was as if God was saying, hush now, and just take in this beauty for a little while before life started up again. Wrapping myself in my robe and finding my slippers, I headed to the kitchen to make a pot of coffee, and then to the living room to start up a fire. This could be a stay in my pajama's day! I opened the back door to let Bug outside and a frigid rush of air greeted us. She was not anxious to go out but she had no choice. With the thermometer hovering around 5 degrees, I couldn't blame her. That was way too cold for a Georgia girl like me! I was mesmerized by the winter beauty, though. Snow was clinging to the tree branches like cotton and coated the bushes like a white shimmering blanket. Taking in this white wonderland, I had to pause and thank God for another of the many ways He showed His love for this world He created. This stark beauty was part of His power that was not lost on me.

Thanks to Sam's tutorial on building a fire, I soon had a blazing warmth welcoming Bug and me. With coffee in hand and a favorite quilt to wrap around us in our chair, we snuggled in when my phone rang. The caller was Sam. What could be wrong? He never called me. "Sam, are you alright?"

"Of course, I am. I just want to let you know to stay inside today. You don't mess around with this kind of cold. The temperature is supposed to drop some more to -10 with wind, so don't go anywhere. I know you like to be on the go, but not today. Do you have enough firewood?"

"Sam, I have plenty of wood and all those Thanksgiving leftovers to eat. Bug and I promise to stay inside. Thanks for checking on me."

"Well, I want you to be safe. Bye." And with that he hung up. I loved that man. He was becoming the father I never knew and maybe I was the daughter he never had. We had found each other and a remarkable bond was growing. I was learning to respect his advice and understand his gruff nature. Under all that toughness was a man who cared about me and knew I needed to be taught the ways of this strange Western world. I thought I had given him a purpose, just like I was trying to do for the people at Haywood House. I wanted him to understand my nature too, though, and my need to be a fixer. The connection I felt to the people I had met since coming to Haywood grew stronger every day. This was where I was meant to be. This was where I could make a difference. I can't do this alone God, and only with Your guidance and blessing can I bring a true light to their lives.

Hours passed and the calmness and serenity of the day seeped into my soul. The need that brought me here, the need to find a deeper meaning to life, the need to heal from my losses, and the need to follow Your plan, God, seemed to be falling into place. I couldn't remember being this happy and this peaceful. Truly, I had found what I had been looking for since Grams passed away. I could almost see her nodding and smiling, knowing I was going to be alright.

Chapter Twenty Seven

In Atlanta, after a ten-inch snow like we had yesterday and the bitter cold temperature, we would have been housebound for a week. Not here in Montana. Jasmine called Saturday morning and said she'd pick me up at 10:00am in her truck. The roads would be cleared and as long as we bundled up, we'd be fine to go shopping in Billings. I had to trust her to know how to navigate this weather and that stores wouldn't be shut down because of a little snowstorm. This was the beginning of winter, and I was finding out how to respect it and also live in it. It was still below freezing and, of course, Bug would stay in the house. Sam was going to check on her and let her out a couple of times because Jasmine said we wouldn't be back till after supper. I wouldn't be surprised if Bug stayed over at Sam's all day. In fact, I hoped she would. They'd be good company for each other. What would I do without him next door?

A million shiny diamonds shimmered outside the house as I opened my front door to Jasmine's horn. I could take in this beauty all day long, but the cold wouldn't let me. I hurried to the truck excited to spend the day with my new best friend and, now, personal fashion expert. She had two thermos bottles of heavenly coffee and, of course, a still warm cinnamon roll for each of us. One could never tire of her cinnamon rolls.

Belted in and ready to shop, we had about an hour's drive to Billings. Luckily, the roads were cleared early in Montana, so we would have smooth sailing.

We chit-chatted about the Thanksgiving dinner and how everything went as planned. Mrs. Blanton was the most relaxed I had ever seen her and that seemed to have a positive effect on the staff and residents. Maybe this would be a turning point for her to look upon the people there more as family. I knew she had to set and enforce rules and regulations, and maintain a professional relationship, nevertheless, she had a compassionate side, too. I'd never heard her mention any family members, and she jumped at the chance to stay for our Thanksgiving dinner. I'd have to ask about family ties. Haywood House might become the family she had been missing.

Jasmine causally asked about Jack and how things were going with us since the dinner and dance date. "He seems to be pretty attentive and available. Up till now, Jack seemed more eager to spend his time with four legged creatures," Jasmine teased.

"I'm not sure where we stand with each other. All I do know is that when we are together, it seems right. Neither of us wants to rush into a relationship. I think we want to see where all this leads. I'm not going anywhere and neither is he, so time is on our side. I do know I haven't felt this way about anyone before. Jack has such a caring and gentle way about him. I can see it in the way he talks about the animals he treats, the way he loves Bug, and when he reminisces about Geraldine and her children. He loves this town and the people here. They have a history together. I'm new to all of this. I need to find my own way in Haywood. I want the people to trust me and know they can depend on me. I want them to know I am here for them, but that will take time. Sometimes I feel like I come rushing in like there is a bee in my bonnet, but I think that is because I know I don't have many years with these precious people.

I learned that with Grams, and that's a lesson I want to remember here. At first, I felt like I had all kinds of time with Grams, even though she went to assisted-living as soon as I left for college. I didn't see or want to acknowledge how much she had declined. I knew there would be time for another visit. I thought, if she could just get over that cold, she'd feel like herself again. I gave her ideas of things to do with her time, and thought that was enough to jump start her enthusiasm and zest for life. Sometimes depression can set in for elderly people. What used to be an independent spirit in them now needs another person to help them find meaning and purpose. I want to make what used to be second nature to them achievable again. Albeit not with the same energy level and productive outcome, but they need to know their value has not been lost. They have not been set aside. Their wisdom is so worthy. You don't live 70, 80, 90 years and not be able to share what made it a good life with those of us who need those life lessons. Oh, Jasmine, do you see why I don't want a day to go by without showing them how much I value them and respect them for those lessons, which makes me a little crazy and why my pace is to have it done yesterday?"

"Claire, you have made an impact on our little town like no one else has. Sam comes in the Sip & Savor every morning to help with my setup, smiling and humming and letting me know how late you stayed up the night before, keeping him from a good night's sleep, all the while knowing he has someone to watch over again. When his wife died and he moved to town, he became pretty much a hermit. He stayed in his house even though he had lived his whole life outdoors. I guess a kind of depression took over and the gruff exterior replaced the confident generous cowboy. He wouldn't let anyone into his sorrow except Jack from time to time. They spent a lot of nights together, two lonesome cowboys. Jack finally convinced him I needed help with my café and that's when he started coming every morning at 6:00am to put the chairs down, set the flower jars on each table, sweep the floors and the doorstep, and grab the first cup of coffee. I didn't really need his help, but seeing him with a purpose, much like what you are doing with the people at Haywood House, meant so much to me. He needed to know that someone depended on him. You and Bug have wormed your way into his heart, and glimpses of the old Sam are showing through now. He's always been tough, but Sandy brought out the compassion in him. When she passed away, he left that side of himself buried with her. He was so lost and couldn't bear to stay out at the ranch by himself. He sold off some of the acreage, but kept the house and surrounding land. People are always trying to get Sam to sell the whole place, but he can't bring himself to do that; however, he can't bring himself to live there either. Living in town is best for him because Jack and I and a few other friends can keep an eye on him. He was a different man before he moved to town, though. It was like the zest for life escaped him."

A thought crossed my mind as Jasmine talked about Sam. Would he take me out to see his ranch? Would that be too painful, or a push in the right direction? I didn't want to lose him as a neighbor, but maybe in the spring he might want to spend time out there, puttering around and rediscovering his purpose. Hmm, another project for me?

"And then there's Jack. Everyone knows Jack. He has grown up here and except for the years he was away for college and vet school, he has only lived here. As you know, Jack is everyone's son at Haywood House. He loves them like parents and does what all good sons do, works hard, lives a clean life, and cares for them. The problem is that Jack cares too much for others and doesn't take care of himself. I have seen a change in him since you arrived. As many times as we have all tried to coax him into joining us for dinner, holidays, ball games, and just general fun get-togethers, he always begs off and goes to check on one of his animals. If you need him, he is there, but if you want him to join the fun, he's gone. It's like he has been afraid to let go and live life, or he just hasn't found the right person to live that life with. Lately, though, he has been more available, thanks to a certain Claire James. It's wonderful to see no matter where it leads. Maybe to just a close friendship and maybe more. We just want to see him happy."

"And what about you Jasmine? What about your happiness?" I asked.

Jasmine hesitated, "That's a story for another time because we are here in Billings and have a mission to accomplish! Get this girl some decent Western wear!"

Chapter Twenty Eight

Billings was the largest city in Montana, but there was no comparison to Atlanta, thank goodness. I was not looking forward to the crazy traffic and hectic driving a big city affords. Luckily, it was not that way in Billings. Big city Billings was still a part of the beauty of Montana. Snow-covered mountains defined this area; however, wide-open spaces were just a stone's throw away.

Jasmine knew her way around and soon we pulled up to a strip of Western shops. Gypsy Wind was the perfect boutique to begin our search for my new look. This store was amazing, totally unique looks with lots of color and girly fashion, just what I wanted. How was I so fortunate to have Jasmine be my stylist? Her eye for design and beauty surpassed my lack of Western fashion sense. Hours flew by and we had about 10 different outfits ranging from super casual jeans and flannel tops to flowing flowery dressy looks. Top all that off with shoes, boots, and jewelry, I was in heaven. She wasn't done yet. Off to SOMETHINGchic, another favorite of hers with really good prices.

I was fading a little so we decided to grab a bite of lunch. At The Sassy Biscuit Co., I took Jasmine's advice and ordered the nana porridge. Never had I tasted oatmeal and granola so deliciously comforting. Maybe I'd better go up one size with my new outfits!

Eating like this was sure to put on pounds.

We talked about Haywood House over coffee and planned our next movie nights. In December, all our movies would be Christmas themed and we would show one every Friday night, so that would mean picking 3. We decided upon *White Christmas*, *It's a Wonderful Life*, and *A Christmas Carol*, all movies of their era. Refreshments of hot cocoa and cookies would be in keeping with a holiday theme.

While in Billings, I wanted to pick up Christmas napkins and small dessert plates. All our brainstorming had me so excited I could hardly wait to implement our ideas. We decided to look for red flannel stockings to hang on everyone's doorknob. Every few days I would put something in the stocking for each person. Our list included candy, of course, lotion, Kleenex, a book mark, pen, notepad, Post-It Notes, keychain, Christmas ornament, small battery-operated candle, soap, calendar, toothpaste, toothbrush, and tea bags. How special it would be for them to find little gifts to brighten their holiday. Jasmine planned to make miniature cinnamon rolls to include in the stockings on one of the days, too. A trip to Laurel later in the month would finish out our list of treasures we couldn't find today. It was so much fun being Santa's helpers!

Jasmine wanted to take me to one more clothing store. At Sagebrush Trading Post in the mall, which had lots of feminine Western wear, I found a beautiful soft blue sweater and pants outfit with jewelry to match and one more pair of boots! I was finding boots were the footwear of choice here as sandals were in Georgia. Boots were pretty comfortable, though, I'd weigh in on that more down the road. I was set for a long time, or at least all winter, with everything we found today.

With still a couple of hours before dinner and heading home before it was too late, we turned our attention to the stocking stuffers. Target was our best place for these goodies, so we loaded up on as much as we could there. I wanted to find some beautiful ribbon to wrap around the quilts I made for everyone. Jasmine was looking for holiday and wintry touches for the Sip & Savor. As happened, when we were together, we had another idea for Haywood House. We could hang a grapevine wreath on everyone's door, and every season or holiday change the decorations to suit the look for that time. For now, we needed red ribbon, some greenery, a cow bell, and pinecones. I bought some extra pieces for Mrs. Darby to use for the centerpieces and the front door wreaths. I would let her and her friends work their magic.

We went to a couple more stores to gather our supplies and then decided to grab a quick bite of dinner before heading home. It was after 6:00pm and dark with the windchill dipping down to single digits. I trusted Jasmine to know when we needed to start home. We ate a delicious hamburger at Montana's Rib and Chop House and now it was after 7:00pm. Jasmine told me to call Sam and Jack to let them know we were on our way home from Billings. I reached Sam on the phone and left a text message for Jack. I was curious about the need to call them. Jasmine said it was important in this type of weather to let someone know your whereabouts and timeline. I was beginning to understand how dangerous winter weather could be if you were not smart and careful. Her truck had all the safety equipment needed for a breakdown in bad weather such as blankets, flashlights, flares, sand, a shovel, water, extra hats, scarves and gloves, and handwarmers. It didn't take long to get in a major dilemma with freezing temperatures, wind, ice, and snow. Letting someone know where you were and when you'd be home lessened the chance to be stranded too long off the road or in a ditch.

"Your job as shotgun is to watch out for deer. They probably aren't moving much in this weather, but it pays to be cautious. Sam and Jack know if we are not home by 8:30, to come looking for us," Jasmine said cautiously.

That made me too nervous to delve into Jasmine's story. I

wanted her to pay attention to the road, so only small talk ensued. We chatted about past Christmases, our favorite Christmas song, family traditions, and traditions in Haywood. The wind picked up and I noticed the truck was having a hard time keeping us warm. Jasmine seemed to grip the steering wheel more firmly and leaned towards the windshield. It wasn't snowing, thank goodness, but the wind was blowing drifts making it harder to see at times. God, be with us and keep us safe. I'm learning about this unbridled land and gaining more respect in each situation in which I find myself.

"Jasmine, did I put us in danger by shopping too late in Billings? We were having so much fun, I never thought about the weather and driving conditions coming home."

Jasmine shook her head, "You did nothing of the sort. First of all, I have lived here all my life and can usually recognize dangerous weather conditions. This is typical of a wintry night but most often later in January. I'm being careful because we have a truck load of killer fashions and Christmas cheer! We have to get all of that home safely. Don't worry, I'm going slowly because of the wind, but we're still making pretty good time."

Just then, movement up ahead on my side of the truck caught my eye. "Jasmine, an animal ahead on the right!"

Jasmine immediately hit the brakes. We skidded to the right just as a deer dashed past the front of the truck, then another. I screamed as the truck slammed into the snowbank off the road and came to a sudden stop. Both of us sat for a second taking in the toll of our situation. We hadn't hit the deer or anything else for that matter. We were just stuck against a snowbank on the side of the road.

"Are you alright, Claire?" Jasmine asked tentatively.

"I'm fine. I didn't mean to scream. I'm so sorry. I just didn't think they would run right in front of us like that," I responded shakily.

"You did the right thing. If you hadn't alerted me, I would have hit them for sure. Now we need to see if we can get the truck back on the road. With all the snow we had yesterday and no chance for any melting, the side of the road on this stretch has a pretty deep bank of snow. We're only 20 minutes from Haywood, so, if we need to call for help, it won't be long."

"Should I call Jack or Sam now?"

"Let me see if I can back out first. Since we missed the deer, we won't have to worry about the truck being damaged.

Jasmine tried to back the truck up out of the snowbank but the side of the road was slick. She rocked the truck back and forth getting a little traction, but still not enough to free us. "I need to put down some sand under the tires to try to get extra traction. Stay in the truck. I'll be back in a couple of minutes. Don't get out. You're not dressed as warmly as I am."

Just as Jasmine opened the back of her truck, another truck slowly approached us on the opposite side of the road. Oh no, two stranded females alone on a deserted highway in the dark with a stranded truck. We were in so much trouble! I jumped out of the truck and yelled over the howling wind, "Jasmine, quick! Get in the truck. Someone is coming!"

The truck pulled over in front of us and stopped. My heart was beating out of my chest. In Atlanta, this would not be a good scenario. Please God, let this be a good Samaritan. At that moment, Jasmine yelled, "Jack, thank goodness you're here. We just missed a couple of deer but found this snowbank. Could you help me attach a tow rope and pull us out of this?"

"Go ahead and get back in the truck and I'll let you know when to back it. Claire, I love coming to your rescue, again!" Jack gave me his irresistible grin, patted the truck door and I asked,

"How did you know we needed help?"

"After I got your message, I just decided to drive slowly toward Billings since it's such a blustery night. I didn't expect you to have a problem, but you never know with wintery weather. Plus, I had already gotten three phone calls from Sam, so I decided to put both our fears to rest. I told him I would find you and follow you home. Girl, you can get into some interesting predicaments. Sure keeps life interesting." And with that he proceeded to free us from the snowbank.

Back on the road I realized how cold I was, as my teeth were chattering and my body was shivering. The heater in the truck was on full blast, but I couldn't get warm. Jasmine seemed fine even though she had been out in the cold while I had been sitting inside most of the time.

"Layering is really important out here in the winter. It's my fault for not telling you what to wear on a day like this. Always wear long underwear, a long sleeve shirt, wool sweater, and a down jacket. I have on wool socks and my insulated boots too. We need to get you home by the fire and warm you up. Next trip we'll have to shop for long underwear and wool socks."

At home in bed with socks, winter pajamas, and my down comforter I was finally cozy warm. Thinking back over the day, I had to smile and thank You, God, for all the good things that happened. Jasmine and I had a wonderful time together. I found a dear friend at last. We connected on so many levels, our love for others, our passion for helping, understanding the needs of the people at Haywood House, our creative minds, and our energy to get things done. You have brought her into my life and me into hers. We're good for each other. We have so many ideas to implement over the next few weeks. Already we have planned a day to get started. And then there was Jack. He cared enough to come looking for us even without knowing we needed him. I didn't remember anyone ever coming to my rescue like Jack had. How did he know? And Sam, he worried like a dad over his little girl. That must be what it feel like to have a dad. I was so blessed.

Chapter Twenty Nine

The first week in December was fun and hectic. Mrs. Blanton helped by hanging all the stockings on everyone's doorknob with the first surprise inside. Seeing everyone's joy over something so small was heart-warming. Mrs. Blanton agreed to have the staff fill the stockings at night every third day. I think she was as excited as Jasmine and I were about our Christmas ideas. The wreaths were all hung on everyone's door with the evergreen and pinecones and the beautiful bows Jasmine made. What couldn't that girl do? Geraldine had started on the three movie posters. The Christmas selections were well received and the holiday spirit was filling Haywood House. Bug and I spent a few hours every day visiting, listening to stories of Christmases long ago, and playing checkers.

I thought we could find enough bridge players to start a table. Grams loved playing bridge which was how I learned by sitting with her friends and watching. Sometimes I filled in when someone was late or sick or left early. I gained enough knowledge of the game to play in college, but didn't know anyone who played when I went to work in Atlanta, so I was very rusty. Mrs. Biggs gathered two other ladies, and our first bridge game was underway. Her cards were pretty worn and not the large print needed to play with some failing eyesight, so I made a note to pick up some new cards the next time

I went to Laurel. I had forgotten how many rules there were for playing this intricate game. We had to establish some guidelines for everyone because it had been a while since any of us had played. Luckily, everyone was just glad to play this beloved game again. Party bridge rules ruled! We didn't need to be cutthroat or use Blackwood or Stayman bidding rules, but we were competitive and loved getting that high score.

I also loved spending more time with Louise and Grace. They were two sisters who hadn't been at Haywood House very long. From what I gathered, they were both spinsters who took care of their parents for many years. After both parents passed away within weeks of each other, the sisters both decided they were worn out from caregiving and were ready to be taken care of themselves. Although neither Louise or Grace had any physical limitations, they appreciated having three daily meals prepared for them, no dishes to wash, no linens to launder, and no rooms to clean. When they found out about the bridge table needing two players, they lit up like a Christmas tree. Now they could share a pastime together. I was totally enjoying playing with these ladies, and I had noticed Mr. Abernathy showing an interest in our card group.

"Mr. Abernathy, I need to leave early today to meet Jasmine. Could you take over my hand to finish out this progression? I really hate to end our game. If you can fill in for me, I sure would appreciate it." I was counting on Mr. Abernathy to know how to play and judging from the interest he had shown when our group met, I was sure he had played before.

"It's been a long time since I held a bridge hand, but I might be able to muddle my way through for you today." And with an eagerness in his eyes, he deftly took over and had now become the fourth regular at the 2:00pm bridge game every day except Sunday at Haywood House.

When I realized how much those four people looked forward to their bridge game each day, I decided to start a Rummikub group. Anyone could play this fun tile game, so having a background of knowledge like the bridge players was not necessary. I checked on Amazon for large numbered tiles and ordered two games. Mrs. Blanton had two card tables set up in the library, and I was able to coax Mrs. Sharp and Ms. Sally into finding four more people to learn how to play. We scheduled playing time for Tuesday and Thursday at 2:00pm.

I realized that lunch at 12:00, then nap time till 2:00pm, was a good schedule. Having something to look forward to in the afternoon kept everyone more involved and interacting with one another. Eventually two more people could join the Rummikub group and then roughly half the residents would have a group activity to look forward to most days.

Not everyone liked this type of involvement. Geraldine was happy painting by herself, but she was where others gathered. Some were content by the fireplace reading. It still saddened me to know about 10 of the residents went back to their rooms after each meal and basically stayed alone. At least the Friday night movies were enjoyed by all. I still needed to come up with some other ways to include the reluctant people. I knew not everyone felt comfortable around people other than relatives, but this was their new home and finding a connection to someone else was vital. Surely there was another link to bring these 10 together for more than a Friday night movie. Maybe Jack and Sam had ideas about the type of activities people who had grown up in Montana might enjoy at this stage in their life.

At home each night I worked on the quilts. It was a peaceful time for me with the amber glow of a fire burning and soft music from Dino playing. *Christmas... A Time for Peace* was my all-time favorite Christmas CD. I remembered Sam's first words to me, "And no loud music!" No, Sam, there wouldn't be loud music coming from my house. Just beautiful instrumentals, gospel music, Broadway soundtracks, and Judy Garland classics.

I had slowly acclimated to the cold and winter white everywhere outside. It just made it cozier in here. I loved to look outside and see gentle flakes falling and the untouched white landscape just after a snow. The quiet beauty took my breath away.

I was down to the last two quilts when I heard a knock on the door. I couldn't believe Sam was going to rake me over the coals tonight, it was only 8:30pm, so I was certainly not keeping him up past his bedtime. I was hesitant to open the door, though. Jack always let me know when he came, so who would be knocking on my door this time of night? Haywood was a safe town and crime was almost nonexistent here, but I came from Atlanta. Opening my door at night back home when I wasn't expecting anyone would just not happen. I shook these thoughts because surely it could only be a friend. When I tentatively open the door, I gasped! "Oh my gosh, Cal?"

"Claire, hi, I'm so glad it's you opening this door. I wasn't sure if I really had the right address, or even the right town, but I guess I do!" Cal exclaimed with relief.

"Cal, what are you doing here? How did you find me? This is crazy. How did you get here? Did you drive? Oh my gosh, Cal, it's freezing outside, come on in and warm up." As I pulled him inside, I couldn't help but give him a big hug and start to wonder what he was doing here? Calvin was a former co-worker from Atlanta, a strapping 6-foot-tall fellow with sandy brown hair that fell in his deep chocolate brown eyes, a square chin that fooled you in to thinking he was the strong silent type, a very good-looking man I always thought of as a younger brother.

"Come over by the fire and warm your hands. If you're going to be outside in the winter in Montana, you have to wear thermal gloves or at least some kind of protection. You have a lot of explaining to do, buddy." Just then I heard another knock on the door. What was going on? As I opened the door, in walked Sam.

"Hey, I just remembered I was going to borrow some coffee from you, cause I'm out. Do you have any?" Sam asked as he stared down Calvin and waited for an explanation of who he was and what was he doing here.

"Sam, let me introduce Calvin Johnson, a former co-worker from Atlanta."

Just then Cal stepped forward, offered his cold chapped hand and said, "Hello, Cal Johnson, it's a pleasure to meet you."

Sam reluctantly shook his hand, "Sam Rainer. I live next door. Just what do you think you are doing here this time of night, barging in on this lady without any warning?"

"You are right sir, it's not very polite to come unannounced. It's just that I've been driving for four days and finally found Claire, and just couldn't wait to see her. I certainly didn't mean to upset anyone. It's just so nice to see a familiar face. Please accept my apology for disrupting the evening. It does make me feel good to know that Claire has a neighbor so attentive to strangers coming to her door. First of all, back in Atlanta, Claire probably would have had a chain on the door if she opened it at all. And secondly, a neighbor would not have come checking on her unless he heard bloodcurdling screams. Thanks so much for watching out for her."

Jack continued to glare at Calvin, "Claire, do you really know this guy? Or do I need to call Jack?"

What in the world was he thinking? "No Sam, you don't need to call Jack. Cal and I worked for the same company back in Atlanta and were friends at work. Let me go get that coffee for you."

"Never mind, I'll just get some at Jasmine's in the morning." He nodded towards Calvin, scratched Bug's ears, and left as abruptly as he came.

"Calvin, let me brew some decaf coffee for us, then you have a lot of explaining to do. Make yourself at home. This is Ladybug. I don't think you ever met her in Atlanta. She seems to like you, or she's just as confused as I am about you showing up here."

Back in the kitchen I was reeling from what just happened. Cal was a nice guy and we had a friendly relationship at work, but never dated. Why in the world would he just appear on my doorstep? And then Sam showed up asking for coffee! He never runs out of coffee at home. He must have seen a strange car outside my house and was worried I needed rescuing again. But really, wasn't I allowed to have someone come visit me? But then, it was so sweet to think Sam was watching out for me. What was that about calling Jack though? I needed to hear this story straight from Calvin's mouth.

"Help yourself to sugar and cream and grab one of these Christmas cookies. I've been trying out new recipes for our cookie swap at Haywood House. That's the assisted-living facility where I am working. We're excited about this cookie swap because there hasn't been one in a long time." I felt like I was babbling but Cal showing up like this had unnerved me. "Now, you owe me a complete explanation of why you showed up on my porch this evening."

"Well, Claire, the short version is I had four weeks of vacation coming before the first of the year, and I have never been out West, so I thought I'd come find you and see how you are doing. Looks like you have really settled down here," Cal slowly gazed around my living room. "I remember dropping by your condo after your heart attack to bring you chicken soup. Your place was so modern, white furniture and glass tables, very minimalistic, but here there's so much color and cozy furniture. This is a stark contrast from Atlanta. You've got your own house and a protective neighbor who knows you, I don't know, you just look so content. I really expected you to return to work after a few weeks, but when you didn't come back or even contact anybody after three months of being gone, I decided to see what was keeping you out here. I closed up my computer, passed any lingering jobs off on Toby, and said I would be back in January. I knew you were moving to Montana and I remembered the town was small and near Billings. Sarah thought you said the name of the town was Haywood or Hampton or something like that, so I started digging around and found a Haywood, Montana. You can get the Haywood newspaper online and I found an article about some positive changes happening at the assisted-living place ever since Claire James was hired as the activity director. I knew it had to be you, or at least I hoped it was, because I wanted to see what it was like to pull up stakes and just set out on your own to a new place with a new job, new friends, and just a new lease on life. It seems this new life suits you. By the way, these cookies are delicious!"

"Calvin, I love it here. I didn't know what I was missing by not connecting with people. Atlanta was so big, and as you know, I'm not an outgoing person. I felt so lost there. The money was good and I do miss my Southern things. You can't get sweet tea here or grits, and weather in the fall was just about perfect in Georgia. But I am adapting to the winter cold which comes early in Montana, and I have met the most amazing people in town and at the assisted-living place where I work. It's a simple life here and one I am trusting to God to make it be the place to stay. I have a girlfriend, Jasmine, who I love talking with over coffee at her place the Sip & Savor. She owns the coffee shop in town and we just clicked the first time we met. We go shopping together because she has this gift for fashion and, goodness knows, I need help with my new Western wardrobe. I just feel like I have found someone with whom I can share my thoughts and dreams in a way I never could or did with anyone back home. Sarah and I went to a couple of bars after work a few times to blow off steam, but we were never close. Life is more than work, money, and things. I realized that after my heart attack. I had a come to Jesus' moment and haven't looked back. But what are you really doing out here? It's a long way to drive to see how I'm doing. You could have called. What's really up, Calvin?"

"I'm contemplating a career change and maybe a move, and I wanted to see how it was working out for you. Plus, I just missed you. I know we weren't bosom buddy close, but you were the only one I could talk to, and no one else has filled that void. I'm not as brave as you are to up and leave everything I have ever known, but I thought you could give me some pointers on change."

"Calvin, I would be more than happy to talk to you about a new life, but as I recall you have quite an extended family back in Georgia. They would miss you and you them if you left the South. I didn't have any family to hold me back. After Grams died, I turned inward. I concentrated on my college courses, graduating early, and then throwing myself into work. It eventually wore me down, and I missed having close bonds with people. When I was alone in the hospital, I realized I only had God to turn to, so I surrendered to Him. He may say I haven't quite done that yet, but I now rely so much more on Him through prayer, and I can't remember a time I was more at peace and happy.

My goodness, it's getting late and if you just pulled into Haywood, you need to call it a night and get some good rest. We can meet up tomorrow. I'll show you around, introduce you to my new friends, and talk some more about a direction for you. It's so good seeing you, Cal. I've missed the Southern drawl! Where are you staying?"

"I've booked a room at the Mountaintop Inn just outside of town. They're giving me a good weekly rate. I am beat though. I think finally arriving in Haywood and finding you has been a great relief. I like knowing I don't have to get up and drive tomorrow. Trying to find you has really taken a toll on me and my adrenaline is spent. I believe I'll sleep well tonight. It's so good to see you and know how happy you are, Claire. And you aren't alone, you have me. As a friend, that is."

"Here's my number. Call me when you are among the living tomorrow. We'll do the town and get you some winter gloves. It's good seeing you too, Cal." He gave me an awkward hug and slipped out into the silent, snowy night.

The fire was about out and there was no need to stoke it. I felt spent after this awkward surprise and should to go to bed soon. I opened the back door for Bug to have one last romp outside and felt the bone-cold air and wondered. God, why is Cal really here? Wrapping my arms around myself I felt just a little off kilter. A chill ran up my back which wasn't just from the cold. Why would he really drive across country to surprise me like this? I was racking my brain to think about our relationship back in Atlanta. We were just work friends, nothing more. At least that's what I thought. Did I, at any time, lead him to thinking anything else? I remembered he brought me flowers when I was in the hospital, but I thought they were from the department. He brought soup while I was out of work for those couple of weeks. He asked about meeting for a drink after work a few times, but I always begged off saying I was tired and going home. I never shared many details of my plans with him about coming out here. I told him it was time for a change and that Montana looked really interesting to me. I told him how much I enjoyed our friendship and to take care. That was it. "Come on, Bug. Let's go inside. It's freezing out here." But the chill lingered even after I snuggled under my down comforter.

Chapter Thirty

The week was hectic, but hectic in a good way. I had always loved Christmas time and what better place to be this time of year than in Haywood. The town seemed to embrace the holiday, too. Lights hung throughout the town. The lamp posts were decorated with greenery, red bows, and silver bells. In the town square stood a huge evergreen tree with beautiful silver balls hung from every bough. The lighting of the tree was set for Thursday night at 6:00pm so families could all be there. You couldn't go anywhere without Christmas carols filling the air. Everyone had the most joyous spirit.

I wanted to take it all in on my own terms, but Calvin followed me around like a lost puppy. Wherever I went, he went. The residents at Haywood fell in love with his boyish charm. He played Rummikub, checkers, poker with a some of the men, and even ate some of his dinners with the ladies. Luckily, he had his own transportation, so in the evening I could just tell him good bye, and I would see him the next day.

By Friday, I was ready for our first Christmas movie night. Jasmine and I brought all the Christmas cookies we had been baking all week over and put them out on beautiful trays. Everyone helped themselves to cookies, then we brought a cup of hot cocoa to them when they were settled. *White Christmas* was our first choice. We thought it would put everyone in a festive mood with the singing and dancing. Calvin motioned me over to sit by him. I was looking around for Jack as he usually came to our movie night if he was free of vet duties. I hadn't seen him all week so I was hoping he would be here. So far, no sign of him. I sat down next to Calvin, and he awkwardly grabbed my hand and said how wonderful this week had been and how he loved being here with me. I was so startled that I pulled my hand away, made up an excuse to go and check on Mrs. Blanton, and quickly left the room. A quick glance back made me realize Calvin was in his own fantasy and I was the center of it. He was smiling as if I had totally melted at his disclosure. Surely, I hadn't led him on these past few days. I'd been very gracious and included him in on everything that had happened this week. We had a couple of meals together and talked a lot about Haywood House. I encouraged him to tell me more about his family thinking he would come to see how much he would miss them if he left Georgia, but that was all. Tears started streaming down my face as I started to think of all I had here and how much I loved my new life. Just then I felt someone come up behind me. No, I will not play into Calvin's fantasy. I needed to nip it in the bud and tell him it was time to head home.

"Calvin, I …" Jack stepped up and wiped a tear from my eye.

"What's wrong? This isn't like you, Claire, to cry on movie night."

"Oh Jack, I'm so glad you're here." And as he took me in his arms I wept. Not just for tonight, but for past Christmases alone, for Grams, my mom, for trying to hold my life together all by myself, for being tired of putting up a good front, for trying to be brave and independent when sometimes I just wanted someone to take care of me. But not Calvin! How had I led him so astray? What was I going to do now?

"Hey, it's going to be alright," Jack reassured me. "I'm sorry I haven't been able to see you this week. Looks like you have been pretty busy playing hostess to Calvin. At least, that's what Sam has been telling me. I understand having a friend from Atlanta come to visit has been pretty exciting. I didn't want you to have to split your time between him and me."

"Jack, I want to go home now. I'm so tired. Could you please tell Jasmine I'm a bit under the weather? She and Mrs. Blanton can clean up after the movie. I'm so sorry to leave like this. This is my favorite Christmas movie and I was so looking forward to tonight, but I can't stay. I know I'm not making any sense, but could you do this for me and send Bug out, too?"

"Sure, Claire. Go home and take care of yourself. We'll manage here, don't worry."

I grabbed my coat and purse, waited on Bug and then hurried out into the cold, lonely night. I did it again, God. I turned away from people and crawled into my shell. More tears fell as I walked to my car in the eerie silence. The crunching of my boots was all I could hear as I walked away, again.

I didn't start a fire in the fireplace. I sat alone in the dark, just a candle lighting the room. I pulled the quilt up around my face to capture some warmth as Bug, my dear Bug, cuddled next to me. I would have to deal with Calvin tomorrow. Whatever kind of relationship he was envisioning, I needed to squelch it now. God, I have so much trouble reading people. Why didn't I set the record straight from the beginning? I never want to hurt other people's feelings so instead I just leave things unsaid. I have to convince him staying here with me is not going to turn into anything. We'll have to have an honest talk in the morning. Please, *God, give me the words, the wisdom, the courage to be frank, to be honest.*

I think seeing Calvin brought back a lot of memories I had buried about my old life. How reclusive I was, unattached, uninvolved, alone. I had changed since being in Haywood. *Please, God, I don't want the change to be surface deep. I want to change down to my soul.*

Please don't let me stay here in my shell. Help me reach out to my friends, to Jack, Jasmine, and Sam.

Just then a knock at the door split the silence. Oh no, please don't be Calvin. I could face him tomorrow, just not tonight. I contemplated not answering the door, but I knew that was a cowardly way of handling things. I gathered my strength to confront him. As I opened the door, there stood Jack holding up the DVD *White Christmas.*

"You said it was your favorite and I happen to like it, too. I have cookies and hot cocoa, or at least we can make it hot. Are you feeling up for a little company?"

I melted into his arms one more time this night. He may not know what to make of me, but I was glad he was giving me another chance to try and find out.

The movie was every bit as wonderful as I remembered. Cuddled up with Jack, a fire glowing, Bug at our feet, I felt a deep sense of love and home. We didn't speak much during the movie, but afterwards he asked me why I had so abruptly left Haywood House tonight. I took a deep breath and decided I needed to be honest with him about Calvin and my past.

"Calvin brought back some issues I never completely dealt with in Atlanta. First of all, he was a friend at work but never a close one. I was floored when he showed up on my porch having driven across country to find me. It was nice to see someone from my old life and we talked a lot about people at work and events that happened in Atlanta. Tonight, I realized Calvin was hoping for more than friendship. I realized his plan was to settle down here and start a relationship with me. A relationship that I did not see in the same light as he did. I thought we were just occasional lunch buddies at work. He was hoping for more. But who would drive all the way across country to see a lunch buddy?

"I am so bad at relationships. I don't want to encourage them, and thought I had done a pretty good job back home of discouraging anyone from getting close to me. I never knew my father, lost my mother when I was 16, and my Grams when I was 19. I couldn't bear to lose anyone else or love anyone else. That worked fairly well for me for about 18 years, long enough for me to learn to depend solely on myself, squirrel away a good bit of money, and become as healthy and fit as possible for a woman in her 30's.

"Then out of the blue came the heart attack. I had just finished a 2-mile run after work, a run that I usually stretched to 6 miles. But something wasn't right. I felt an enormous pressure in my chest and a tingling in my arms, nothing I had ever felt after a run. I also felt very nauseous. For some reason, I knew I had to find help right away. I drove myself to the ER and explained my symptoms. The doctor treating me administered fluids and said I was probably de-hydrated after my run, but when I told him and the nurse treating me about my mother dying of a heart attack in her 30's, it got their attention. Immediately an angiogram was ordered which is the only way to diagnose SCAD, spontaneous coronary artery dissection. Thank goodness that particular doctor and nurse were aware of the possibility of a SCAD heart attack because many women have been mis-diagnosed or not diagnosed at all with a heart condition. Long story short, I stayed in the hospital a few days on blood thinners and luckily did not have to have bypass surgery. The dissection healed on its own. I did have to change my lifestyle though. No more running, no heavy lifting which was not really a problem, and reduced stress in my life. That's when I turned to God. Through lots of prayer, He helped me realize Atlanta was not the place for me if I wanted a stress-free life. Also, I needed love in my life, and I got Bug! I needed to move somewhere I could slow down but fulfill a passion growing inside me to validate my Grams and others like her in the twilight of their years. That is way more than you bargained for when you asked me why I left Haywood House this evening."

"Claire, I had no idea you were recovering from such a life changing event. So, you think your mother died from SCAD? Can this happen again?"

"It's a little hard to know about Mom because her heart attack happened over 25 years ago and very little was known about SCAD. But she had a lot of the triggers: lots of stress, poor health overall, and ignored symptoms. It's also most prevalent in young females. I do remember she had trouble breathing and was nauseous the day she died. But she refused to have an ambulance called or go to the ER until it was too late. It's not likely for this to happen again to my heart, but it could. Moving here removed the everyday stress I was experiencing in Atlanta. I must say I have had a couple of incidents here that caused a bit of worry, like the ladder fall, the mountain lion, and the blizzard! But overall, I have trusted God to watch over me and help me through any more valleys, and He has."

"Claire, you amaze me. To go through all that alone, then make the major decision to move here sight unseen where you know nobody and completely change your vocation. That takes a lot of courage and faith."

"I was never alone through all of that. God has been with me all along. I just didn't acknowledge Him until the heart attack. Then He got my attention! Coming to Haywood has been the best decision I have made in my life. I still have a lot of things to sort out, and I'm trying to go slowly, which is so against my nature. Calvin showing up, though, brought to light some things I was hiding from you, Jasmine, and Sam. If I'm going to make it here, I need friends, close friends. I don't want the Calvin kind of friendship, where everything we talk about or share is surface talk. I have to know I can share deep thoughts at times as well as my shortcomings. That's why I'm bearing my soul now, I guess. You can bail if this is too much information."

"I'm not going to bail. But you do have to let me be a little more protective. I know you're not fragile and I won't treat you that way, I am concerned for your health and I want to be the one you call if you're out of sorts. I'm saying, Claire, I want to be part of your life. We'll go slowly if that's what you want right now, but I'll be here." And with that he pulled me into his arms, kissed me, held me, and assured me he meant it.

Chapter Thirty One

I knew I had to confront Calvin today. The sooner we had this out in the open the better. Plus, he needed to head home to his family and reassess his own goals. They just couldn't include me. I called him at 10:00am and asked him to meet me at Jasmine's for coffee. I was nervous about being blunt with him, but that's the most direct way. I had skirted around relationships my whole adult life. After all Jack and I talked about last night, I had to have the courage to be honest and let Calvin know I didn't want to lead him on anymore.

When I walked in Sip & Savor, Calvin was already there. I took a deep breath and asked God to help me find kind words. As I sat down, immediately Calvin grabbed my hand and asked if I was alright. He said he was so sorry I felt ill last night, but glad I looked fine today. I slowly pulled my hand away.

"Calvin, I want you to know how touched I am by your visit and the interest you have shown in Haywood. The people at Haywood House have so enjoyed getting to know you. You're so at ease with older folks. It's time for you to go back home, though. This is not your dream, it's mine. You are clearly not embracing the winter here, and it will get worse before it gets better. I love the winter weather. I'm excited when it snows and I see ice crystals everywhere. I'm learning how to dress for this season; however, you, on the other hand, have been miserable outside. I've seen how your fingers turn blue even when you have been wearing gloves. You need the sunny South. You also are an amazing graphic artist and your talent can best be appreciated at a large company or at best a large town. Your family must miss you so much. If I remember correctly, you have quite a few nieces and nephews, and your mom and dad are in the Atlanta area, too. Family is important. I had no family back home, so it was easier for me to break away from that life and find a new place to put down roots. No one is missing me back there. Calvin, our friendship will remain just that, a friendship. You came a very long way to find that out, but I don't want to lead you to believe there is any future for us. I'm happy here. I have new friends who mean a lot to me. I have a job that I am passionate about, and I am closer to God than I have ever been. This is where my focus is; this is what I want. And I think this is where God wants me to be, too."

Calvin hesitated for a moment and finally said, "Claire, I don't know quite what to say. I thought we were getting along very well and everyone seems to like me here."

"Of course, they like you, Calvin. You are a fine man. You fit in well with any group of people. But settling down here and trying to find a niche for your talents does not seem plausible. You thrive on the hustle and bustle of a big city. Haywood is small and slow, and after a while you would sorely miss your family, I know you would. You used to talk about them all the time to me. There was always a family gathering you would tell me about. What are they thinking about your trip out here?"

"They are wondering when I'm coming back. My niece Allie called me on the phone the other night and said I had to be back in time for Christmas Eve because it wouldn't be Christmas without me. I do miss them, but I had to find out if there was an us in the future. It had been on my mind day and night since you left. I know we were not an item back in Atlanta, but I had to find out for sure if it was a possibility. I never got to tell you how I felt. You just left so suddenly, and I thought maybe given a few weeks you would be back. Then I didn't know how to get in touch with you except that you went to Montana, so I researched towns and got lucky with the article in the paper about you being the new activity director at Haywood House. Claire, are you sure there's not a chance for us to get to know each other better? I'm willing to stay here and brave the cold."

"No, Calvin. This is not the place for you, and I am not the woman for you. Go home. Embrace your family, enjoy Christmas, and maybe do some looking around for another company in need of a graphic artist. You have a long drive back to Atlanta. Do some brainstorming about what you really want to do, but your God-given talent has to be part of it. It has been good seeing you and hearing about everyone back home. Please tell them hello for me and tell them I am happy and content and staying here."

As I stood up to leave, he did too. He tenderly kissed my cheek, and as I turned to go, I grabbed his arm and said, "Be safe, Calvin. Go find your own special dream and let me know when you have. I truly care." I blinked away a tear and walked out of Sip & Savor into a bitter, cold wind with the hint of snow in the air.

Chapter Thirty Two

The next couple of weeks flew by. A weight was lifted from me when Calvin left. It was so hard to confront him that day at Jasmine's but it had to be done sooner than later. He did let me know when he got home, and that the drive was very cathartic. I told him to stay in touch and let me know his new direction in the coming year. Without worrying about Calvin anymore, I was able to throw myself into everything Christmas.

Every Sunday morning in December was special in a unique way. The first Sunday brought out the advent candles and many favorite Christmas hymns at Trinity. That night everyone was invited back to the church for hot cocoa and cookies and an old fashion sing along with favorites such as "Oh Holy Night," "Silent Night," "God Rest Ye Merry Gentlemen," "Oh Little Town of Bethlehem" and others. The second Sunday, the children treated the congregation to the reenactment of the Christmas story complete with a donkey in the sanctuary and a live baby Jesus! His mother was close by. The third Sunday was a beautiful cantata that had us all in tears through its message of the birth of our glorious Savior. I could never go through another Christmas season without this holy reminder of the real reason for celebration.

Haywood House was a showcase of holiday cheer: wreaths, stockings, more twinkling lights and greenery everywhere, our movies every Friday night, and cookies lots of cookies!

Jasmine and I had quite a few afternoon talks over coffee after she closed the Sip & Savor. I felt I could confide in her about Calvin and about Jack. We also talked about doing something special for Sam. She said he always seemed so melancholy during the holidays. He missed his wife and life on the ranch. I wondered if there was any way to have a wagon ride out there like he used to offer when he and his wife hosted the town at Christmas. Maybe we could keep it on a small scale this year, but think about a bigger celebration next year. I didn't want to over step my bounds, but maybe Jack could find a couple of horses to hitch to a wagon, and Sam could drive us around. Jasmine and I could plan refreshments and music. Would it open up old wounds? Now I was excited and again wanted to plow straight through someone else's life.

I'd have to talk to Jack about this when he came for dinner tonight. Since the night he brought over *White Christmas*, we had been seeing or talking to each other every day. Tonight, I had planned chili and cornbread. Sam would come and eat with us, but he usually left early, and that would give me a chance to talk to Jack about my idea. I invited Jasmine too, but she had a date with her oven and some fruitcakes she made every year.

Jack and Sam filled me in on Christmas Eve in Haywood over dinner. Of course, all the churches had services, but before that everyone gathered downtown near the decorated tree to sing Christmas Carols and enjoy holiday refreshments laid out on tables in the square. Dressed up elves would make a brief appearance to remind all the children to scurry to bed on time and to sleep tight so Santa could come in the night. The unified chiming of all the churches' bells at 7:00pm created a glorious sound and announced the beginning of Christmas Eve services. I was so excited to be a part of such a wonderful tradition.

After Sam left, I approached Jack with my idea for reliving Sam's Christmas gift to the community, but on a much smaller scale. I was so excited about the idea that I hardly caught Jack's reluctance.

"Jasmine and I can go out to his ranch and decorate as much as possible. We can have the hot cider in thermos jugs and bring Jasmine's famous fruitcake. Then we can play some Christmas carols, I'm not sure how to do that yet, if we can't get inside Sam's house. And you can hitch up..."

"Whoa, slow down. Claire, no. Not this year, maybe not ever. That was a memory Sam has held close to him for many years. I don't think he's ready to open up again. It would be so different for him and maybe even painful without his wife. No, I'll have to nix this idea, I'm so sorry. I know you want to make all things happy for Sam but this won't work. Well, listen, I need to be going. I have to check on some horses out near Pete's house. It will take the rest of the evening to get out there, make sure they are alright, and get back. I was hoping to spend the evening with you, but we'll try again, maybe Tuesday night?" Jack gave me a quick kiss and a hug, rubbed Bug's ears and was gone.

What just happened? The evening was going so well. It was just a few days until Christmas and I was alone on a Saturday night feeling like I just messed up big time. God, am I too pushy? I know I haven't grown up here and don't know everyone intimately, but I really just wanted to bring some joy to Sam this Christmas. Why did Jack leave so suddenly? Was he trying to tell me something in a backhanded way? Did I overstep my bounds by wanting to bring back a Haywood tradition? One I have never been a part of but would love to be?

Tears started to gather behind heavy eyelids, my heart started to hurt, and I had to clutch a pillow to stop the trembling. Oh, God, I don't think I belong here either. I jumped in where I was not wanted. How could I face Jack again knowing he was disappointed in me?

And Jasmine and Sam, did they think I was too pushy? Did they wish I would go back to Atlanta now that I had tried out my little pipe dream? A sob escaped and Bug jumped up into my chair and laid in my lap. I'll always have you, Bug, but I thought I'd found a family. Tears flowed like a dam had been breached. All my past Christmas emotions swelled up to the surface, because I thought this Christmas would be perfect. God, do you really mean for me to be alone? How did I miss the signs of my overbearing personality poisoning relationships here? Things seemed to be working at Haywood House. I thought I was making a lot of friends there and making a difference in their lives. Their happiness seemed genuine. Maybe Jack was meant to be a bachelor and Sam would just continue to wallow in memories this time of year. I did think Jasmine and I were hitting it off really well. Should I call her? No, I'm going to slip back in my shell, it's safe there. I'll go through the motions of Christmas, especially for the folks at Haywood House. Then after the first of the year, I'll give my notice to Mrs. Blanton and pack up and head back to Atlanta. I can get lost in the humongous impersonal life of a big city, and as long as I have Bug, I'll be fine.

Hours had flown by and I was still mesmerized by the fire and lost in my sad world that I failed to hear a knock at the door. Sam appeared in the open doorway, and Bug jumped down to greet him. I knew my face was a mess with dried mascara under my eyes, not on my lashes, and red blotches on my cheeks. A pile of used Kleenex had gathered next to me. Could I pull off a cold?

"Hey, I saw your lights still on and it's getting late. Is everything all right?"

"Of course, Sam. I'm just reminiscing and sometimes it makes a few tears fall. I'm just fine. Thank you for reminding me of the time. Off to bed for both of us. Hurry home, I know it's cold out there."

Sam looked at me a little longer than I'd like. I didn't want him questioning me too much, I might just fall apart. I gave him a brave smile and quick hug and then gently pushed him towards the door. How would I be able to leave this wonderful man who was like a father to me? I wanted so much to be a daughter to him. It was just not going to happen. I had to accept that I couldn't make things happen just because I wanted them that way. Such a hard reality. *God, I promised to trust You and accept where You led, but surely not this.*

Chapter Thirty Three

Sunday was hard, but I muddled through. The church service was beautiful, full of anticipation for Christmas on Thursday. I enjoyed the Christmas music, the heartfelt message of hope, and the beauty of the sanctuary. After the service, I begged off lunch with Jasmine saying I thought I was coming down with a cold and wanted to nip it so I wouldn't carry anything to Haywood House on Monday. If she noticed my red swollen eyes, then at least the possibility of a cold made sense. I hurried home and tried to concentrate on the special coffee cakes I was making for Christmas Eve breakfast. This recipe made a lot so I would have plenty for the residents, one for Jasmine, Sam, and Jack. It helped keep my mind occupied because while I may be a pushy person, I was also a caring person. I wanted to do things for others. That part of me would never change.

Monday was busy with everyone needing help wrapping packages for their family. Christmas cards needed delivering to friends at Haywood House as well as ones being sent by postal service. I told Mrs. Blanton I wanted to bring the coffee cakes by early on Christmas Eve. I also reminded her I wanted to put a special gift at the foot of everyone's bed late Christmas Eve. I had written a personal note to each resident reminding them of their unique gift. I needed to go home and finish that job and wrap each quilt with ribbon.

Jack called Monday night and asked how I was feeling. He said, "Jasmine told me you were coming down with a cold."

"I'm feeling better and have so much to do before Thursday I'd best not talk long. I hope you won't have any vet emergency to take you away from celebrating Christmas."

"I always try to treat myself this time of year to a few days off when the office is closed. Of course, that doesn't mean some emergency can't come up, but usually I have some down time. I was hoping you would go with me to the Christmas Eve activities I was telling you about the other night. Are you free?"

No, no, no crying right now! "Sure, Jack I would love to go. Just let me know when. Bye."

I'd have to talk to him about going back to Atlanta, but not this week. Christmas could not be ruined.

Tuesday brought more hustle and bustle at Haywood House. Everyone was in such a good mood I had to join them. We sang Christmas Carols, talked about our favorite Christmas as a child, and, of course, ate cookies. So many of the stories centered around simple acts. Agnes remembered the first Christmas she got her own ball of yarn and knitting needles. Mrs. Sharp said she would never forget opening up the last present under the tree and finding it was *The Secret Garden*, the first brand new book she had ever owned. Mr. Evans remembered always going to chop down a tree with the whole family. One year they over-estimated the size of the tree they brought home. It was so big they had to put it on the porch. The kids were so worried Santa would not leave any gifts because he wouldn't be able to find the tree. He did find it, and the Christmas tree on the porch became tradition.

"What was your favorite Christmas as a child, Claire?" Mrs. Collins asked.

"I always loved dolls, and my mother or Grams would surprise me with a little Betsy Bits or a Barbie doll each year. One year I wanted so badly Victoria, a Madame Alexander doll. She was beautiful and had a soft pink gown with a matching bonnet. She looked like a real baby. She was also very expensive, so I told Santa I didn't want anything else, just that baby doll. I remember trying to be extra good that year helping my mother with the dishes and sweeping the floor every night. I think Grams must have been Santa that year because under the tree was a signature blue box with a big ribbon around it. I remember holding my breath and hoping the Victoria doll was inside. And it was! I loved that doll many years past the time to still hold on to baby dolls. Okay, who's next?"

The afternoon went on with so many heartfelt stories and memories. I loved sitting around getting to know everyone a little bit more. And then I had a reality check. I wouldn't be here after New Year's. I just wanted to enjoy the moment. And I did. Bug and I took off for home a little after 4:00pm. It had started snowing and the walk home was heavenly, snow gently falling through the air, glistening on the ground, the silence that it caused, and the chill that warmed my heart. I was going to miss this beauty. I was taking in everything around me as if for the last time. Haywood was a special place with old homes families still inhabited, big trees, wide streets. It had a quaintness that spoke of solid roots, not a willingness to tear down and rebuild, but hold onto the past and embrace the present. This was what I wanted, but maybe not what I was supposed to have.

My phone rang as we approached my house. It was Jack.

"Hi, I'm planning on grabbing a sandwich for supper. How about you and Bug joining me. I can pick you up in half an hour. I know you need to eat something and hopefully you haven't started fixing anything yet. My treat. Oh, and we might want to take a walk in the snow afterwards, so dress warmly."

"Sure, we'll be ready. Thanks!" A bit strange but he knew I loved the snow, so I'd dress accordingly.

When Jack knocked on the door, Bug and I were ready. As I opened it, he leaned down and kissed me so gently. I just wanted to stay in this moment, but I pulled away not wanting to make the parting in January any more difficult and heartbreaking than necessary. Light heartedly, I said something like, let's get going, I'm starving. In the truck I started telling Jack about my day and all the Christmas memories shared. He talked about the happenings at the clinic. Just chitchat, then I asked where we were going because it seemed like we were leaving town.

"I thought we'd drive around a little. It's early to be eating and I don't think you've been out to this part of Haywood. It's kind of nice to get out of town and just see open spaces. Sit back and enjoy the view, or at least what you can see in the fading light. I thought we'd drive by some of the ranches where I take care of horses. This is really a pretty part of our little world."

I leaned back and looked at the view. Snow covered fences, evergreens with shimmery boughs, ranch houses with lights in the windows, and smoke curling out of chimneys. It all looked so peaceful. Then Jack turned down a lane that led to a house with a host of mini lights hanging from trees and the roof of the porch. Lights in the house indicated someone was home. He must be checking on someone's livestock before we eat. What a perfect place! It was a huge log cabin that invited you to come warm by a fire or sit around with family and friends sharing dreams. When he pulled up to the front of the ranch house, the door opened and there stood Sam. What was he doing here? And then Jasmine stepped out. Where were we, what was going on?

"Welcome, this is my ranch," says Sam.

I was speechless. Jack ushered me into a room filled with

a roaring fire in a large stone fireplace, a mantle with candles glowing in mason jars and a regal elk head mounted over it. Deep brown leather couches and chairs and a braided rug with warm earth tones sat in front of the hearth, on dark honey-colored pine flooring. Hanging from the vaulted ceiling, the chandelier was the attention getter with a whole host of antlers and small lights. It was gorgeous. I had no idea Sam's ranch house was still livable. I thought since he lived in town that his ranch was boarded up just ready to be sold one day.

"Sam, this is exquisite. I don't know what to say."

"Well, I hope you'll say you're hungry because Jasmine has a pot of soup on the stove and homemade bread in the oven. Jack was supposed to bring the pie and you are our guest of honor."

"I've got the pie, so let's sit down, and I can explain all of this to Claire. You have been doing so much for everyone in Haywood since you arrived and have really made a positive difference in so many lives in such a short time. We have been trying to come up with something special for you, when you mentioned to Jasmine about Sam taking us on a hayride like he and his wife used to do at Christmas for so many years. Jasmine told Sam and me about your idea, and we decided to turn it into a gift for you, but that meant throwing cold water on your plan when you suggested it to me. Believe me that was hard. The look on your face broke my heart, but we really wanted to surprise you, complete with a hayride after supper."

"I have to admit, at first, I wasn't keen on the idea. I didn't think I could do it without Sandy, but then with all of us getting together out here to hang lights and clean the house and fix up the sleigh, I've gotten excited for the first time since she passed away. It's small scale this year, but next year we can invite the town again. It's a tradition I don't want Haywood to lose," Sam's husky voice told me how emotional this was for him.

The tears started flowing again and I didn't care. Throwing my arms around Sam, I cried happy tears and my heart felt as light as a snowflake and as warm as the glow from the fire. They wanted me here.

The delicious dinner was followed by a magical hayride, with snow falling gently and the bells on the horses' reins jingling softly. Jack and I were tucked under a quilt in the back of the sleigh while Sam drove and Jasmine sat beside him reminiscing about past Christmas rides. I could see how this was a favored tradition for the townspeople. Leaning my head on Jack's shoulder I said a prayer to God thanking Him for bringing me to Haywood and surrounding me with this new family. Back at Sam's, enjoying a mug of hot cocoa, I confessed about leaving Haywood after the first of the year. I was not good at gauging other people's feelings. I think it was part of my trust issues. I apologized for not believing in their friendship.

All three of them started to fuss at me for ever doubting their friendship, but it was in such a loving way that I had to take my reprimand and promise not to ever waver again.

Back at home as Jack walked me to my door, ending my now most favorite Christmas, he reached into his pocket and handed me a small velvet-covered box. I looked at him as if this night could not get any better.

"Open it," he whispered.

I opened the box, and laying in white satin was an exquisite necklace, a delicate silver angel with an intricately cut pearl. I gently took it out of the box. "Oh Jack, it's the most gorgeous necklace I have ever seen."

"It's a guardian angel, Claire. It's just a symbol but I want you to know you are being watched over always, because I'm falling in love with you."

I looked up at him and knew how special this man was to me.

How lucky I was to have him in my life.

"Oh, Jack, me, too." As I reached up to touch his cheek, he gathered me in his arms and kissed me gently at first and then with a passion I had only imagined in my dreams. This was truly the best Christmas ever.

Chapter Thirty Four

Christmas Eve service was everything I hoped it would be. We sang the familiar carols, "Oh Holy Night," "Oh Little Town of Bethlehem," and "Silent Night." After hearing the familiar, yet, touching story of so long ago, the congregation celebrated in a darkened church with all of us holding a single lighted candle, remembering the birth of a babe, brought to earth to change the world. It was indeed a silent night, a holy night. God, Your Son came to us so humbly that we might understand what a gift You gave, love wrapped in swaddling clothes, a precious gift of love. How clueless we are at times, and yet to be more like Jesus, we just need to give love humbly and completely to all God's children. I was learning that holding back and protecting my heart was not the life God planned for me. I'm here to care for and love your people, God. I'm blessed.

As I walked out of the church, I viewed the twinkling stars on the night canvas. Only God could paint such beauty.

Mrs. Blanton quietly opened the front door at midnight. Ladybug had to stay home because I couldn't risk her waking any of the residents. I felt like Santa! I had all the lap blankets and hand written notes to put at the foot of each bed. I hoped when they awakened Christmas morning, each one would feel a little more loved by me as they discovered my special gift to them. One more blanket to deliver. I quietly tapped on Mrs. Blanton's door. She called me inside and I handed her a quilt of turquoise and yellow squares, one of my favorites.

"Mrs. Blanton, you believed in me even when I wasn't so sure I should be here trying to make a difference in these people's lives. You gave me a chance; my heart is full to bursting. I can't thank you enough, and I hope you know this was made with love just for you."

Mrs. Blanton gently fingered the blanket I placed in her hands. Looking closely, I detected a tear gathering in her eye, "Claire, I have to admit you have brought life to our little community. I was skeptical at first, but something told me to let you hang in there. It's not often that someone, as genuine as you, comes along and wants to help our most vulnerable citizens. I wanted to protect them, keep them from getting their hopes up that you would stay for the long run. That happens you know. People come here and want to help all in good faith, but a new charity comes along and off they go. I think you are good for our people. You have an old soul inside of you that understands aging. I want to continue to partner with you into the new year with new ideas to awaken purpose in each resident. So, with that being said, I'd like to offer you a fulltime position at Haywood House as Activities Coordinator and Life Enrichment Leader. I was going to wait until the first of the year, but it seems fitting to inform you tonight as sort of my Christmas present to you,"

Trembling, I whispered, "Mrs. Blanton, thank you so much! I don't know what to say!" I couldn't help but hug her and then regaining my composure, I shook her hand.

"No need to talk tonight about the new responsibilities that will be involved. Take the time off you had planned between Christmas and New Year's. We can discuss hours, insurance, and other benefits in January, as well as all the brainstorms I'm sure you will come up with for our little community. Merry Christmas, Claire."

I walked out into the frigid night, but felt strangely warm and secure. It was clear and crisp with the stars shining like crystals in a pitch-black sky, and the moon, a perfect crescent, the way it might have been in Bethlehem that first Christmas Eve. God, I can't begin to know how Mary felt this night so long ago. My heart is full and I know it's Your love that has filled it, just like You filled Mary's heart. I never want to forget this feeling. I reached for my guardian angel. You give us so many ways to show a Christ-like love for our family, for friends, for a new love, and for our vulnerable. No holding back now. I have found the place to open up my heart and give my love unconditionally.

Chapter Thirty Five

How swiftly this week between Christmas and New Year's had flown and yet I rested, walked, planned, cooked, and spent time with my favorite people. Sam was touched by the quilt I made for him. I noticed it took up a permanent residence at his favorite chair. Jasmine and Jack appeared to love their scarves, as they were snuggly wrapped around their necks every time I saw them. Since the weather took a turn for the worse, woolen scarves were one essential for being outdoors. A lot more snow and bitter temperatures arrived. Dressing properly for it though made all the difference in the world. I didn't feel like I had to be a hermit when the weather was bad. I bundled myself up, and I have to admit, I bundled Bug up in a fleece coat, too, and off we went for our daily walk. I was not going to complain about winter weather. It was beautiful to me. It was a major factor in this dramatic move of mine. I knew spring and summer would be very welcomed when they arrived, but now I liked the white, glistening, quiet, and peaceful winter.

I'd been brainstorming ideas to bring a healthier lifestyle to Haywood House. Exercise was one area that was lacking here. I hadn't seen anyone doing much more than walking to the dining room and back to their bedrooms on any given day. A walking program in the winter was a challenge, but I might be able to map out a walking route in the facility and measure the distance in steps. Studies showed that physical activity in older adults improved overall health and lessened the risk of falls. Our people needed at least 3,000 steps a day beyond their normal walking to and from their rooms. We should be working on a goal of 5,000 steps, or even more for the people who weren't compromised with knee or hip issues. I knew some people had breathing issues and a couple of our residents were in wheelchairs. I would work on individualized plans for them. We wanted to shoot for 30 extra minutes a day in exercise, but that could be broken up into three 10-minute segments. Stretching and lightweight strength training were also important, but somehow, I needed to make that part of exercising fun, easy for starters, and worthwhile. Music had to be part of it, also. Everything was more fun with music.

My notebook was brimming over with exciting possibilities. Jasmine could lead a cooking or baking class. Not that any of the ladies or men needed to be taught to cook, but sometimes it felt so good to create something new in the kitchen. When was the last time any of them cooked a meal or just a dish or dessert? Maybe those interested could dig deep into their family recipe boxes and share a favorite dish from the past. Grams was known for her scrumptious macaroni and cheese recipe. It was always the first empty dish when there was a potluck supper at church. I could share that for starters. It wouldn't make the healthy foods list but certainly would be on top for comfort food.

We could start a book club by picking out a book to read or listen to on tape and then discuss. I'd need to check on available books on tape since many have failing eyesight and would need to listen rather than read a book. I had some thoughts on good books to hook them. Jan Karon wrote the *Mitford* series and Olive Ann Burns wrote *Cold Sassy Tree*. Both authors painted a warm, inviting view of the South that just screamed sweet tea, fried chicken and buttermilk biscuits. I would love for my new friends to have a glimpse into the world from which I came.

Geraldine could teach some basic drawing and watercolor classes. Pastor Michael, from Trinity, could start a Bible Study as long as he agreed to no homework! We could schedule game day once a month and play Scrabble, Clue, Hearts, Rummy Royal, and Canasta. I wanted to get a knitting group started and possibly have the knitters make children's scarves for the Hope Shelter. We could use size 10 needles and bulky yarn to make it easier on their fingers, and it would stitch up quickly, too. A guest speaker could come in once a month and talk about something of interest on which he or she was an expert such as Western history, wildlife, or current events. I had so many ideas that I couldn't wait to implement. I did remember what Mrs. Blanton said about slow and easy. I didn't want to overwhelm anyone, but time was not on their side. I'd share these ideas with Mrs. B on Monday, and then start introducing a few at a time. It would be a wonderful new year.

Chapter Thirty Six

Monday was another icy, cold, snowy day, but Bug and I were determined to go to Haywood House and see everyone. It had only been a week, but I missed my dear friends. As we blew through the door, we found our familiar group chitchatting and staying warm around the fireplace. Everyone started talking at once when they saw us walk in and motioned for us to join them.

"Claire, the quilts you made are gorgeous!" said Mrs. Sharp.

"Oh, my yes," exclaimed Mrs. Collins. "We all brought ours out to show each other. And when they aren't being used to keep the chill off our old bones, we agreed to put them on the end of our beds so when we walk by the rooms, they are on display! Claire, we just want to give you the biggest hug and thank you from the bottom of our hearts."

Standing there being enveloped in their loving thoughts and arms I flashed back to Grams and how she would have loved being a part of this caring community. This was for you Grams. All I am doing here was for you. I wished you could have known this kind of place. Sad and happy tears trickled down my cheeks, and I felt I now had a whole family of new grandparents to dote upon.

As I looked around, I noticed someone is missing. "Where is Geraldine?"

"Oh, my dear, she is under the weather and hasn't been out of her room for a couple of days now. I heard Mrs. Blanton say she might have to call EMS to take her to Doc Linder's and see what's wrong," Mrs. Darby said as she wrung her hanky, clearly worried.

"I'll go check right now and let you all know how she's doing."

I hurried to Mrs. Blanton's office and just as I approached her door, EMS workers came through the front door. Mrs. Blanton directed them to Geraldine's room three doors down the hall, and they disappeared for what seemed like hours. We all sat in the main room not saying much. No one wanted to see friends leaving in an ambulance. Pretty soon they wheeled Geraldine out on a stretcher hooked up to oxygen. She looked very pale and her eyes were closed. The ambulance took off with our sweet friend all by herself in the back. I rushed to Mrs. Blanton's office to see what she knew.

With a worried tone in her voice, Mrs. Blanton said, "I think Geraldine is very sick. She had a cough and the sniffles starting a few days ago. She wanted to rest in her room so we brought her meals to her and checked on her often. This morning she took a turn for the worse. I need to get in touch with her daughter. She should be here in case health decisions need to be made."

"Mrs. Blanton, I'm going to the hospital if that's okay with you. I may not be able to see her, but at least I can be near and maybe get some information on how she is doing." I told the other ladies my plan, and that I would let them know what I found out as soon as possible.

"Claire," says Mrs. Darby. "Please take the quilt you made for her. She hasn't let go of it since Christmas morning when she found it at the foot of her bed. I think it will bring her a lot of comfort."

Mrs. Blanton said it would be alright for me to take it from Geraldine's room. While I was in there, I saw by her bed, the photograph of Bug I had given her. I took that, too. No other picture was on her nightstand or dresser. I wondered about her daughter, her daughter-in-law, and her grandson. Surely, they kept in touch somehow. How could a family just dissolve into thin air? I would have to ask Geraldine when she was stronger about these family ties. They couldn't have been severed completely.

Chapter Thirty Seven

Geraldine had been in ICU for two days now. I'd been tied up in knots, as I awaited word from the nurses and/or doctors. It had been touch and go, and I hated to leave the hospital each night worrying that she would be worse the next morning. I divided my time between the waiting room outside ICU and Haywood House trying to keep things as calm and normal as possible for all her friends there. Thank goodness Sam had been willing to keep Bug at his house when I was at the hospital. I arrived as soon as the doors opened each morning and sat or paced in the waiting room hoping that she would be moved to a regular room any moment so I could see her, hug her, and give her the quilt. Right now, only family was allowed in ICU, and I was not family. Unfortunately, her daughter was not around. Geraldine's doctor assured me that she was resting comfortably and knew I was here. My prayers to God seemed endless, and at times, I went to the chapel to make sure He heard me. Geraldine had a nasty case of pneumonia that they were trying to get under control.

Just as I returned from the canteen with another cup of coffee, oh how I longed for Jasmine's brew, a tall, willowy, gorgeous woman with long curly chestnut hair, deep brown eyes wearing clothes fit for a movie star (over the knee leather boots, camel brown cashmere coat, a scarf of Sonoma colors, and a Gucci bag slung over her shoulder), whisked by me into the ICU unit. This woman had to be Cassie.

After a short while, Cassie came out and looked to be in a hurry. I stopped her though, and asked if she was Geraldine's daughter.

"I am, but who are you?" Cassie asked, clearly annoyed.

"My name is Claire James. I'm a friend of your mother. Do you mind my asking how she is doing today?"

"Well, nobody tells me anything. She didn't open her eyes, even though I know she heard me talking to her. I'm going to check into the Lodge and rest up a bit. I'll be back later today. I hope she leaves ICU soon. I have a movie shoot in LA and can't afford to be gone long. They're holding everything up for me right now as it is." With that she left in a whirl of high dollar perfume and an air of entitlement. I thought Geraldine kept her eyes closed on purpose!

Later in the day, Geraldine was finally moved to a private room. It was such a relief knowing she was making progress. This also meant I would be able to see her and sit with her. She needed to know someone was close by. After the nurses settled her in her room, I slipped in and quietly sat beside the bed covering her with the quilt she had become so attached to in such a short time. I was saying a prayer for her improvement and asking God to continue to watch over her and heal her completely when I heard a weak voice, "Claire, you're still here."

I gently caressed her forehead, "Oh, Miss Geraldine, you don't know how happy I am to hear your voice. You gave us quite a scare. Everyone has been praying for you and asking about you. Bug is beside herself whenever we go to Haywood House because she can't find you. You're a pretty important person, you know. How are you feeling?"

Slowly fingering the quilt and smiling ever so slightly, she quietly whispered, "I'm not sure, but I am glad I'm awake. I know you have been here Claire. I felt your presence and the nurses talked to me about the different people that have come by, Jasmine, Jack, Sam, Mrs. Blanton, Pastor Michael. Mainly you though. That means a lot to me."

"Miss Geraldine, you're very special to me. And I didn't want you to be alone. Your daughter is here. Did the nurse tell you? She arrived this morning and said she'd be back later today. I know you must be anxious to see her. It's been a while since she's been home, hasn't it?"

Geraldine sighed, "Cassie hasn't been home for 10 years, since her brother's funeral. She was home long enough to make arrangements for me to move to Haywood House, put my house on the market, and check with my lawyer to see that he would handle all my legal and financial matters. I knew she was here this morning and was a bit surprised, but she won't be here long. I know Cassie."

"She's a beautiful woman and apparently successful. I'm so sorry she hasn't been here for you very often."

Geraldine closed her eyes and I knew she was tired. I reached for her thin translucent hand. She squeezed mine and gave a little smile. "I have you," she whispered.

Nurses came and went checking her vital signs but mainly letting her sleep. It was getting late, and I needed to get home for Bug. Her daughter should be coming sometime soon. I gave her a soft kiss on her forehead and slipped out of her room.

Down the hall, I could see Jack coming into the hospital from the parking lot. I hurried to let him know the good news about Geraldine. As I neared the entrance, Cassie appeared from the waiting room and boldly approached him throwing her arms around his neck. Somehow, I knew this wasn't a chance encounter. I held back a little and watched as an intimate conversation seemed to be taking place. Cassie was gorgeous and worldly and confident. I remembered now how Jack talked about her when they were growing up. He had a crush on her. Or did he love her? Was that why he hadn't found anyone else. Was he waiting for her to come back? My crazy imagination was working overtime. He didn't see me in the hall because his eyes were fixed on her. My eyes were suddenly filled with tears of hurt for being ignored, thankfulness for Geraldine's recovery, and sadness for realizing Jack's true feelings were for someone else, even if he didn't know it himself.

Escaping out of the side door, I couldn't get to my car fast enough, tears blurring my vision. All the way home I pounded the steering wheel, sobbed until my chest hurt, and cried to God for blindsiding me. Why did You let me fall in love with Jack when he has always been in love with Cassie? I couldn't compete with a woman like her and the past they shared. I pulled into my driveway and sat, unable to move. I continued to weep for all that had happened in my life. What a pity party I was having! I cried for my mom and my Grams, I missed them so much, for my heart condition that hung over me like a wrecking ball, for the chance I took starting my life over in a completely strange place, for Geraldine's mortality and all my frail friends at Haywood House, but mostly for Jack. I thought we had a future together. I had never felt so deeply for anyone else. He was compassionate, kind, caring, funny, dedicated to his work to a fault, but that just made him more charming. He loved animals, those beasts that loved unconditionally. We had so much in common. We passionately loved those most vulnerable. His animals, my seniors. God, how could I have missed this part of him that had been dormant all these years. Why didn't he tell me he still had strong feelings for Cassie?

A rap at my car window jolted me out of my misery. Only then did I realize my teeth were chattering from the cold and my body was shivering.

"You had better get out of that car before you freeze to death. It's in the teens and not fixing to get any warmer anytime soon. Plus, your dog is about to go crazy waiting for you to come get her." Sam had a way of showing me his tough love. He was my bright spot. Thank you, God, for Sam.

"Sam, I'm so sorry. You're right, I am freezing out here. What was I thinking? I better rescue Bug and start a fire."

"I happen to know you're not crying because Geraldine has taken a turn for the worse. I called the hospital to check on her. The nurse said she's in a room doing better, and her daughter came by to see her for a minute. Seems like Cassie had some catching up to do but not with her mama. Is that the reason for your blotchy face and red eyes? Do you want to talk about it?"

We reached Sam's porch and let Bug out. She greeted me like I had been gone for days instead of hours. What love this dog had for me and me for her. God, just when I think I can't handle life, you unleash this furry ball of love to melt my pain away, at least for the moment.

"Sam, I can't compete with Cassie. And when she leaves, as I'm sure she will, her ghost will remain. That will be an even stronger hold on Jack."

"Don't give up on him. He'll see the light through that thick head of his. He's a good man." With those words of wisdom, he kissed my head and walked us to my door. "He loves you, Claire. He'll figure that out real soon."

The emotional drain I felt from worrying about Geraldine gave way to exhaustion. Knowing she was out of the woods and on the mend was a great weight off my heart, but it was all I could do to start a fire and climb into my comfy jogging pants and old Atlanta Braves sweatshirt. I fixed a cheese and crackers plate and a glass of wine and settled into my chair in front of the hearth. Bug lay at my feet curled up on her own soft blanket, content that we were home and all was right with the world.

My first prayer was one of thanksgiving for Geraldine. She

had become such an important person in my life. She had so much wisdom to share. Her life had not been easy and some of her choices, she readily admitted, had not been good ones. But she learned and grew from past mistakes. She also turned back to her God given gift, the gift of beauty through art, and had shared it with those whom she had allowed to become her family.

God, here in this quiet place I understand what You might possibly want me to learn. It's enough to love unconditionally. I don't need love to be reciprocated. I have enough love for Geraldine, Sam, Jasmine, and Jack, and of course my Bug. My family. Maybe in some other life, Jack and I would fall in love, get married, have a family and live happily ever after. But I didn't move to Haywood to find a husband. I moved here to find a life given over to You, God, to fulfill Your will for my life. To use the gifts and talents and parts of me that most glorify You and honor others. To lead a selfless life and cherish those who cross my path for however long they may be with me. God, I trust Your infinite wisdom and timing that my life here is meaningful, purposeful, full of joy, and love. I softly touched the guardian angel hanging around my neck and knew it is all about trust.

Such a peace came over me as I grew in the grace God gave me, and I accepted it. With Geraldine improving and a new year moving along, it was time for me to look ahead. Gazing out the front window, I saw snow gently falling. A new beautiful white blanket reminding me of fresh beginnings and of being wrapped in the security of home. I had found a home at last.

Chapter Thirty Eight

I couldn't wait to tell everyone at Haywood House about Geraldine's improvement. I knew she wouldn't be coming back soon because she was so weak, but we all needed hope in due time she would be back with us strong and healthy and we would welcome her. I remembered how hard it was on Grams when one of her friends didn't return to the assisted-living facility because of needing therapy and then went to skilled nursing. Grams missed her so much. While Haywood did have a nursing home, I truly prayed that Geraldine would recover enough to return here and not go to a place that just took care of physical needs.

Walking through the door, I saw my dear friends gathered around the fireplace talking up a storm. As Bug and I approached the ladies, a hush came over the group and they all looked at me, anxiously.

Giddily, I jumped right in with my update on Geraldine, "Did you hear the wonderful news? Geraldine is out of ICU. The doctor said she is making great progress, although she is very weak and won't be back here for a while. Why are you all looking at me strangely?"

Belva spoke up, "Cassie is in town. Jack brought her by last night to see Geraldine's room. It's the first time Cassie has been back since her brother's funeral. They didn't stay long and she hardly spoke to any of us. I don't know what he sees in her."

"Belva! I can't believe you said that in front of Claire. You know she and Jack are seeing each other," whispered Doris.

Hoping my face was not turning fire engine red at this moment, I replied, "Jack and I are just friends. I know he has a history with Cassie. I'm glad they are having a chance to catch up on the last few years. Oh, excuse me, I need to run in and see Mrs. Blanton. We need to talk about the upcoming schedule of activities I have planned." And with that I made a quick exit before the tears puddling in my eyes overflowed.

Talking over all the ideas I had for this new year with Mrs. Blanton was just the distraction I needed from the picture forming in my mind of Cassie and Jack together fanning an old flame. Thank goodness my plans peaked Mrs. Blanton's interest as she started offering more suggestions to go along with mine. She thought the walking program was a good start and gave permission to map out a walking path in the building. She even suggested we give the route a name, Happy Trails, and put up ¼ mile markers with incentive messages to encourage our new walkers. She said she'd check with the Parks and Recreation Office to see if they had pedometers for a reasonable price. A few years ago, they promoted a healthy lifestyle program that included a walking plan in the park. Pedometers were offered to walkers for $15.00. The incentive was to log 10,000 steps daily. If there were some left, the Parks and Recreation Office might reduce the price for us. I couldn't help but smile at the sparkle in Mrs. Blanton's eyes as she busily made notes on who to call about promoting Happy Trails at Haywood House.

I decided to call the hospital to check on Geraldine. I really wanted to go see her and sit with her, but I wouldn't take up time that Cassie needed with her mother. When I called, Sue, at the nurses' station, said Cassie had already been there and left, she thought to head back to California. That was odd. I told her I'd like to come by in the afternoon. Could she think of anything Geraldine needs?

"She needs someone who loves her to not brush her off and plead her busy life. She needs you, Claire. Just come and be with her."

"I will."

Checking my phone for messages, I saw a text from Jack:

> Hey You, miss you. Let's get together
> one night this week. J

My return message:

> Super busy this week,
> maybe next week. C

What a chicken I was! I needed time to process all that had happened in the last 48 hours before seeing Jack. And I had a feeling he might need to think about what just took place as Miss California breezed in and out.

Geraldine's eyes were closed. She looked so frail lying in the hospital bed, hooked to tubes, a blood pressure cuff, and oxygen. God, please give her the strength to get better and come back to Haywood House. I quietly sat down and carefully put her hand in mine. Such a strong gifted woman with so much heartache in her past. I would love to be a light for her present and future. To bring some love to her twilight years. To bring some joy back into her life. At that moment I felt her squeeze my hand.

"You're here, Claire. I'm so glad."

"I can't think of another place I'd rather be." I leaned over, kissed her forehead, squeezed her hand, and settled back to just be with her.

Chapter Thirty Nine

My ideas were having to take a backseat to all the sickness going around Haywood House. I knew winter was a difficult time for the flu and respiratory illnesses, especially for the elderly, and it had really hit hard this year. Visitation at Haywood House had been limited to just workers and care givers. Mrs. Blanton said I might best use my time checking on those in the hospital. Geraldine had been there two weeks now, but was making great progress. I'd been able to see her every day and kept her filled in on how everyone else was doing. Morning and afternoon I took her for laps around the hospital floor in her wheelchair. She had even dabbled a bit with the sketch book I brought to her. Louise and Grace, the spinster sisters, both had to be hospitalized as did Ms. Sally. The sisters' recuperation was steadily improving, but I was worried about Ms. Sally. She slept a lot and did not want to get out of bed. Sarah, the sweet kindergarten teacher from Haywood Elementary, had come to visit her after school each day and filled her in on everything happening in her classroom. Seeing Sarah so animated talking to Ms. Sally made me imagine what Ms. Sally might have been like as a young teacher so many years ago. Ms. Sally perked up during those visits, ever the teacher of young minds. I believe she felt at peace now that she had passed the torch of learning to Sarah. Both their lives had been enriched for knowing each other.

Doc Linder came out of Ms. Sally's room as I was about to leave for the day. I asked how she was doing and he shook his head. "Her body is wearing down and her heart is very weak. I'm afraid it's time to call in the family."

"May I go sit with her until her family comes?"

"By all means. I think she considers you family, Claire. You will be a comfort to her." Paul gave me a slight smile. I knew this was hard on him. I thought maybe doctors in a small town had a harder time dealing with the loss of a patient because the patient was like extended family. He had known Ms. Sally all his life. I reached for his hand and passed on an understanding of how hard it was to lose a loved one, even when it was a long life well lived.

As I entered her room, I thought back on our first meeting. How I wished I had been one of her students back in her days of teaching. Some teachers made life-changing impressions on children. She was one of those special people. She imparted knowledge, enthusiasm, wonder, and wisdom, loving each and every child in her care. Sitting with her now, I knew she had fought the good fight and was ready to rest. But, God, it's so hard to let go.

Chapter Forty

I was young when my mom died and I barely remembered what was said at her funeral, all the while holding Grams' hand tightly in mine. Grams took care of all the details. I did remember beautiful comforting music, kind words being shared, and Bible verses being read. But a 16-year-old girl shouldn't have to bury her mother. Then at Grams' funeral, I was so sad and numb, that again, very little stood out to me. Two deaths within 3 years of each other. I knew then I was totally alone in the world. Oh, there were some friends, but no more family. The pastor read some of Grams' favorite scripture as well as his own. Again, beautiful music was sung and some flower arrangements decorated the church. I had daisies covering her simple casket, just the way she would have wanted.

Now, sitting in the church waiting for Pastor Michael to begin the service for Ms. Sally, I felt a peace come over me. I was ready to hear those words and understand their meaning for the passage of this life to the next. He began by talking about the house with many rooms that has been prepared for us. He talked about the good and faithful servant Ms. Sally had been and the wonderful welcome she had received from all the friends and family that had gone before her. It was a beautiful celebration of life. A humble, beautiful life lived by a woman of faith, of wisdom, and of love. I was so blessed to have known her for the short time I had been in Haywood. I was thankful I had a chance to bring back the memories of her days as a teacher and help her pass on her gift.

After the service a gathering was held in the church parlor. So many of the people there had been taught by Ms. Sally. As I wandered around the room, I heard snippets of stories from the classroom where she had formed lives. Stories mixed with humor, because Ms. Sally always wanted joy and laughter to be part of learning.

Sarah came up to me and grabbed my hands. "If you hadn't brought me to Haywood House to meet Ms. Sally, I would have missed the most important lessons I have learned about teaching. She imparted so much knowledge that is not gained from education classes or textbooks. I only wish I had more time with her. You know we met every Thursday afternoon after you first introduced us. She said I reminded her of herself as a young teacher, full of excitement, energy and wanting to conquer the world of the classroom. But she reminded me to slow down each day and live in the moment of a child's wonder. That's what we are here for to bring the wonder of learning to young eager minds. And to love the children, especially when they are most unlovable. When you do, they will know your love is real. I will miss her so much," a sob escaped as she hugged me and I held her with an understanding of kindred spirits that were able to find each other just a short time ago.

I walked home from the church slowly as snowflakes silently fell on the passing of a dear soul. How fitting that God was shedding soft tears for those of us left behind. In the quiet and the beauty of this place called Haywood, I thought of the many times I sat with Ms. Sally and listened to her share heart-felt memories. The memories of a life lived to the fullest. Not because she was able to travel to exotic places, or live in a big house, or have tremendous adventures. Ms. Sally found joy every day in the little children she so loved. Because her joy was genuine, for a short time in their lives, she gave those children a year of childhood that all children should experience: innocence, love, curiosity, and the time to be carefree. Like Sarah, I would miss her terribly, but how lucky I was to know her.

Chapter Forty One

The residents and I moved into a slow but predictable routine. Most days I was able to be at Haywood House; however, the extremely snowy icy winter caught me off guard a couple of days, and I just stayed at home instead of risking my Southern driving skills on slick roads. We did start our indoor walking program, and the One Mile Walker group was formed. Pace was not important, just making that mile each day was something we all looked forward to achieving as we gathered at our starting point Monday through Friday mornings. Afterwards, we met in the dining room and made sure we drank water and ate orange slices.

Six people showed interest in our first book club meeting, which was encouraging. I suggested starting with the first book in the Mitford series by Jan Karon. It surprised me no one had read any of her books, but I knew they would be a hit. The setting was a small town in North Carolina and the main character was Father Tim. This would be a warm light-hearted read, perfect for our group. I ordered the first book, *At Home in Mitford*, for everyone, and we agreed to meet back in one month to talk about the book and choose the next one. I secretly hoped they would want to go through the whole series, but we'd wait and see.

Next on my idea list was our knitting group. Today I was going to meet with Agnes about a simple scarf pattern for our first project. When we talked earlier in the month, she was excited about leading this group. Once a knitter, always a knitter. She knew just the type of yarn to order to knit soft washable scarves for the children at Hope Shelter. Agnes decided to choose bright colors in the Sassy Skein line. It was not the bulky yarn I thought would be easiest to work with, but I let the expert make the call. The Sassy Skein yarn with its vibrant array of color choices would be perfect for children.

I talked to the director at the shelter and found out there were 5 girls and 6 boys ages 3-15. It was hard to imagine 11 children from this small town did not have a home to live in and needed to stay at Hope Shelter. Then I learned that some of the children were from towns 50 miles away. Haywood was the only town close by with such a facility. I was quite impressed with the place. It was very clean and homey looking. The older children were in school and the 3 younger ones were in the day care section. I was here to talk about the scarves, but I planned to come back and find out about other needs. Wouldn't it be great to develop a grandparent/grandchild relationship between the shelter and Haywood House? My wheels were rolling.

But something else was missing from all my ideas. I had covered the social aspect of Haywood House, physical activities in place, and lots of hobby outlets for the residents. What is missing, God? Oh, my goodness, You are! Pastor Michael conducted a Bible Study once a week, but I didn't think that was enough. How could I be so blind as to miss the one area of life so important to me and the main reason for me moving here? A deep personal relationship with You, God. I knew most everyone here had a past filled with church activities and regular church attendance. I had heard them talk about church socials and quilting bees in the church basement and how their children grew up in the church. But now being physically removed from a church setting, made it harder to connect to God like they did in the past.

I knew of another way to make a connection. Everyone loved music. I had heard Louise and Grace often singing to all the songs from our Broadway movies with beautiful voices. I wondered if either of them could play the piano? If so, I'm sure I could find one to put in the living room and we could have gospel sing night. Singing always lifted people's spirits, and the old favorite hymns were known to all denominations. I put this idea on the front burner. I needed to check with Louise and Grace, first, and see if they were interested in leading a group sing-along every week. I could find the music and bring in hymnals.

When I pitched my idea about a group sing to Mrs. Blanton, she was very much in favor of it, but at a loss for coming up with a piano. She would do some asking around though. Prayers were answered when I went to Louise and Grace. They had been missing the music they enjoyed at their home. Grace was an accomplished pianist, and they both loved singing. And they still had a piano at their old house! They hadn't wanted to get rid of it or sell it just yet, so it was sitting idly at their family home. Maybe it could be brought to Haywood House? How perfect.

God, if I just listen for Your still small voice and reach out to Your people, miracles happen. This isn't an earth-shattering miracle, but two people are given back their love of music and chance to share their talent with friends who will now be able to enjoy singing His praises and having a closer walk with Him. That's a pretty good win-win all around.

One morning in late January, I walked into the living room at Haywood House and saw a stranger talking with the men by the fireplace. I went to greet whoever was visiting and found out he would soon be a new resident.

"Claire, meet Hank Brenner. Hank grew up in Haywood, but took off for greener pastures and roamed the world while taking photos of anything and everything," said Mr. Evans.

"Hello, Mr. Brenner. I'm Claire James. It's so nice to meet you. Will you be staying long in Haywood?"

"Well, I kind of hope so. I'm back home to stay and plan on moving in here the end of the week. I'd love to buy my old house back, but I'm not able to get around very easily anymore. I think this is just the place for me. Plus, my cooking leaves a lot to be desired, so three-square meals a day cooked by someone who knows their way around a kitchen and will clean up to boot, sold me. I'm just catching up with some old acquaintances, then Mrs. Blanton is going to show me the available room."

"I'd love to hear about your photo adventures after you settle in. We just might put your skills to work here capturing our activities on film for an album one day. We do have a resident artist, but not a photographer."

"Who is your artist, if I may ask?"

"Ms. Geraldine Cline is a fantastic artist and paints our movie posters. That one over there is for our next movie night. We're starting our Western series with John Wayne in *True Grit*, a week from Friday. I hope you will join us. Movie night is lots of fun with delicious snacks too."

Mr. Brenner's face seemed to drain of color as he reached for a chair to sit down. "Geraldine is here?"

"Yes, do you know her? She just returned from three weeks in the hospital with pneumonia. She's pretty weak, but we're all so glad she's back home with us now. She's been staying in her room, but today, I was going to coax her out by the fire. She scared us being so sick, but Geraldine's a trooper and is slowly getting her strength back. You'll have to catch up with her after you move in and reminisce about old times."

"Geraldine may not want to do that. You see, long story short; we were young and in love when I left on my first shooting assignment.

I thought I'd be back soon, but more jobs in fascinating places kept presenting themselves, and I took them. So many of my photo shoots were in Africa. I started out in Algeria and worked my way through Sudan and Kenya and finally settling in South Africa as my home base. I had a lucrative position with *National Geographic*. I thought I was living the life, and I was if I wanted to be a loner. After a couple of years, the letters stopped coming from Geraldine, and I heard she had married. There was definitely no reason to come home then. Years became decades, and we both continued to lead separate lives. I heard bits and pieces about her life. I knew she had two children and became obsessed with her art after her husband died. I haven't had a chance to talk to anyone about her since returning, but I did go by her house and realized she no longer lived there. I had no idea she was here at Haywood House. She may not want me here."

Just then a quiet voice said, "Oh, yes I do." Sonia was pushing Geraldine's wheelchair out to the living room. Geraldine sat regally; delicate artist's hands clasped together over the quilt I made for her. Even with tears in her eyes, she, none the less, looked beautiful.

As if they were the only two people in the room, hesitantly she took Hank's hand and looked up at him with a mixture of sadness and longing. "It's been a very long time, Hank. I never thought I would see you again. I tried to follow your adventures for a while, seeing your photographs in magazines, but I lost track of you when my own life filled with children, and then my art. I think we have some catching up to do if you think you'll be content settling down in sleepy Haywood."

It took Hank time to realize Geraldine was really here before him, "I can't think of a place I'd rather settle in than here. I've had the high life of jet-setting around the world. I've seen beautiful cities, the poorest of communities, and God-created places in nature. I've been extremely lucky with my life and my job, but very lonely. It was time for me to come home. I never thought in a million years you'd still be here, but I hoped you would. I am very ready for some catching up time with you."

We all had tears flowing after witnessing such a heartfelt reunion. Oh my, this is just what Geraldine needs to give her life meaning again. After Cassie coming and going so abruptly, I was afraid her selfish daughter took all the hope out of Geraldine's life. *I believe the timing for Hank's return is Your doing, God. And if only for a renewed friendship, then thank You.*

Chapter Forty Two

Jack and I slipped back into our comfortable relationship. He never said anything about Cassie, and I didn't bring up the fact I saw what appeared to be an intimate embrace that day in the hospital before she left. With her back in California, Cassie didn't seem like much of a threat. I was kind of waiting for Jack to say something though. Would she be back? Was he planning on visiting her out there? Was it any of my business? Throwing myself back into the happenings at Haywood House kept me from thinking on this too much. Jack and I were still new at our relationship. I didn't want to become a possessive, jealous woman. I didn't quite know how to navigate our lives moving forward. I wanted to be a part of his though, so we'd hopefully continue to take it slowly and steadily.

The weather was doing its part to keep us from seeing each other much. I had never seen so much snow! Careful what you wish for Grams always said. I wanted to live in a place with lots of snow in the winter and here I am. Sam said he remembered only one other winter this bad, back in 1977. Luckily, I had plenty of wood for the fireplace and, so far, we hadn't lost power. Bug liked to romp in the fresh snow and didn't seem phased by the cold temperatures unless it dipped below zero. Then she was out and in quickly which was fine with me. Tonight, we were home with a pot of vegetable soup on the stove and cornbread in the oven. I'd take some to Sam in a little bit.

Sam had his routine in the evening. During the week he watched old Western TV shows. *Bonanza* came on first, then *Gunsmoke*, *Rawhide* and ending with *Maverick*. He probably had seen them all countless times, but they were like old friends. It was a comfort to him. I had to get dinner over to him before Ben, Hoss and Little Joe found themselves in some sort of predicament.

My choice of evening entertainment was sometimes a Hallmark movie, sappy, I know, but I could get a lot of knitting done during the same old scenes or I might have chosen a first-rate can't-put-it-down book. Tonight, I wanted to finish the quilt I had been making from Grams' favorite fabrics, so I chose love songs by Michael Bublé to play on my CD. Grams loved color, especially brilliant reds, forest greens, golden yellows, and cornflower blues. I started the scrappy quilt pattern with these colors back in Atlanta. Working with the fabric she had picked out and used for quilts she made over the years made me feel closer to Grams. She loved quilting. Grams and her friends made many quilts during their sewing days together and gave them all away. She would never take any money for one, even though they all looked professional. I wasn't there yet, but I loved working with my hands like she did. Hand piecing the top allowed me to work on the quilt anywhere, any time. The time I spent at the hospital waiting for news about Geraldine and then later sitting in her room in the afternoons afforded me lots of quilting time. I'd even taken blocks to Haywood House and pieced them together while visiting by the fire. The ladies were always anxious to see how far along I was and made me promise to bring the finished product for them to see. This evening I was at a point to finish hand quilting the three layers together, thanks to the many snowy nights we'd had since Christmas. Then I could stitch the binding, and I'd be ready to wrap up in the memories of Grams for the rest of this cold winter.

It was so easy to lose track of time when in my sewing zone. My phone rang at 10:00pm. It was Jack.

"Hi there, I hope I didn't wake you. Just wanted to let you know there's a big storm blowing in tonight and tomorrow. Please don't plan to go to Haywood House in the morning because your car could easily get snowbound. I checked on Sam. He said he has enough vegetable soup to see him through a couple of days, thanks to you. He'll be fine, so don't try to go over and check on him. This really is supposed to be a whopper. I was afraid you hadn't heard the weather forecast."

"You're right, I haven't listened to anything on TV. I've been working on Grams' quilt and time has gotten away from me. I didn't even realize it's after 10:00pm. I guess I'd better let Bug out. Please tell me you're not going anywhere either."

"No, I have a lot of respect for this type of storm. It's going to dip down into the single digits, be windy, and dump a couple of feet or more of snow tonight. Just to be on the safe side, have a flashlight handy and some candles ready in case you lose power. Do you have enough wood inside?"

"The fire is getting low, but I'll keep a little burning through the night. I'll bring in some more wood before I go to bed. You're sure Sam is okay?"

"Sam knows how to stay safe in this kind of weather. He's lived in it all his life. It's you I'm concerned about. Best thing for you to do is find a book you've been wanting to read, curl up under a blanket in front of the fire with a mug of hot cocoa, and enjoy Mother Nature in all her majesty. I wish I was there with you."

"What a perfect setting that would be. I'll hold you to that wish some other time. Stay in and stay safe. Bye, Jack. Thanks for calling and checking on me."

After we hung up, I went to the window and looked out on a glorious scene of winter beauty. The snow was falling and swirls of glistening flakes shone in the light of the streetlamp. The ground was covered with a fresh blanket of white wiping clean any trace of footsteps that might have lingered in the front yard. I stepped out on the porch and immediately felt the drop in temperature, but I loved the quiet of a snowy night, so I stood shivering in awe of God's world.

I must have fallen asleep a little after 2:00am, because I awoke late at 8:00am disoriented from sleeping in on a weekday. Embers were still glowing in the fireplace, but the chill in the air told me I'd better quickly stoke the fire back to a warm blaze. Snow was still falling outside. The fact it covered the porch steps, indicated, it hadn't let up much last night. Bug was anxious to go outside, so I let her out the kitchen door where there was a small covered area and the snow wasn't so deep. She hurried out to do her business and was glad to be back inside the cozy warmth of the kitchen. The thermometer read 8 degrees, no melting today. Before I planned out my day, a big pot of coffee was in order. One of Jasmine's cinnamon rolls from the freezer would be a snowy day treat. While the coffee was brewing and the roll heating, I put on some comfortable warm ups and my favorite Atlanta Falcon sweatshirt. I've had this sweatshirt for 25 years. It was just about worn-in perfectly. Today was that wonderful snow day that we Southerners loved. As long as you had milk and bread, you could stay hunkered down for a week. No one could drive on those snowy, icy roads. The South didn't have snow removal equipment so we just waited for it to melt. It usually didn't take too long, but in the meantime, we played hooky from school and work and felt like a kid again—sledding, having snowball fights, making snow angels, and eating snow cream, the best.

The fire warmed up my cozy living room again. Sitting in my favorite chair, I set out to make my to-do list. Some things would be must-dos, but mostly fun things. After all this was an official snow day. Laundry was top of the list since I still had power, then unpacking one more box from my move. I thought these boxes multiplied while I was sleeping. Fun things today included finishing my quilt, starting a jigsaw puzzle, baking bread, and watching *When Harry Met Sally* with a full bowl of popcorn. I was pretty comfortable being by myself most of the time, but a little twinge tugged at my heart and made me wish I wasn't alone. Silly me, I have Bug and I could always talk to God.

Laundry and emptied box checked off the list, now time for some fun. As I was setting up the card table by the window in the living room to work a jigsaw puzzle, I saw Sam outside attempting to shovel snow off the front walk. What was he thinking? It was way too cold to shovel heavy snow. He'd have a heart attack!

Then I grabbed the snow shovel from beside the back door and quickly put on my boots, a heavy jacket, a scarf, and my toboggan. To my friends down South, a toboggan was a sled. But in this neck of the woods, it was your trusted warm woolen hat. Pulling on my gloves, I headed outside making Bug stay in the house much to her dismay.

"Sam, what are you doing out here. Don't you know you could have a heart attack moving this heavy snow? Let me at least help. Some physical exercise might feel good right now since I've been pretty much lounging around all morning."

Sam paused to catch his breath and leaned on the snow shovel, "You don't need to be out here in this weather. I've lived here all my life and this is just one more snowfall I'm trying to get ahead of. Now you go back inside before you get frostbit."

"I can at least help a little so we can both go back inside sooner." And with that I started shoveling a path with Sam. This snow was different from others this winter or maybe it was just so much had accumulated over a short span of time. After shoveling a few loads, it didn't take very long for me to become winded. I wasn't about to let Sam know I was such a lightweight. Stopping for a moment, I looked around and realized there was no one else outside. No cars moved along the street either. I wondered when the snow plow would come to our neighborhood. I liked this peacefulness, though. I hoped it would continue throughout the day.

"Sam, I think..." a sharp pain gripped my chest followed by continued pain in my arms and my jaw. I knew this pain. Oh, please no God, not another heart attack! I dropped the shovel and grabbed my chest. The pain was sharper than I remembered during the first one, especially in my arms. Beads of sweat popped out on my forehead and quickly froze. I couldn't pass out. I had to tell Sam what was happening.

I turned to Sam and he immediately grabbed me when he saw the look of terror on my face. "Sam, I'm having a heart attack," I whispered. I was almost afraid to say it out loud as if not saying anything would make it go away. I flashbacked to three years ago. I was running and suddenly it felt like I was dragging a ton of bricks. I hit a wall after only 2 miles. Usually, I was invigorated after a run but this time I was spent. I remembered thinking I must be coming down with something. I felt a little nauseous and so tired. That night my chest started to hurt and pain radiated down my arms. This wasn't right. I remembered my mom having the same symptoms, but shaking them off. After I drove myself to the emergency room, the doctors quickly assessed I was having cardiac problems. I eventually made it to the CCU with a cardiac doctor familiar with SCAD. I was lucky then; would I be lucky again?

"Girl you just over-did it out here. Come on let's get you inside. I could use a little break right now, too."

"No, Sam. This has happened to me before." A heaviness overtook me and I could hardly stand, let alone walk to Sam's house. I didn't want him to carry me because we just didn't need two heart attack victims! "Sam, you need to call Paul and tell him I am experiencing

SCAD, spontaneous coronary artery dissection. He may not know about it, it's pretty rare, but he can look it up and see what tests to order. Sam, I'm scared."

Despite my protests, he picked me up with ease and quickly trudged through the deep snow to his front door. Inside his house, he gently sat me down on his couch and grabbed his phone to dial the hospital. I heard him in the background whispering in the phone.

"Paul says for you to take some aspirin and lie down. He's sending an ambulance, but it might take a while because the roads aren't cleared yet. He said to call back if you have any other symptoms or feel worse. I'm going to let Jack know what's going on."

"No, Sam. He told me to stay inside because this wasn't the kind of weather to fool around with. He'll be mad I didn't listen to him."

"You're darn right he'll be mad and so am I! I never would have let you shovel snow if I knew you had a heart condition." Sam started pacing and running his hands through his hair and then knelt down next to me. "Listen, we love you Claire, and don't want anything to happen to you. You have to trust us to take care of you. And that means letting all those people who love you know you need them right now. I'm calling Jack and Jasmine."

He left to go get the aspirin and tears welled up in my eyes. I didn't want to leave these wonderful people. *God, please help me though this. Give me strength and courage and always faith.*

Sam came back and handed me the phone. "Someone wants to talk to you. I'll be right back." I knew it was Jack.

"Claire, oh kiddo, what have you gone and done this time? Hey, gal, I'm going to stay on the line with you until the ambulance gets there. Okay? I'm going to act a little bit like a doctor right now. Just bear with me. Is any of the pain worse than when you first experienced it?"

"No, in my chest there's just a dull ache. My jaw hurts some though. I'm so tired. I don't think I can walk to the emergency room."

"Claire, don't try to get up or go anywhere. The aspirin will help prevent blood clotting and Paul will have all the tests ready for when you arrive at the hospital. I'll meet you there. Sam will stay with you, for now. You're not alone."

The front door opened and Sam came in with a snow-covered brown bundle of fur and wiggles. Bug sensed something was not right and instead of her boundless energy when she saw me, she quietly came over and put a paw on my arm. Seeing her brought a fresh gush of tears. She curled up beside me and we waited for the ambulance. Sam stayed on the phone with Jack and reported on my condition. Right now, I just wanted to sleep. Sam jostled me every few minutes, I guess to see if I was still alive! I was not going anywhere. A siren sounded in the back of my mind. Was I in Atlanta? Why was this happening all over again?

So much took place in such a short time and yet I felt like I was in a slow-moving fog. As I was being moved to the ambulance, I felt faint and about to black out. That was the last thing I remembered. I found out later that my heart stopped and the EMS worker started CPR. To Sam, minutes that seemed like hours went by, and finally the paramedics restored my pulse. In the ambulance I was hooked up to all kinds of lines. Sam stayed with me and patted my hand saying over and over, "Hang in there, girl." Once we reached the hospital, Paul took over. Before I went for the tests he had ordered, Jack was by my side. I tried to apologize for not following his orders to stay inside, but everything was fuzzy. One minute he was beside me, and the next I was being wheeled down the corridor.

A strange calm came over me as I surrendered to Paul's expertise. I didn't need to be in charge any more. He knew what he was doing and by the mirage of tests he had ordered, I could tell he was on top of everything. Since this was my second cardiac event, Paul called in a cardiologist from Billings to take the lead on this. I was taken to the ICU after the angiogram determined where the tears were in the arteries to my heart. Two more heart attacks took place while waiting for the specialist. I was in the right place though, and if it was not my time to die, Paul would do whatever was necessary to keep me alive. When conscious, the pain was excruciating. Something was definitely different from last time. God, is this when I make another bargain with you? Just let me live through this, and I will be totally yours. But I realized God was not in the bargaining business. I would be okay with the outcome. I was trusting and fully loving those who had come into my life. If I didn't see tomorrow, I had had many todays that had been blessed.

The beeping was the first thing I was aware of when I woke up in a white and steel, sterile room. I looked around at all the bags hanging on poles, the monitors with numbers changing on a regular basis, and the white board on the wall with names scribbled by phone numbers. I felt a tube going down my throat, the blood pressure cuff on my left arm, and the pulse oximeter on my finger measuring my oxygen level and heart rate. I was alive. Then I looked over at the man slumped in the chair beside me. I squeezed the comforting hand holding mine. Jack opened his sleepy red eyes and said, "Hey there, I sure am glad you're back."

Ten days in the hospital was a gracious plenty. Recuperating from a triple bypass procedure would slow a person down but not out. It took that to repair the arteries to my heart and keep it from being further damaged from the heart attacks. I was so anxious to get home, but my incredibly loving and over-protective extended family had seen fit to not let me go home by myself. So, it was decided, why not stay at Haywood House just long enough to regain my strength and health? Mrs. Blanton assured me that there was a room available, that no one would be put out because of me. That way, I wouldn't be alone, I'd have regular meals, and someone would look in on me day and night. My objections to this plan fell on deaf ears. I would stay at Haywood House for two weeks, then undergo another check-up. If everything looked good at that point, I might be able to go home.

I said there was no way I'd leave Bug any longer. Already I had to rely on Sam to take care of her while I was in the hospital. I couldn't ask him to continue two more weeks. Mrs. Blanton offered me an alternative plan. Bug could stay with me during the day at Haywood House with different staff members gladly volunteering to take her outside for exercise. At night, Sam or Jack would come get her and take her back home with one of them. She would love this because aside from me, they were her two favorite people. This was an argument I wasn't going to win.

And truth be told, I was a little relieved not to be alone after being discharged from the hospital. A scare like this, my second SCAD event, put a lot of things in perspective. I admitted to being apprehensive about living alone right now. I also appreciated the love shown me by so many people. I'd been given an incredible gift. Another day to be grateful, to be surrounded by friends who loved me and shared the joy God so freely gives to all of us. Okay, I'd be a Haywood House resident for a couple of weeks.

Chapter Forty Three

It was true. Being needed brings a whole new level of energy to a person or persons. My first day at Haywod House brought everyone to my room to just say hi, to give me a peck on the cheek, to pat my shoulder, or to squeeze my hand. They were advised to not stay and visit so as not to wear me out, but just check in to make sure I was okay. I loved it. Sam stayed in the room with me to keep the flow of people moving. Every once in a while, he said it was time for me to rest and would step out and close the door giving me a bit of privacy. After two days of this bedside manner, I assured him I would take it easy and call someone if I needed anything. He could go socialize with everyone and retell the snow shoveling story. Since then, my friends at Haywood House had been at my beck and call throughout each day I'd been a resident here checking to see if I needed some water, more blankets, or something to eat. Though I haven't really needed them for anything, I wouldn't ever let them know their concern was not appreciated.

Paul checked on me daily, although I knew it was above and beyond his normal duty as an ER doctor. I was just so grateful for him believing me about SCAD and his quick thinking in ordering the angiogram and echocardiogram and having the operating room ready for the cardiologist. It was a rare condition and presented itself differently with each individual. Precious time could have been lost if he had taken a wait-and-see approach. Sometimes that works, but this time I needed repair immediately. I believe God was watching out for me, too. Because the snowstorm created bad driving conditions, the ambulance could have been hampered from picking me up as well as the cardiac doctor seriously delayed coming from Billings. All turned out well, though. Sam took care of Bug and Jasmine made sure both Sam and Jack didn't go hungry. Jack never left the hospital from the time I arrived in the ambulance until I woke up from the surgery. After that he would just go home to sleep at night when he was assured the nurses would hover while he was gone. Mrs. Blanton came daily to get an update. She said the residents at Haywood House would not be content until she saw me in the flesh every day and reported back to them. Cards were delivered along with flower arrangements, but the most touching gesture was that Grams' quilt was finished and brought to me when I moved to a private room. I didn't know who completed the binding, but the stitches were impeccable. I was thinking Mr. Abernathy with his talent for sewing had the biggest hand in that. Jasmine brought the quilt and laid it over me. I immediately felt a connection with Grams. She was watching over me. Jasmine knew the healing effect it would have on me.

As the days went by, I glimpsed into the inner workings of an assisted-living place. Even before the residents woke up, the staff was busy with meal preparation, medication distribution, laundry, general cleaning, and assignments for care. Some people needed help with showering, dressing, making the bed, and getting to the dining room for breakfast. For a few days I was one of those in need. I didn't want to take any of the workers away from the regular residents, but I had lost a lot of strength while I was in the hospital and had to rely on the staff to help me up and start the day. It was very humbling to require help with the basics of walking to the bathroom, getting dressed, and leaving your room to go to the dining area. I was very appreciative of the help, but so embarrassed to need it. This whole experience brought empathy to mind.

In Atlanta, I came out of the hospital fairly quickly with just an order to take it easy for two weeks. This time I was recovering from major surgery. I could relate to my friends here who not long ago, were living very independent productive lives. Then, all of a sudden, independence was taken away. You couldn't do anything the way you used to do it. Maybe you were a morning person and you got up early, fixed your coffee and while it was brewing, took a walk in the neighborhood or around the ranch. When you came home you ordered your day according to chores that needed tending such as, shopping, lunch with a friend, yard work, or whatever your gift was that called for a few hours of your afternoon. Then you planned dinner and prepped for it, maybe enjoyed a glass of wine at that time or later, had a quiet meal with or without someone, then curled up in a favorite chair and lost yourself in a book or movie of your choice. When you lived in a retirement facility your choices were limited. Not gone completely, but limited. You may no longer have a car, so that spur of the moment idea to run to the store to pick up that forgotten ingredient, or drop by to see someone with a plate of warm cookies, or take in a movie on a rainy afternoon was no longer an option.

I knew my time here was brief. That this wasn't where I would spend my future. I would be going back home soon to my independent life and all my own choices. How could I use this experience to further enrich the lives of everyone at Haywood House? I started writing down how my life had changed over these past couple of weeks and set up a meeting with Mrs. Blanton to go over my new ideas. First though, I made it a point to list the positive accomplishments already in place. Top of the list was the caring staff. They went out of their way to help but not demean any resident because of their inability to take care of everyday tasks. The facility was every bit as clean as anyone's own home. That was not an easy job because of the size of the place and so many residents. The chef and kitchen workers offered a variety of very good meal choices. Breakfast could be a hot meal of eggs your way, bacon or sausage, toast or bagel, or cereal and fruit. Every week pancakes or French toast or muffins were prepared. Lunch was different soups, sandwiches, and salad. Dinner had a meat, two or three vegetable choices, salad, bread, and always a dessert. The kitchen staff was aware of healthy guidelines, yet still managed to make the food tasty and appetizing. The different activities I introduced were ongoing and totally supported by the staff. Happy residents made for happy staff members, and vise-versa. But there was still something missing. I would continue to be observant and take my ideas to Mrs. Blanton before I left which would be soon.

Jack surprised me when he came by at 5:00pm right before it was time to go into the dining room for dinner. I'd seen him almost every day, but usually he came in the morning before he opened the clinic or around lunchtime.

"Hi, Jack. What a nice surprise! What's in the bag?" I asked curiously.

"You and I are going to have a quiet dinner by the fireplace when everyone else goes into the dining room. I brought Brunswick Stew, cornbread, and baked apples. Jasmine threw in two of her decadent brownies for dessert. You, my dear, are going out for dinner with me but with the convenience of never leaving the facility. I even brought a flower for the table." He pulled out a bud vase with a beautiful red rose and babies' breath surrounding it and set it in the center of a card table after he covered it with a white tablecloth and two cloth napkins. He left for a minute and brought back two soup bowls, two plates, silverware, and two glasses of ice water. I think Mrs. Blanton had been in on this, as she winked when passing by on the way to the dining room.

"Jack, what's this all about? Hopefully I'll be home in a few days. We could have this surprise meal at my house."

Jack took a moment to give Bug the attention she was vying for by her wagging tail and circling around his legs. When she had gotten enough loving from him, she was content to lay down under the table.

"I've missed talking to you. We see each other for a walk around the building or a few minutes here and there, but there is always someone around. I love visiting with all the people here you know that, but tonight I'm being selfish. I want you to myself. So, with Mrs. Blanton's help I have your undivided attention for a whole hour. She has planned a little after dinner activity for everyone in the dining room so we won't be disturbed."

"Jack, this is perfect!

"Claire, ever since Geraldine was hospitalized, we have both been so busy that we haven't had a chance to talk about Cassie."

I knew this moment would come, but I wasn't ready for it to be brought out into the open. Not tonight. Let's just enjoy one more time together. Oh please, Jack. I'm not ready to give you up.

"Claire, Cassie has been part of my life for as long as I remember. We grew up together and I always thought we had a future together, too. When she went off to California, I threw myself into being the best veterinarian I could be for our community. It gave me a purpose and helped with the loneliness. I hoped she would tire of that life and come back sooner or later. Then the years went by. I would hear from her just enough to keep my interest and hope alive that one day we would marry and live here in Haywood. We talked about it, but she just said she needed to follow her dream of success in Hollywood before she settled down. I was okay with that for a while. Like I said, I was pretty busy with the life I had built here and certainly didn't want to move to Los Angeles. I would fly down to see her a couple of times a year, but she never came back here except for her brother's funeral and then when Geraldine was so sick. Up until this last visit I was okay with our arrangement. We were both doing what we loved and enjoyed seeing each other from time to time."

I was taking all of this in and trying so hard to be strong, but I couldn't keep tears from betraying how I really felt. They left a trail of sadness down my face. Jack tenderly wiped a tear off my cheek, reached for my hands, and held them tightly.

"Claire, when I met you in September, I felt alive in a way I hadn't felt with Cassie. You totally caught me off guard with your helplessness that night in the emergency room. Not to mention how I fell for Bug right off the bat. I wanted to be the one who kept you safe and you gave me plenty of opportunities to do so. What kept me wanting to know you better was the unselfish nature that came through in all you did for a community you didn't know at all. I was taken by this woman who drove across the country alone to start a new life, a life that brought joy to others so easily. I knew I was falling for you, but I hadn't severed my long-distance relationship with Cassie. It was easy to put her out of my mind since we didn't communicate on a regular basis. Then she showed up when Geraldine was hospitalized. The stark difference between the love and concern you showed Geraldine, being at the hospital hours on end, sitting with her, talking with her, holding her hand, and the breeze-in and breeze-out nature of Cassie with her mother almost at death's door, was the deciding factor. My eyes were opened at that moment to Cassie's selfish personality. A personality that wasn't going to change. If she couldn't spend more than 24 hours with her mother who was in critical condition, then nothing would make her want to come back home for good. I thought her dream of making it in California was worthy and exciting, but it came with a price. I told her our on-and-off again relationship was over. I couldn't see a future with someone so callous. She really wasn't like that growing up. She was adventurous and fun loving, the life of the party, so to speak. I gave her room and time to come back to live in Haywood, but that's not going to happen. I told her at the hospital before she left not to call anymore, and that I wouldn't be flying to Los Angeles this spring either. I think she was surprised, but she didn't try to talk me out of my decision. She just said it's been fun, but Haywood is just too small for her. She needed the pace and excitement L.A. brought to her life. I feel for her because it sounds like a life just trying to blot out real feelings. The hectic pace keeps her from facing a life of meaning and commitment.

"So, Claire, I have been wanting to tell you this since Cassie left. We kind of missed each other for a couple of weeks. I think you were trying to distance yourself from me. Was it because of Cassie? Then I got the heart-rending call from Sam about your heart attack. I have never been so worried in my life waiting for you at the hospital and, then, seeing you lying there so helpless and scared. I wanted to make it better, but I had to just rely on Paul and the heart surgeon to fix everything. And they did. Now I can see our future together as nothing but perfect."

By now, I was a puddle of tears, happy and sad. Happy that this wonderful man sitting here holding my hands was everything I hoped for in a companion. He had cleared up all my doubts about Cassie and had made me believe that we could move forward together. But then, the sad. I was not a whole woman. I came with scars and flaws and the inability to have children. I couldn't saddle him with this future. Right now, he was being protective but, in a few months, or years would he feel the same? I had to tell him.

"Jack, you are the kindest, most gentle, and sincere person I have ever known. You deserve a complete life with a healthy full-of-energy woman. One who could give you a family. Jack, I'm damaged goods. I've had two heart attacks and have been told to never have children. I can't rob you of that incredible joy of having a family. I love you. I love you so much I have to let you go. I am not freeing you to go back to Cassie. She is not the woman for you, but someone else out there is. I'm so incredibly sorry I didn't tell you how serious my medical problem was in the beginning. We could have been good friends, but not fallen in love. I think I'm meant to be alone and I'm trying to come to grips with that. God and I have had many conversations about my role in this world. I have found such joy being here in Haywood and working at Haywood House. My friendship with you, Sam, and Jasmine will be enough. Until this second attack happened, I was starting to believe I was invincible. Most of the time SCAD only happens once to a person. I wanted to leave that part of my past in Atlanta and chalk it up to the stress and the pace of my life back there. I'm now realizing I have to live with this condition the rest of my life. While I may never have another episode, living in Atlanta was not what caused this to happen. It's the way I was made."

Shaking his head, Jack chuckled, smiled and said, "I understand your uncertainty right now. You haven't completely healed from your surgery, let alone gotten over the shock of this happening again. But Claire, I'm not looking for some perfectly healthy woman without issues. I have fallen in love with you, flaws and all. I don't know what the future will bring as far as a family is concerned, but not being able to have children is not a deal-breaker for me. I love you. We may just have a passel of dogs, or we could adopt. We can work that out. Right now, I just know I want to spend the rest of my life with you, but you have to know I love my job, too. I might have crazy hours such as leaving in the middle of the night to birth a colt or calf. Being the only vet around here means long hours at times. Could you live with that?"

My heart was bursting at this moment. Jack loved me flaws and all. I wanted to let him off the hook, but he wanted to stay around.

I threw my arms around his neck and felt the security and love I had been searching for since losing Grams. I didn't want to let him go. But just then the dining room doors opened and our intimate dinner was now quite public. Oohs and aahs and a bit of clapping brought by our friends interrupted our intimate setting.

"Let's continue this conversation when I am released from rehab, but just so you know, love for your job and long hours is not a deal-breaker for me!" Breaking from our embrace with a tender kiss, we greeted our dear friends and were immersed in the chatter of the wonderful ordinary life inside Haywood House.

Chapter Forty Four

I was being released from rehab and Haywood House. I still needed follow up with some physical therapy, but Paul had given me a clean bill of health to go home. I had mixed emotions. Yes, I was totally happy that I could go back to my home and independent life. I would have my privacy, ability to make my own meals, chance to come and go as I pleased, and use of my car. All the things I had missed, and that I knew everyone at Haywood House missed, also. But it could be lonely at home.

Here, at Haywood House, there was always someone to talk to, play cards with, and eat meals with. Someone was always checking on you. How could I make that an even more positive part of assisted-living? While I was here, I noticed all the ways the staff worked hard to make living conditions so homey, but I kept thinking something was missing. I thought I knew what it was. I wanted to go home and work on this idea, run it by Jack and see if I was on to something.

Jack came to take me home. I couldn't wait to have Bug to myself curling up in our favorite chair by a roaring fire. I definitely missed my little brown dog in our own home. You would think I was leaving and never coming back by the sad faces and clinging goodbyes I was getting from everybody. A tightness in my chest momentarily caught me off guard. Tears gathered, as often they did, when my emotions tended to surface. These people had been family to me. It was hard leaving them.

"Please come by and see us from time to time," said Mrs. Darby through tears and hiccups. "We have just gotten so used to you being here with us so we can keep an eye on you and make sure you are alright. You're like our daughter and we don't want to let go."

"Oh, Mrs. Darby, everyone, I'll be back next week, same as I was before this incident happened. My hours may be a little shortened at first, but you are going to be seeing plenty of me, don't worry. I'm going home, but not to stay. Just long enough to tweak some ideas brewing in my mind to bring back to all of you. There's no way I'll stop being a part of Haywood House. I love you all. You're my family."

Everyone let out a big sigh of relief, as if they had all been holding their breath wondering if I would vanish out of their lives. I didn't realize they thought I wasn't coming back. I hoped that was enough for them right now, to know that I'd be back next week. No one ever left assisted-living to resume their normal life. I had to make them understand about new chapters in their lives, just like I would be understanding about a new chapter in my life. God, the changes we have to adapt to can be viewed positively or negatively. We all have mountains and valleys to navigate, and if we are lucky enough to live a long life, we can help others down their path with wisdom gathered from our journey. Maybe it was time for all of us to have a deepened conversation about life when our hopes and dreams took a detour. I promised to see them next Monday, and with that I was able to give my last hug and kiss and wave goodbye.

Bug was wild beyond belief. I had never seen her so bonkers. When Jack opened the door, she came flying out to the porch, shook her little body all around me, whimpered and almost howled to let me know what she had thought about my absence from our house.

I knew how she felt though. We belonged together because of all we had been through these last three years. I could barely sit down before she was in my lap daring me to move without her attached. Jack and Sam could only stand there watching with laughter. Sam had been a Godsend taking care of Bug all this time. What would I do without them, either of them?

As Bug calmed down, I started to feel a drain on my energy. I knew I had to take it easy, but I didn't know I would feel this weak. Jack immediately picked up on how I was feeling and ordered me to put my feet up while he and Sam took care of moving in my luggage and getting a fire started. Something smelled scrumptious from the kitchen and I knew Jasmine must have had something to do with that. I closed my eyes for a moment and reflected on the last few weeks. Fear and worry had been replaced by sureness and love. I'd be taken care of here. I didn't know what the future held, but I did know I was not alone. What a blessed feeling.

Chapter Forty Five

Home was the medicine I was missing. I felt stronger every day. Even though I could not go outdoors because of the cold and continued snow, I was able to exercise inside and work on my plan for Haywood House. I walked around the house and took in the things that made it home for me. I was able to choose the wall colors, colors that made me feel a certain way. Yellow in the kitchen made me happy and awake, blue in the bedroom was calming and secure, soft terra cotta in the living room brought out my love of earth tones and was warm and inviting. Artwork on the walls was also meaningful to me. Some pieces I brought from my home in Georgia, and others I purchased here to surround myself with my new life, depicting scenes of the mountains and rugged plains. I loved having my afghans, quilts, and pillows bringing texture to the rooms along with candles and vases of flowers which added personal touches even in the winter. I was surrounded by colors, scents, and the feel of what made me happy; what made this place a home for me, not just a dwelling place or house.

This was what was missing at Haywood House. The individual rooms were spacious and clean and, yes, most of the residents had their own furniture. But something was missing, and I felt it the short time I was there. Almost like I was living in a nice hotel room with lots of amenities, but nothing was really saying, "this was your home now." A hotel room implied stay here a while, but don't put down roots. And that was all well and good because you didn't plan to stay long in a hotel. But when you moved into an assisted-living facility, you might stay a long while, and almost always wouldn't be going back to your home. Nobody liked to stay in limbo. Your roots may not have had time to grow very deep, but they must be put down. Do you remember going on trips and having a wonderful time, but there was always something special about coming home?

This would be a hard sell to Mrs. Blanton. She ran a very neat, clean, well-managed facility where everyone was taken care of, fed good meals, and now had a lot of activities to enjoy each day. I felt positive about the changes I had helped bring about to make Haywood House feel more like home. To help the residents become more engaged with each other, Mrs. Blanton had come through for me and my ideas so far, so maybe, just maybe, she would go for this one, too. I'd run it by Jack tonight, when he came over for dinner and then be ready to present this idea to Mrs. Blanton in the morning.

Leaning back in my chair after a delicious dinner I said, "Jack, you are spoiling me. Dinner together three times this week and you have supplied them all. It's my turn."

"You'll have lots of chances to cook for me, right now, you are to rest and get stronger. Going back to work tomorrow might be a little premature. Please promise me you will only go there for half a day. In fact, plan on a half-day all week."

"Jack, I've been cleared to start my normal routine except for running. I'll be fine. Plus, I think there will be about 20 mother hens watching over me all week. If I so much as hiccup, I will be ordered to sit down and put my feet up. I'm ready to jump back in and start testing my new ideas which I wanted to talk to you about tonight. I really feel like Haywood House has to take on a more permanent meaning for everyone, albeit, more short term. When I was there, I felt like a guest in a nice hotel, just passing through. And I was just passing through given my circumstances. The residents there are not passing through, there's no going home. Yet, I don't get the feeling that it is home for anyone."

"How are you going to change that concept? It's like that in most assisted-living places. People know they can't live alone anymore, and most of them accept this is the next step."

"What if they had more ownership in their room. They pick the paint color for the walls, put up more pictures, make a sitting area with a favorite chair, and a rug. Right now, their rooms are neat and clean, and except for the bedspreads and quilts on the foot of the beds, they pretty much look alike. Surely, they have some furniture at their home or in storage they could bring to make each room unique and homier. What if they had carpet instead of linoleum? Jack, I really think Haywood House could become Haywood Home."

"Claire, I am the last one to want to burst your bubble, but all that takes money and the residents just don't have a lot of extra to spend that way. And there is a turnover of people. Not very quickly, but we're talking a few years, not decades."

"Jack, I know when a room opens for a new resident, the walls get painted, but why just a light beige? Why not green, or blue, or coral, or yellow? And surely a carpet would be warmer and maybe even safer than a slick floor. The rooms at Haywood are very large. I think they can be turned into more creative living areas with just a little ingenuity."

"Claire, don't you think that is a decision for the families to make? How are you going to implement this make-over?"

"I don't know if the families even realize something can be done to make homes out of these rooms. That's what I want to talk to Mrs. Blanton about tomorrow and also, I want to have a serious discussion with everyone about accepting and embracing change.

I thought a lot about this during the weeks I spent at Haywood. I knew I was going home and my life was going to be different. After my heart attack, I could either wallow in pity and wish for a different scenario or look for new ways to accept God's plan for my life. I'm afraid many of the seniors are not accepting this new chapter in their lives. They are hoping against hope that they will be able to go back to their home, or they have given up on finding the joy in their new circumstances. For Grams, assisted-living was a holding pattern for her. She was content, but not joyful. I don't want Haywood House to be just a holding place for the people there. Do you think I can convince them to live more in the moment than in the past?"

"I don't think you give yourself enough credit for what you have done already. There is a lot more joy at Haywood House now than six months ago. You have made a difference. You won't be able to change everyone's outlook. That's just human nature to cling to the past or wish for a different set of circumstances. But you might be able to reach one or two people. In fact, I think you already have. Look at the sparkle in Geraldine's and Mrs. Darby's eyes. You have brought joy back into their lives. That being said, I think sharing your story of how life has thrown a monkey wrench into your plans can only help them sort out feelings for their future at Haywood House. I say go for it with Mrs. Blanton. She has mellowed over the past few months. You are having a very positive influence on her. She wants the best for her people, but she must consider the management side of running this business. You see the compassionate side. From her standpoint though, these changes are not in the budget, and I can't see her raising the monthly charge. How are these decorating ideas going to be financed?"

"Jack, back in Atlanta, I had a very good job and made a nice salary. The best thing I did was invest. I lived fairly frugally and put my money into stocks. It has paid off and continues to grow. I can foot the bill for paint and carpet and, like I said, as the rooms turn over, new residents can choose a paint color rather than beige. Good carpeting can be cleaned as needed. I would be a silent partner, though. I don't want the residents to know I am paying for this if it is accepted."

"Claire, that is such a noble gesture, but you might need the money in the future for your own situation. Don't put yourself in a bind over this. You've got too big of a heart, and that can be a problem down the road."

I had to smile at that thought. Taking Jack's hands and bringing them to my heart I said, "My heart is forever fixed to give. There's no problem too big that God can't fix one way or the other. I trust Him completely."

Jack brushed my hair back and looked in my eyes trying to imagine how we had come to be. His kiss was tender and full of the love I knew he had for me. Tears of happiness began to fall and as he wiped them away, I told him, "I'll love you forever."

Chapter Forty Six

The reception I received Monday morning from my friends was crazy! You would have thought I had been gone for months instead of days. Well, I guess technically, I was gone from my job a number of weeks, but now things would start to get back to normal and at a good time, too. Mid-winter was a dreary time of the year anywhere, but here with the cold and dirty snow and lack of color outside, we were all in kind of a funk. That's why I hoped my idea could take root and maybe we could liven things up around here.

I couldn't believe how nervous I was about presenting my idea to Mrs. Blanton. I think it was because I wanted so much for her to accept it and be excited. I had done a lot of research into type of paint for the walls that would be easy to keep clean. Also, the best carpeting for the money that would be safe, durable, and again easy to clean. I contacted Tab's Hardware and could order the paint and carpet through them. Manny, who painted my house, could find painters willing to work so that many rooms could be painted at the same time to hasten the process. I knew things would be disrupted for a while, but maybe we could have more activities in the living room and dining room during the day to keep people entertained while out of their rooms. That was right up my alley so I could easily make it happen.

If I could walk on air, I'd be floating right now! Mrs. Blanton bought my idea lock, stock, and barrel! She said she had always wanted to fix up the individual rooms, but money constraints kept her from being able to do anything. She also admitted she didn't have a very good eye for decorating so she was glad someone else was willing to step in to make Haywood House the warm welcoming homey place I was describing. I couldn't wait to get started, but first I had to talk to the residents. While I couldn't imagine them not being excited about redecorating, Mrs. Blanton warned me they could be a hard sell. If they viewed their time here as temporary, they might not see the need to fix up their rooms. That was where my other idea had to be accepted. This was their home now. I would have that talk tomorrow. Right now, I was feeling the effects of my first day back to work and my energy level was not matching my enthusiasm. Time to gather up Bug and let everyone know I'd be back tomorrow.

At home, I started jotting down thoughts to share tomorrow about how life throws you a curveball, and if you wanted to keep playing the game, you had to learn to adjust. I wanted to share my story first, and then I hoped others would share, too. I think I'd have to have some boxes of Kleenex handy!

Tuesday morning, most everyone had gathered in the dining room, and while it was not the most intimate of places to have a serious discussion, it afforded us enough room to include all residents and some staff members. I began my story.

"I am so happy that you all have come here this morning with open minds to some possible ideas that will directly and positively affect each of you. First, though, I want to share the road that has led me here today." I took a deep breath, said a little prayer, and jumped in.

"Growing up, I lived with my mom and grandmother, but was closest to my Grams, Mom's mother. My mom worked many hours a week to keep us in a comfortable home with enough to eat and access to a good school. Grams lived with us at that time, and since she didn't work, I was with her most of the time I wasn't in school which was why I had such a close relationship with her. When I was young, my mother died suddenly, or what I thought was suddenly, of a heart attack or what at that time was called heart complications. I later realized my mother had died from SCAD or spontaneous coronary artery dissection. I know this because that is what I have experienced twice. Once in Atlanta, and once here. SCAD is what made me completely change my life from living downtown Atlanta and working in corporate America to moving to Haywood and finding the life God had planned for me from the beginning. The life that was nurtured by my dear Grams. I thought because I was free from the stress of my former life, that I would never have to worry about my health again or at least not for a very long time. I was wrong. Without going into a lot of detail, SCAD entered my life again with more devastating effects. I am fairly young, but my heart has been compromised. It is not working at full capacity, and I will never be able to have children because of the strain it can put on my body. This is not the way I wanted my life to go. Don't so many of us look forward to getting married and having a family? I did. But now the family part is not possible and getting married with this damaged body does not bode well for me. Not the life I had planned. But I have had many conversations with God in prayer, and He constantly reminds me that I am in His hands. That I need to trust His goodness and plan. Only today is promised, not tomorrow, and I need to make the most of today. I've kind of simplified things this morning but I want to relate my life to yours. Like me and my limitations, you are not where you planned to be at this time of your life. And because of this, it seems like you are just passing through right now or even in a holding pattern in your life. When that happens, we stop living and do more existing. Being here at Haywood House should not be viewed as the end of the line. We each wake up every morning to a new day that God has given us. We can enjoy reminiscing about the past, but not get stuck living in the past, or wishing for things to be the way they were.

"I have wrestled with God a lot over this. In the end, I keep going back to His love and unique design for my life. He made me this way, flaws and all, for a specific reason. I'm hoping I am on the same page as He is by being here, loving all of you and wanting the best for you each day." The Kleenex boxes were circulating around the room. I think they were listening.

"I want to help make Haywood House your home. It's not a hotel in which you are temporarily staying. It is now your home, albeit, not like your home growing up, or even the one you raised your family in, but it is now your home. I want to help make it just that for you. I have some ideas to propose to you and I want to get your ideas and thoughts, too. I presented my ideas to Mrs. Blanton and she is on board. Any questions or thoughts before I go on?"

"Claire," says Mrs. Darby, "I'm worried about you. Can you continue working here in your condition? We don't want to cause you to have any more heart problems. Is this job too much for you?"

"Mrs. Darby, thank you for your concern, but I assure you this job is not putting a strain on my heart. There may be some days I work shorter hours, but there is no stress here, and it's where I want to be, with all of you."

"Claire, should you be living by yourself in this condition? Wouldn't it be better for you to come back here and live so you can be watched over?" asked Mrs. Collins.

"Mrs. Collins, I was so grateful to have a chance to live here while I was recuperating, but I've been cleared by my doctors to live at home. I have regular visits with my physical therapist and have scheduled quarterly doctor exams. I'm okay. With Sam next door, there is no way I will not be watched over, I assure you!"

"Now about my ideas for a home setting here at Haywood House, I have proposed to Mrs. Blanton that your rooms be redecorated with paint color of your choosing and carpet. If any of you have pictures from home to hang on the walls or want to purchase some pictures, that will be included in the renovation. Your rooms will be yours to fix up to your taste. Any ideas for making the common areas, such as living room, dining room, or library homier will be welcomed. This renovation will not affect your monthly fee and none of the redecorating will come out of your pocket or your family's pocket. The work will be done by people here in town and, that way, can be done in a timely manner."

Right now, as I looked out at the residents, I was seeing blank faces, not the response I was hoping for and certainly not the answer to my plan. Was I totally wrong in wanting this for these dear people?

"Claire, let's give everyone a chance to think all of this over. It's quite a surprise, I am sure. Plus, it's almost lunchtime, so how about we revisit this tomorrow after thinking through and sleeping on all these wonderful ideas," said Mrs. Blanton. She gently escorted me from the dining room as the staff busily brought out the lunch plates.

"Oh, Mrs. Blanton! Have I made a big mistake? Have I over-stepped my bounds? Did I in some way offend them? I thought they would be so excited. The last thing I wanted to do was come in here and tell them what needed to be done, but that's just what I did isn't it. Oh, sometimes I just don't realize how overwhelming I can be. I just want to make a positive difference, but I plow right ahead forgetting to accept things as they are because they are okay the way they are. Am I making any sense?" Those dreaded tears began to fall, and I searched for the Kleenex box.

"Claire, you did an amazing job explaining how life takes unexpected turns for all of us. And sometimes people just need time to absorb the truth in all of that. I think right now you need to go home and rest and let everyone here think about all you said. Give them a chance to get excited for themselves. Remember, you've been thinking about this for a while but they just heard about it today. It's hard to adapt to changes when you get older. Change requires energy and that is not something they have an abundance of at this stage of their lives. Give them some time to wrap their heads around the ideas. I think you will find with time they will all come around to your idea of home. Now, off to your home and don't worry a bit about this anymore today," Mrs. Blanton gave me a reassuring hug and escorted me to the door.

God, please tell me I haven't alienated myself from them. I love these people and only want the best life for them. Please, God, let me know I didn't mess up.

At that moment, Mr. Gaston asked me if he could have a word with me before I left. I was so distraught over the reaction my proposal had on the residents that I almost told him I would have to talk to him tomorrow. But something nudged me into following him back to the living room. We settled off to the side in two chairs, and he took my hands in his. Leaning towards me, he began, "Claire, your story and your courage touched me deeply. Also, your close relationship with God has been evident since you began working here. I've watched you interact with the people here, and only from a profound sense of sincerity and love can anyone genuinely touch their hearts as you have done. God is mysterious and awesome and full of grace for each of us, always. I know because I was a minister for 50 years. I loved my calling and all the churches I served and the people I came to love along the way. But one day, I woke up burned out and lonely. You see, when you tend the sheep, sometimes no one tends the shepherd. Or, so I thought. I never married, and thus never had a family. While I had many good friends, I missed going home to someone each night. But that was not in the cards for me because I truly followed God's plan for my life. Somewhere along the way, though, I stopped trusting Him.

"I've been at Haywood House nine months now. No one knew me before I came, as I lived and worked in Kansas. I just wanted to live out my life alone and on my own terms. Mrs. Blanton knows a little about me, but she has been very respectful of my privacy. I didn't want anyone to know I was a minister because if they did know, so much would be expected of me. I had no more to give. Over the last few months, I have been observing you. Your selflessness, kindness, enthusiasm, and gentle spirit has started to renew in me the love for people and mostly my love for God. After hearing your story and witnessing your genuine surrender to God and His plan for you, I felt God awakening in me my life's calling again. I'm ready to rejoin the human race now. I'm not sure how to do it, but all your wonderful ideas for the people here might want to include a devotional time, Bible Study, or even some Sunday sermons. I can't promise a lot, because I don't have the energy I had years ago, but I have a willing heart. Maybe we can work something out, the two of us."

God, how could I have been so blind? This was exactly what had been missing at Haywood House. You in the form of Mr. Gaston, Your humble servant. I guess, God, I didn't mess up after all.

"Mr. Gaston, you and I are two very lucky people. Somehow, we both have had the patience or have been given the patience to listen for that still small voice leading us in the right direction. I truly believe your gift to Haywood House of sharing God's word is the missing piece to complete our puzzle, what we need to bring us all together in love and friendship, to take one day at a time, and find pure joy in every step. Thank you." I leaned in to kiss his cheek, knowing God was in the house.

Chapter Forty Seven

Mrs. Blanton was right. I waited two days before going back to Haywood House for a couple of reasons. One, I didn't realize how exhausted I would be after my first day back at work, so an extra down day was needed for my strength. Also, I was afraid to face the residents and their thoughts that I was meddling in personal areas of their lives and needed to back off. I was shocked when I walked in Wednesday and was greeted by people showing me paint swatches and pictures of room arrangements. What color will the carpet be? When will the painters get here? Whose room gets started on first? Can I hang more than one picture per wall? Is it okay to have a small table in my room? Can I bring my favorite chairs from home? The questions seemed endless and so upbeat. The excitement in the air was tangible, and as I looked over at Mrs. Blanton, she just winked and said "I think you're going to be awfully busy pulling off this latest idea!"

Over the course of the next two months, Haywood House was transformed. Painting was done first and everyone picked the color that spoke to them whether it was one from a room in their former house or a favorite color. The painters and I did convince them to go with lighter shades of their choices as color bounced off walls and could become intense. Carpet came next which was a light color tweed to compliment all the rooms. It was also a low pile like indoor-outdoor carpeting, making it easy to move a walker or wheelchair. Everyone commented on how much quieter their rooms were with the new carpet. I knew spills would be inevitable, so quarterly cleaning of all carpets was factored into the project. Gradually pictures were hung on the walls, and a few added pieces of furniture completed the homey feel. We decided to have an open house to show off the new look to the community, families, as well as each other as everyone was being very secretive about their transformed rooms, not letting anyone see how they chose to make their own rooms special. Mrs. Blanton and I were the exceptions and went in every room to help with the placement of pictures and furniture. So many different personalities came out with this project. You thought you knew someone by learning about their past and visiting them on a daily basis, but sometimes surprises were in store when dreams came alive. Giving everyone a carte-blanche slate, for the most part, allowed on a very small scale, each resident to imagine their dream room and have it realized. I understood that feeling because that's what I was able to do with my house. For almost 20 years, I lived with a modern colorless décor thinking I was being very sophisticated and uptown. When I moved to Haywood, I completely surrendered to my love of color and coziness. My house was my dream home.

I was giddy with anticipation the day of the open house. Jasmine helped with the refreshments and table decorations. We decided to serve punch and cookies in the dining room where people could sit and visit a while. She made the most delicious lemon sherbet punch that looked as good as it tasted with dollops of sherbet and slices of lemon floating in icy lemon-lime soda. No one could stop at just one of her cookies, so we met at Sip & Savor after hours earlier in the week and baked dozens of vanilla shortbread, oatmeal cranberry, and peanut butter cookies. On each table was Jasmine's signature mason jar vase with yellow gingham ribbon tied around the lip of the jar and blue cornflowers with baby's breath teasing us with the coming of spring.

The turnout was much more than I had expected. Family members came of course, but also a lot of people from town, too. Our teaser in the local paper that Haywood House was being transformed must have worked. Now seeing so many smiling faces and hearing such glowing reports of how beautiful and individualistic each room turned out warmed my heart. That was exactly what I envisioned, a place of cozy charm and unique personality evident in every room. As I moved from room to room, I saw a person not a place.

In Mrs. Sharp's room there were walnut bookshelves from the library where she worked for so many years filled with her favorite books against warm, tawny walls. A small table with an antique lamp and two high back wooden chairs with floral seat cushions filled the corner. Next to that area was a beautiful mahogany leather recliner with my quilt lying over the back. She'd spend many hours there reading her beloved books.

Mr. Abernathy had chosen a heather green wall color with an ornate tapestry, brought from his home hanging on one wall. Curtains made of beautiful fabric from his collection drew you into his room. A high back chair covered in a houndstooth pattern sat next to a small round table. The coordination of all the different fabrics could only be achieved by someone such as he, a master of his trade.

Mr. Gaston's walls were a blue gray with white shutters at his windows that when opened allowed the soft morning light in and the dusty haze evening light, too. He had a twin bed in the corner so that most of his living space could be used as a sitting area for his devotion time. Up to five people could sit at his round coffee table for prayer time or Bible study. He liked the intimacy of a smaller number of people gathering away from the hustle and bustle of the main living room. Pastoral pictures and beautiful crosses on the walls brought a serenity to his room. What a wonderful addition to the life of Haywood House. A peace and acceptance of this next chapter of their lives could be felt here.

Mrs. Collins' room was a bit of a surprise to me. She had chosen a dusty rose paint color for the walls, lace curtains with a matching dust ruffle, and a gorgeous floral comforter. There were multiple pillows of various colors on her bed and a white chair in the corner by the window with my quilt draped over it. When I complimented her on her room, she said she raised three sons and everything about her earlier life was rough and tumble in shades of brown and denim. She was ready for a total feminine look. I got it!

Geraldine's room was my favorite. She went with a soft creamy white on her walls in order to display her beautiful art work. Cassie let Jack know there was a storage unit holding all of Geraldine's paintings from the past. Her work was amazing. She had sweeping landscapes of Montana showing the changing seasons, delicate wildflower watercolors, and hauntingly beautiful portraits of mountain men and women seeming to carve out a life in the wilderness. Also, brought from that storage unit was the easel she worked from all those years ago. The easel now stood in the corner with light coming in from the windows. A perfect place for her to continue using the God-given talent she had never lost.

I was speechless over the transformation I saw here. Not only in the rooms but in the people, too. There was a pride and ownership for their new surroundings. And while I didn't want them to retreat to their rooms and not interact in the common areas, it was heart-warming to see their excitement and anticipation. It will be like asking a neighbor over for a cup of coffee or spending one-on-one time with a friend or two. It'll give a whole new dimension to their life, a bit of independence they thought they had lost.

Mrs. Blanton called for everyone to gather in the living room.

Our two-hour Open House had flown by and it seemed no one wanted to leave. Jack joined me along with Jasmine and Sam as we quietly celebrated the success of this hairbrained idea. I couldn't have done this without their encouragement and support. They believed in this project as much as I did.

"Thank you all for coming here today to see the remarkable renewal of our facility. I personally want to thank Claire James for her vision, tireless effort, and enthusiasm for seeing this project through from beginning to end. I loved the idea when she brought it to me, but thought it might never come to fruition. I was thinking of the obstacles in the way but Claire was confident this could work. I think we can all agree the impact of this dream is far reaching. Please join me in giving Claire a big thank you from our hearts." Mrs. Blanton initiated a rousing round of applause. My smile couldn't be any wider for the happiness I felt at this moment.

"One more thing we have to address before everyone leaves today. Geraldine, will you do the honors?" Mrs. Blanton stepped aside and Geraldine wheeled up next to the fireplace. I didn't notice before, but there was something draped in a sheet leaning against the hearth. I was trying to rack my brain about something we had left out of our plan for this Open House. Jack took hold of my hand and I looked up at him curiously.

Geraldine in her quiet authoritative voice began, "Almost nine months ago, this young spirited stranger along with the cutest bundle of chocolate brown fur walked through the doors of Haywood House and they proceeded to work their way into our lives and our hearts. Claire has brought life to a weary group of old folks who were well taken care of but not living to the fullest. She tapped into what made our lives rich in our younger years and brought that spark back for so many of us. She made us believe in having fun again and in realizing there are all types of families in our lives. We grew up with a mom and dad and siblings. Then many of us went on to have families of our own, spouses, children, nieces and nephews. Many, many years have passed and brought us to this new family. Throughout our lives we have known home as a place of love, security, and people who mean so much to us. Haywood House has become that place for us now and so it should reflect our feelings. This is no longer Haywood House; it is now Haywood Home." Geraldine pulled the sheet from the object leaning against the hearth to reveal a beautiful sign, *Haywood Home Where Wisdom Lives*. Jack squeezed my hand as the room erupted in another round of applause. It seemed like everyone knew about this but me. The faucet of tears had been turned on again, and Jasmine stuffed Kleenex in my hand.

Someone yells out "Speech!" I looked at Mrs. Blanton and she was smiling from ear to ear and encouraged me with a nod of her head to say something.

"I am not often at a loss for words, but you have truly surprised me today. This amazing community of people has always been here with their talents, their passions, their love for each other and this special town. As an outsider I could see that and wanted to be part of it. I just helped bring out what has been here all along. From the beginning, this crazy Southern girl with a bit of an accent, love for sweet tea, and a special little brown dog has been accepted into your family. You have become for me what I have missed for so much of my life. I love you all from the bottom of my heart. And Mrs. Blanton, you took a chance on me, a complete stranger, coming in here and disrupting the apple cart. Thank you for giving me this chance. I am so grateful to you."

Another round of applause and I become engulfed in hugs and kisses from my new family. A feeling of belonging was a powerful emotion. As I looked over at Jack, he was smiling and looking at me in a way that melted me to the core. Another strong emotion took over and I felt helplessly, hopelessly in love.

Chapter Forty Eight

Spring in Montana was nothing like spring in Georgia. I was used to steadily warming days with a good amount of sun, a few thunderstorms, and the beginning of the most colorful season of all. Pale pink to fuchsia blossoms, intermingled with light green leaves, dotted the dogwoods and redbuds. The azalea bushes popped out white, pink, purple, and red blooms everywhere in people's yards, in landscapes around downtown buildings, parks, and green spaces. Flowers couldn't wait to compete with the dogwoods, redbuds and azaleas. Daffodils paraded out first, then low growing crocus, followed by tulips, irises, and hyacinth. I did love Georgia in the spring.

Wildflowers marked the coming of spring in Montana. Bursts of color appeared everywhere in their natural habitat. Going for a walk or hike meant you would probably spot brilliant flashes of yellow, red, and blue nestled in the grasses. All this could disappear with a heavy snowstorm which happened a lot in the spring. I was enjoying getting outside more often. I'd never complain about the snow because I absolutely loved the beauty of it, but everyone needed to soak up the sun and warm breeze that April and May brought.

I heard a strange bark coming from Sam's yard. I paused

sweeping my front porch to see Bug bounding over to check out the new playmate. A beautiful white and black pup with a tail wagging two-forty met Bug halfway between our houses. Lots of tumbling and tussling occurred with yips and playful growls letting us know they were really getting along. Sam came over and called to the pup, "Scout, come." With that single command, the cute black and white furball ceased play and bounded over to Sam.

"Sam, are you dog sitting for someone? That sure is a pretty dog. He and Bug look like they could become great pals." I walked over to Sam's yard and Scout came over to me as friendly as if we had known each other forever.

"Every time I have to send Bug to your house after watching her for a day or an evening, the house gets quiet and empty. I miss the companionship. I asked Jack to be on the lookout for a border collie needing a home. Scout was one of three pups at the Morrison's ranch. They had been looking for someone to take one of the dogs because with Clyde Morrison laid up from a nasty fall, Jane Morrison was having to run the ranch and keep up with three young pups. They hated to break them up, but knew I would take good care of the runt of the litter when Jack told them I was interested in having one of them. I had border collies all the years I lived out on my ranch. They are the smartest dogs I know and very loyal. One thing I'm a bit worried about though is that they need constant stimulation and exercise. I guess I need that too. I figured Bug could help me out some in the stimulation department. We'll give it a go and hope we are a good match."

'Sam, I'm so excited for you. What a perfect companion. He's just beautiful and well mannered. How old is he?"

"Just shy of a year. He's had professional training so I am lucky to bypass the puppy stage and stubborn learning part. I've been going out to the Morrison's for a few weeks now so he can get to know me and to see if we are compatible. Looks like we are. I plan on taking him out to my ranch now that the weather is getting better. I didn't realize how much I missed being out there, and now with Scout, I have a good reason to go more often. I was hoping he and Bug would get along because I'm sure he misses his litter mates."

"What a great idea, Sam. Any time you want to have Bug out at your ranch, let me know. I'll be glad to bring her out. She would love the run of the place, too. You are a beauty, Scout."

Scout wagged his tail and seemed to love getting scratched on the ears as much as Bug. I was so thrilled for Sam to finally take another step toward living. The past years with him mourning the loss of his wife and leaving his ranch had been existing years, not living years. I understood the mourning period and how it could last a very long time, but Sandy would want him to move ahead and find joy again; I was sure. I believed this black and white bundle of energy might just be the spark he needed to rejoin the human race.

And so, as spring slowly unfolded her beauty and warmth, we all found time to enjoy this splendor on Sam's ranch on the weekends. Scout and Bug were inseparable. They explored every inch of the ranch loving the freedom to run and stir up new life hidden in the grass. Lots of baby jack rabbits, gophers, and field mice kept the two of them on the go.

Sam had renewed energy; he was like a different person out here in his element. He had projects galore that couldn't get done fast enough, although he did appreciate the free labor the three of us offered. Paul occasionally chipped in when he wasn't at the hospital. He brought his kids out here and they loved playing and exploring much like Scout and Bug. Jasmine came out after she closed the coffee shop on Saturday and always brought us cookies or cinnamon rolls that were left over from the morning. We felt the sugar rush was a good tradeoff for the manual labor put forth. A lot of weekends she or I would cook up a pot of venison chili or vegetable soup with cornbread to have in the evenings before we headed home. We often ate outside around the firepit. It didn't get much better than that.

The fourth person that often joined us was Daniel Anderson. Jack had been looking for someone to help him at the animal clinic and with ranch calls. Up until this year, he had been content to handle everything himself. It had been his life. He had a love and passion for animals, and without a family, this life suited him. He would hang out with Paul or Sam when he had some free time, and he thought that would be enough until Cassie moved back to Haywood, but that was not going to happen. Then I came along and offered more to his life than animals. So, Jack reached out to his alma mater in Colorado, Colorado State University, where he graduated from veterinary school, and posted a position for an assistant. Enter Daniel.

Daniel went into the army right out of high school in Colorado. He didn't have the money needed to go to college and frankly wasn't ready to settle down and work towards a career. After completing two tours in Afghanistan, he realized the army was not going to be his career. He fulfilled his military obligations and left to go to college and then on to veterinary school in Fort Collins, Colorado, on the G.I. bill. Like Jack, he had always had a connection with animals. Growing up, he took in strays that were hurt or undernourished and brought them back to good health. As a young teenager, he just didn't see the long road to becoming a vet right out of high school. The road he took was the best one in the long run. He needed to grow up and mature. The army did that for him.

Daniel answered the ad Jack put out for an assistant as soon as he graduated in December. The two of them seemed to have a lot of things in common and hit it off immediately. Jack didn't sugar coat anything, though. He told him the hours would be long, the pay minimal to start with, and the town slow and sleepy, but the people genuine. As far as living in Haywood, it was God's country.

Daniel rented a house close to the clinic. He showed up before Jack in the morning and left after Jack at night. He shadowed him a lot the first couple of weeks when he went out to different ranches to treat livestock. Daniel seemed to have that innate ability to calm animals and diagnose the problems they were having. Ranchers could see how well he took care of their animals, just like Jack. It didn't take Jack long to realize what a gem he had in Daniel. After a month, he doubled his pay and gave him some accounts of his own. He became especially valuable when I ended up in the hospital with my heart attack. Jack was able to leave so much of the clinic appointments and ranch calls to Daniel without hesitancy.

Daniel had a problem that turned out to be one of the best things that happened to him in Haywood. He couldn't cook. With his meager salary, he had to be frugal with grocery money. He existed on apples, ramen noodles, hard boiled eggs, and venison jerky. His love for coffee, though, brought him to Sip & Savor. Every morning before work he would run in and get a large coffee, and twice a week he would treat himself to Jasmine's soup for lunch. Looking back, he admitted that the coffee and the soup weren't the only reasons for his new routine. Daniel was taken with the beautiful girl with the blue streaked hair, lots of earrings, and a love for Frank Sinatra music. Daniel and Jasmine were brought together in an unlikely way and we said, "That's a God thing!"

They didn't get off on a good note when he first entered Sip & Savor, though. Daniel was so focused on his new job that he forgot to pay for his coffee the first day. What was worse, he was so distracted that when Jasmine introduced herself and welcomed him to Haywood, he spilled his large cup of coffee all over the counter and ended up calling her Jackson thanking her for the second cup of coffee and leaving quickly after trying unsuccessfully to help mop up the mess. Believe it or not she let him in the shop the next day and their banter went a lot smoother. Daniel and Jasmine had spent most of their free time together and a lot of that time had been out at Sam's ranch. I was so happy for Jasmine. She deserved to have someone give her some special attention. She was always looking out for other people, it was time someone looked out for her. He was caring and funny and complimented Jasmine in that they were opposites in some ways. She was quirky and a throwback hippy where he was strait-laced and down to earth. But they both had big hearts. Having Daniel at the ranch that particular Saturday, might have been the reason I was able to survive the most frightening day of my life.

Chapter Forty Nine

So far, for me, it had been a real toss up to choose a favorite season in Southern Montana. I loved the fall when I first arrived in Haywood. The mornings and evenings were cool and crisp and the sunny afternoons brought just enough warmth to want to be outside and witness the beautiful autumn changes. Then came winter with the silent snow and ice crystals and bitter cold which prompted fires every night and hot cocoa or hot toddies. I loved the winter despite the harshness. But now we welcomed spring, and after a long cold winter it became my favorite season. I loved seeing nature unfurl itself from hibernation. This season was, of course, still new to me but I was ready for color and warmth.

This weekend was the warmest one so far, and we had taken advantage of being outside all day at Sam's ranch. I weeded the old vegetable garden with Jasmine's help when she arrived after work. Sam was working on a corral that needed rails replaced. Jack and Daniel showed up just after five and started pitching in with Sam. Scout and Bug had been in and out of all of our projects and occasionally off to chase a varmint. As the afternoon slipped away, the temperature started to drop and clouds gathered quickly in the northwest. None of us had paid attention to the weather. It could change quickly out here.

Jasmine and I were so close to having a sizable plot of garden ready for planting that we refused to stop even when a few pellets of rain came down. Surely, we could finish this one area, but the pellets turned into sleet and soon it was a deluge of freezing rain. Sam yelled for the two of us to head to the house, then whistled for Scout and Bug. Jasmine and I gathered up our tools and ran to the porch. I couldn't believe how fast this storm came up. We went to the kitchen and heated up the chili and began making cornbread for dinner. I didn't think about Bug because I knew she was with Scout and probably in the barn with the guys by now.

There were always logs laid in the fireplace so I lit them knowing the fellows would be pretty chilled and ready to relax in front of a warm crackling fire this evening. Outside the storm sounded fierce. Looking out from the porch, I saw the wind was whipping sleet and rain with occasional snow mixed with it. It was so cold. This was spring in Montana! With the chili heated and the cornbread baked, I rang the dinner bell out on Sam's porch just to let the fellows know supper was ready when they were.

Usually, Bug came running at that sound, but she must be playing with Scout in the barn, or they were both exhausted from the day's romp. It was not like her to not check in with me by now, though. I was chilled to the bone so I reluctantly went back into the house. I didn't have a good feeling. Something was not right. I wished the guys would hurry up and come from the barn. God, I'm working on my tendency to worry too much. I need to shake off this inclination that something is wrong. I'm working hard on trust and faith, but God, this gut feeling…

A few minutes later stomping on the porch let us know the guys were ready to dry off, warm up, and eat. The table was set, the fire was blazing, and Jasmine and I had decided to break open a bottle of wine to enjoy with dinner. The door opened with a rush of cold air and three wet men, but no dogs.

"Are you banishing the dogs to the porch until they dry off?" I kidded with Sam.

"No, we thought they were here with you. They're not around?"

The panic that started as an inkling was about to be full blown.

"Jack, they shouldn't be out in this storm. Something bad has happened to them, I just know it." My voice began to quiver and I grabbed my chest. My face drained of all color, and I felt myself start to collapse.

Jack immediately grabbed me and took me to the couch to sit down. "Are you alright? Is it your heart? Claire, talk to me!"

"Jack, this isn't like Bug. She would never stay out in a storm like this. Something is really wrong; I can feel it."

"We'll find the dogs, they're okay, but I'm worried about you. Do we need to go to the hospital? Please tell me what's going on!"

I took a deep breath and tried to calm myself. I didn't feel the same sensation in my heart that I had when past episodes had taken place. There was no pain radiating up my arms either. I was okay. "I'm alright, just scared that the dogs are in trouble. Please let's go look for them."

Sam put on his heavy slicker and boots and handed slickers over to Daniel and Jack. "The storm is letting up; we'll go and call for them. If they have held up some place during the worst of the storm, they should answer our call now. You and Jasmine stay here in case they come back on their own. Ring the dinner bell three times if they return. Come on fellas, let's go find those critters."

"Sam's right. You don't need to be out in this. Bug will come to my call or Sam's. We'll have her back before you know it. Have that chili and a pot of coffee ready for us when we come back." Jack wrapped me in his arms holding me tight and secure and kissed me. I had to trust he was right. *God, be with them and keep them safe. It's still wet, cold, and slick out there.*

Sam gathered flashlights for each of them and the three men

strategized their plan. Sam knew the property best so he'd take Daniel with him in case there was a need for first aid. Jack was very familiar with the land as well, so he went in the opposite direction. Just as they split up, they heard a bark and saw Scout running towards them. He was drenched and muddy and all alone. Where was Bug?

"Hey buddy, where's your friend?" exclaimed Sam. Scout kept barking. "Scout, where's Bug? Can you show us, boy?" Scout started running back in the direction he had come. He must have known where she was.

Sam ran to get the ATV from the barn and the three of them climbed in and followed Scout. It was slow going because of the mud and rough terrain, but they were soon out of sight.

Jasmine tried to convince me to come inside by the fire to get warm, but I insisted we wait out on the porch so I could call to Bug immediately when she came home. We both wrapped up in blankets, settled back in the rocking chairs, eyes strained in the dark hoping to see my little Bug or hear two different barks any minute.

After a while, Jasmine brought out two steaming cups of coffee and two extra blankets. My teeth were chattering and my hands were ice cold. The mug warmed them but couldn't completely squelch the shivering that was both cold and worry. God, please watch over Bug, please don't let anything happen to her. Keep the men safe, too. They were out in this nasty weather and I just didn't know what I'd do if anything happened to one of them.

As we anxiously waited on the porch each minute seemed like hours that Bug was missing. Worrying about her was killing me. I have wrung my hands so much they were beginning to chap. I started pacing the porch and wanted so much to run out into the night, but Jasmine kept her wits about her for both of us and tried to reassure me that Scout knew where Bug was and the guys would follow his lead, but because of the weather it was slow going. *Please, God, keep her safe and bring her home to me.* We heard the distant sound of the ATV getting closer. Soon, we saw the lights coming across the field. Oh, please have Bug! Please make sure she was alright.

Sam and Jack pulled up to the porch but not Daniel or Scout. Jack ran over to me while Sam headed to the barn. "We found her. Scout led us right to her, but she has fallen down an embankment and can't climb up. She might have injured her leg, but she is conscious. Daniel stayed back with her to keep her calm so she won't try to scramble up. Scout was amazing. He knew exactly where to lead us to find her. Sam is getting the tractor. Since we can't reach her and risk her falling farther or hurting herself more, I'll hook myself to a rope that is tied to the tractor and repel down to her. I can assess what is wrong and then bring her back up with me. We'll bring her home soon."

"Jack, I want to go, please!" I pleaded with tears running down my face.

"No, Claire. I'm afraid if she hears your voice she might try to move and come to you, and there is not a lot of room on that ledge. We've got a good plan. It will work. Now have that chili ready and some towels. There will be wet men and dirty dogs coming home soon." He gave me a reassuring hug and ran to the tractor.

"Wait, Jack. Take this blanket. You might need to wrap her up when you get her. Please be safe." I handed him the blanket and gave him a quick fierce hug. "Sam, bring them home to me."

"Will do."

Jasmine convinced me to go inside to help get dinner ready and stir up the fire. Bug had been found and she was alive. I was a bit more at ease now that I knew she was not lost or, heaven forbid, taken by a bear or mountain lion. Jasmine kept up a steady stream of chit-chat to keep us both distracted and help the time go by until they came home.

One topic she circled around to a lot was Daniel. And what a positive distraction this conversation was for me. Jasmine admitted she was taken by him from the very first time they met, even though it resulted in spilled coffee. She said he had the most tender heart of anyone she had dated and that they shared the same love of old movies and romantic songs. He didn't have a lot of free time right now as he was getting to know all the clients and wanted to gain as much experience as he could. She appreciated that work ethic and was content to see him when she could which was pretty much whenever he was not working. I loved seeing her dreamy-eyed. She needed someone in her life like Daniel. Two special people with such giving souls.

I was beginning to get more concerned and agitated as over an hour had passed since they came to get the tractor, but then we heard the distant sound of both the ATV and tractor and ran out on to the porch. Sam led driving the tractor to the barn with Scout in his lap. Jack pulled the ATV up to the porch with Daniel holding a bundle of blanket and wet brown fur in his lap. I rushed over to him and saw Bug's beautiful honey-filled eyes looking at me as if to say "Please make it better!" I heard her whimpering, but her tail was wagging two-forty because she just couldn't help being happy to see me. Thank you, God.

"Oh Bug, you darling dog. You had me so worried. Is she okay? Do you know what is wrong with her?" I checked over her head and shoulders and wanted so much to wrap her in my arms, but I didn't want to move her just yet.

Daniel said, "It appears to be a broken leg. We checked her spine but didn't detect any breaks or sore spots. We need to take her to the clinic and make x-rays. She's going to be okay thanks to her best bud Scout. Scout knew exactly where she was, and I think stayed with her until the storm eased, and he could come back here and then lead us to the rescue. He is one smart dog. Sam is bursting with pride over him. I think this little one was awfully glad to hear your voice and see you, though."

"You three are soaked to the bone and have to be frozen. Come in and dry off and warm up by the fire. Can you take a minute to eat some chili before going to the clinic? I can hold Bug and she'll be still. I want to hear about her rescue."

The three of them toweled off as much as possible leaving their boots and slickers by the door. Sam dried Scout but wasn't about to deny him a place inside, not the hero! Everyone settled down by the fire. Coffee was all anyone wanted for the time being.

Jack began the account of the rescue, "Scout knew exactly where to lead us. Apparently, Bug fell off of a narrow path probably because of the rain and sleet. Luckily, there was a ledge about 20 feet down that she landed on, but the fall broke her back leg. When Scout brought us to the spot where Bug fell, we realized we needed the tractor to plan a rescue because of the distance down to Bug, the slick ground, and rough terrain. Daniel stayed with her while Sam and I came back after the tractor. Luckily, Daniel had his vet bag in his truck, so we were able to bring it back with us. When we got back to the path where she had fallen, Daniel, adept at rope rescue from his military training, made a couple of knots in the rope, secured it around his waist, and rappelled down to Bug. When he reached her, she was alert but in pain so he gave her a shot of Metacam to relax her. He carefully put her in a sling. Backing the tractor was tricky, but we were able to pull the two of them up slowly, with Daniel holding Bug in the sling against his body. Luckily, we had brought some bags of sand and that really helped with traction. Thank goodness the worst of the storm was about over, too"

Fighting back tears I looked at each one of them, "I can't thank you all enough. I've never been so afraid in my life. If anything tragic had happened to Bug I don't know what I would do. She is so precious to me. She's been with me on this journey the past three years, and until I met you all, she was the only one I felt close to. God answered my prayers." Bug was safely in my lap drifting off to a drug-induced sleep to ease the pain, and I was surrounded by the best friends I could ever have.

Chapter Fifty

Keeping Bug quiet for six weeks while her leg healed was a challenge, but we were about over the hump. Now she could get around with a splint on her back leg. Scout and Bug had become inseparable. Where one went the other followed: my house, Sam's house, and the ranch. With two vet friends, Bug's broken leg had been monitored very closely and healed nicely. Fortunately, it was the only damage from the fall.

Jack was coming over tonight for supper. I wanted to make something special for him so I had Beef Bourguignon simmering on the stove, homemade bread, a caprese salad, and brownies with ice cream for dessert. We'd both been busy with work these last two weeks so I was really anxious to see him. The dining room table was covered with an antique lace tablecloth, candles, and Grams fine china. The nights were still chilly even though we were well into spring so I had a fire in the fireplace, more candles lit on the mantle, and a favorite CD of Judy Garland's romantic music playing in the background. The doorbell rang, and as I opened the door, Jack greeted me with a bouquet of beautiful red roses and a bottle of red wine. Perfect!

"It could be that I am just hungry for a home cooked meal, but whatever is happening in your kitchen smells out of this world!"

Jack pulled me into a tender kiss and a hug that I never wanted to end. So much had happened these last few months. I just wanted to stay in the arms of this wonderful man feeling safe and protected and loved. But he was hungry and dinner was ready so I ushered him into the dining room, found a vase for the roses, and selected two crystal wine glasses.

We had so much to catch up on over dinner. He filled me in on the latest happenings at the clinic, and how Daniel was fitting right in with everyone in Haywood. He had a real knack working with horses. I shared the latest news from Haywood Home. Everyone was enjoying the warm weather and spending time out in the courtyard. Mrs. Blanton had approved the plan for putting large planters around the patio filled with native flowers, purchasing new cushions for the chairs and rockers, and stringing lights around all the trees and trellises. It was so inviting and cozy. Having a beautiful place to gather out in the fresh air was a boost to everyone's morale.

We brought our coffee and brownies into the living room and settled in by the fire. I loved the times we spent with our friends, but this evening was special, just the two of us. It was so comfortable and so right being together. The music had stopped so I went to change to an old Carpenters' CD of love songs. When I returned to the sofa, Jack was sitting there with a small blue velvet box in his hands. I reached for the guardian angel necklace that he gave me, that I never take off. I didn't want anything to replace it. I sat down beside him, and he gingerly opened the box. In it was the most exquisite diamond solitaire.

"Claire, will you marry me?"

A million thoughts raced through my head: I'm damaged goods, I can't have children, you deserve a family, you don't need to take care of me, I might have another heart attack, but I love you more than life itself…

I looked at this amazing man through a waterfall of tears and couldn't for the life of me understand how lucky I was. But it's not luck, is it God? You have orchestrated this moment from the fateful day I arrived in the ER with blood gushing down my face only to gaze into the most beautiful, kindest blue eyes I had ever seen. Gazing into those eyes now, I had only one answer.

"Yes."

Chapter Fifty One

The next few weeks went by in such a flurry. We decided to get married sooner than later, but some things required a little planning. I wanted a church wedding, so we needed to check with Pastor Michael on the availability of the church. Our wedding party would be small. I asked Jasmine to be my maid of honor and Jack asked Sam to be his best man. Both said most heartily, "Yes!" I didn't think either one of them was surprised. Big wedding or small, there were still certain aspects that couldn't be left out. Jack wanted this to be my dream wedding. I just wanted to be Mrs. Thompson. I agreed to some traditions including wedding invitations, a rehearsal dinner, church wedding, wedding reception with music and a cake, and a honeymoon. Jack was in charge of the honeymoon.

When I walked into the lobby of Haywood Home on the Monday after Jack proposed, I wanted to gather everyone together and make the announcement that Jack and I were engaged. I didn't have a chance. The ladies sitting together knitting by the fire must have seen my ring. Mrs. Darby let out a shriek and started clapping. The rest of them started laughing and crying and asked me a million questions. They just knew Jack would pop the question soon.

My dear sweet friends would not be left out of the planning.

They insisted the reception be held at Haywood Home and they would take care of the decorations and food. Thus began the most activity this place had ever seen. Mrs. Sharp was a natural leader and born organizer. She gave everyone a task to complete and, of course, met with Mrs. Blanton daily to authorize the plans. A beautiful reception was in the making.

On Friday, two weeks before the wedding, I walked into Haywood Home and no one was in the main room. I found that very odd because every day I had been coming here there was always a group large or small gathered by the fireplace chatting, drinking coffee, or reading. Today the place was empty and quiet. I had a sinking feeling that something was very wrong. Bug started sniffing around looking for his buddies, and I went in search of Mrs. Blanton. She was not in her office and none of the staff was anywhere to be found. What was going on here? Just then Bug started whimpering at the dining room door. I walked over there and opened it, "Surprise!" and I sure was!

Everyone had gathered around the tables that were adorned with flowers, confetti, and gifts. All the residents and staff were there along with Jasmine, June from the animal hospital, Paul's wife Meg, the kindergarten and first grade teachers. I was speechless! Mrs. Blanton came over and directed me to a chair in the middle of the gathering.

"We planned a surprise Bridal Shower for you and I think we pulled it off!" she said with a wink. Bug seemed as surprised and happy as I. She wagged her tail and limped along from chair to chair until finally settling down beside Geraldine.

"I can't believe you all kept this such a secret. I had no idea. Not one slip up. I thought you were concentrating on the wedding reception. You've done too much." And the tears started forming and falling unchecked as I gazed around at all the loving faces of my Haywood family. True, I didn't have any blood relatives here, but I couldn't have had a more loving group of people to help me celebrate my upcoming wedding.

"Let's have Claire start opening the presents!" Mrs. Collins exclaimed excitedly. "I can't remember the last time I've been to a Bridal Shower."

And so, I began opening presents handed to me by Jasmine. She also was my secretary writing down each gift and the giver. So many thoughtful gifts were for our new home: a beautiful pottery vase made on one of the reservations in Montana, wind chimes with the most delicate of tones, etched wine glasses, a gorgeous wooden picture frame, a beautiful metal family door sign with *Thompson* in the center, a wooden cheese tray, and a love and luck horseshoe. Then came the personal gifts including the softest, silkiest white negligee and robe, delicate fleece slippers, along with lavender body wash and lotion. The last gift handed to me was quite large.

"We all chipped in on this, Claire," said Mrs. Darby.

I slowly opened it up and discovered a stunning quilt with fabric I recognized from the quilts I had made for each of the people at Haywood House. The pattern was the traditional nine patch, so each block was made from two different fabrics. The border, binding and backing were a delicate watercolor design of blue wildflowers which looked like they were picked from the fields just beyond Haywood. How did this happen?

"I don't know what to say. This is the most precious gift I have ever received. How did you do this?"

"Well, you didn't make it easy for us planning your wedding so quickly, but with everyone either cutting, ironing, or sewing, we managed to get it made on time. Jasmine sneaked into your house with Sam's help right after you announced your engagement. She found all the scrapes of material from the quilts you made for us and brought them here. We decided the nine patch would be the easiest and quickest pattern to make, so we all got busy cutting squares and sewing the blocks together. Mr. Abernathy knew a lady in Billings who had a long arm quilting machine. She was able to quilt and bind it for us in record time. We just couldn't think of a better gift from all of us. One that we could all have a part in making for you and Jack. One that shows how much we love you," Mrs. Blanton said as her voice cracked and tears gathered.

I jumped up and hugged her and then Jasmine. My heart was so full at that moment I thought it would burst.

"Thank you just doesn't begin to express how I feel right now. When I decided to come here, almost a year ago, I trusted God to help me find my place and to find people to be my family. It was a pipe dream, and one I wasn't sure would come true, but I had to try. I never thought I could be so lucky and so happy! But it wasn't luck. I believe God knew all along that you were the people I needed to find and that Haywood was the place I needed to call home. I'll admit, early on, there were times I thought I should just pack up and go back to Atlanta. I wasn't cut out to be a Western girl with only strangers to talk to and a new lifestyle to learn. No grits or sweet tea. Bug settled in a lot quicker than I did and trusted the people she met from the beginning. And when I realized how accepting you were of her and me, I felt God giving me permission to accept back. I love each and every one of you from the bottom of my heart. I can't wait to show Jack this labor of love!"

Mrs. Darby wiped away tears just like the rest of the ladies and said, "Oh, my goodness, we're turning into a bunch of biddies! Let's eat. Jasmine has made the most delicious sandwiches, tea cakes, and punch. Claire, you are the guest of honor so you go first."

Chapter Fifty Two

Time was of the essence. First, Jasmine and I had to go shopping for my wedding dress. Due to the time crunch, we had to find something in stock and in my size. Jasmine knew just the place, an upscale vintage clothing store in Billings. She often shopped there for herself and knew the owner so she asked her to be on the look-out for a size 6 wedding gown. At this late date, I couldn't be choosy, but every girl wanted the perfect dress, so fingers crossed, we started our quest. We arrived at 10:00am, both of us taking a day off from work. Suzanne, the owner, greeted us with the flair of a 1950's debutant. She was excited she was able to find three dresses from the 30s and 40s. I was a little hesitant about the era and the age of the dresses, but I trusted Jasmine's faith in Suzanne. The first dress was very flouncy with a lot of tulle. We all agreed that wasn't my style. The second one was very sophisticated and lacy. It fit nicely, and I didn't dislike it, but I also didn't melt when I saw it. The third one she held back for last. She said the dress had been made out of a bridegroom's parachute from WWII. It had a fitted bodice with lace at the off-the-shoulder neckline and capped sleeves. The dress was A-line ankle length with covered buttons down the back. It was exquisite. I could only hope when I tried it on, that it would be the one. It was. It fit to a tee and made me feel beautiful. Jasmine and

Suzanne gave it four thumbs up. Oh, my goodness, this was really happening. I had only dreamed of walking down the aisle in a gorgeous wedding gown, and now it was going to be a reality.

After purchasing the dress, we had to find the right pair of shoes since they would be showing. This search took a while, but Jasmine, the stylist, knew exactly what to look for, and we finally found the perfect white satin-heeled shoes with a narrow ankle strap.

We went back to Suzanne's store after lunch and found a light blue bohemian style sleeveless dress for Jasmine to wear as my maid of honor. It was so Jasmine, willowy with tiny blue flowers and a blue satin ribbon at the empire waist. She already had sandals that would complement the dress, so our mission was accomplished. We left for home with a promise that when, not if, she married we'd do this all over again in reverse.

Jack and I had decided he would move into my house after the wedding. While it was small, it was recently painted and redecorated. Jack's home, though plenty large, was over the animal clinic and not very intimate for newlyweds. Jack did not need to be so accessible to work now that he had Daniel assisting in the practice. Plus, the decorating at his house left a lot to be desired. Daniel and Jack worked out a good deal so he could move into Jack's place, as it was perfect for one of them to be close to the clinic. Down the road we would look for another house, but, right now, I didn't want to leave Sam, and Scout and Bug were inseparable. Scout would be at our house or Bug at Sam's or both out in the backyard laying in the sun together. We would have to introduce Jack's dog to the pair, but they had played a lot together at Sam's ranch, so I doubt three would be a crowd.

I never would have envisioned this happening a year ago. All I could hope for last year at this time was finding a small town that would welcome me and help me put down new roots. I wanted to find a job that would turn into my passion for helping the elderly still live vibrantly and with purpose. I wanted to honor Grams and my promise to her to not let their later years become just existing years. People who have lived a lifetime had experiences and wisdom that must be shared. And we as the next generations should listen and learn from them. The people at Haywood Home had taught me so much in such a short time. I still had a lot to gain from being with them, and I hoped in the coming years we would all enrich our lives for having crossed paths and shared in this wonderful institute of life in all its many phases, none more important than the last.

What I didn't see taking place here was Jack. I remembered the first time I saw him in the emergency room after the disastrous fall in my kitchen. I couldn't have been any lower then, embarrassed, scared, hurt, dependent on strangers, and yet I saw in him the kindest eyes and gentle spirit. A person who jumped right in to help clean up the huge mess of my making. In a small town like Haywood, we were bound to cross paths from time to time. But each time seemed a bit orchestrated by God. Jack always appeared to be there when I needed help, never judging me, just wanting to make things right. His love for Bug, right from the start, certainly didn't hurt the relationship. It was so hard to establish an actual dating life because he was so busy with his veterinary practice, and I was holding back because of my heart condition. No way could I saddle someone with my medical problems especially after my second trauma shoveling snow. Two episodes of SCAD pretty much guaranteed I could never have children and, possibly, not a long life. Jack deserved so much more than that. My love for him made it necessary to curb any strong feelings that were forming between us. I couldn't imagine that wonderful giving man without children and a family that would reach into those golden years like my friends at Haywood Home. God and His mysterious ways had different ideas. He brought us together and nothing could tear us apart. There were many types of families and ours may be one formed with our love for the seniors in our town and for our pups. A teeny tiny part of me hoped that one day we might look into adopting a baby. Right now, we had each other, and we would take our days one at a time and cherish them completely.

Thursday afternoon, as I was leaving work, Geraldine stopped me and asked if Jack and I could drop by later in the evening for a minute. She had something she wanted to give to us before the wedding. I told her we would certainly be back about 7:00pm.

Jack and I strolled hand-in-hand into Haywood Home and were greeted with smiles and laughter and even a whistle from Mr. Abernathy. I think my friends felt they had a hand in bringing us together, two of their favorite people. I couldn't wait to see them all at the church on Saturday. Mrs. Blanton had rented a bus to transport everyone including the staff. Then we would all come back here for a beautiful reception in the dining room and out on the patio. The weather forecast was to be a perfect summer day in Montana, upper 70's, with a gentle breeze. The beauty of Western wildflowers would be everywhere in mason jars on the tables and the surrounding landscape of meadows and mountains, a perfect setting.

We found Geraldine in her room. Both Jack and I leaned down to give her a hug and a kiss.

"I wanted to give you something special for your new life together. I wanted it to embolden the beauty of our part of the country and the beauty of a new and long-lasting marriage. As I sat looking out over the countryside and saw the peaceful artistry, I pictured the two of you going out into this world together. Two loving people blazing their own trail together and impacting so many lives along the way. I hope you like it." Then she pulled the sheet down from the picture on the easel.

We were both speechless. Before us was Geraldine's watercolor painting, a scene with a meadow of wildflowers in an array of blues, yellows, and whites, with green grass stretching out to the mountains, their splendor and majesty adorned with lavender and grays. Snowcapped peaks looked as if clouds had nestled down over them. In the meadow, hand-in-hand, walked two people moving towards what could be a new life together, and beyond them were dogs playfully frolicking in the flowers. One was white and black with long legs and a furry tail, the other chocolate brown with floppy ears and a perky short tail. The sky was a deep blue haze with wispy clouds and the rays of a setting sun casting pink, orange, and purple streaks. It reminded me of the first time I saw Haywood. How could she have known?

"Geraldine, this is just the most beautiful painting I have ever seen. Jack, it has to go over our fireplace so we can see it every day to remind us of this perfect place and this wonderful woman," I said through tears and a husky voice.

"I couldn't agree more. Geraldine this is a gift we will cherish for a lifetime. Thank you." Jack had caught my pension for tears and hugged Geraldine for a long time.

"Off you go now, and take this with you. I need some beauty sleep if I'm going to show up at your wedding on Saturday. I love you both."

"Geraldine, I love you too. Thank you for this priceless gift." I gave her another hug and kiss realizing I had a hand in awakening the talent God blessed her with again.

Chapter Fifty Three

Planning our wedding gave me an inkling that Jack and I would be good together. Our thoughts and ideas were very much the same when it came to the service. I wanted the traditional wedding march, Canon in D Major played on the organ as I came down the aisle. Pastor Michael would read the scripture about love 1 Corinthians 13: 4-13, Love is patient, love is kind. Grace would sing "Surely the Presence" while Louise accompanied her on the piano. Before lighting the unity candle, Pastor Gaston would offer a prayer to bless our new life together. Then we would recite The Lord's Prayer with the congregation. Then Grace would sing "The Prayer" right before our vows. Our vows would be simple and repeated after Pastor Michael. We would exchange rings, then Michael would tell Jack he could kiss his bride. Finally, we would be introduced as Dr. and Mrs. Jack Thompson. God, it almost seems like a dream, but I pinched myself and it was not.

I gazed out at the church, packed with everyone from Haywood Home, Jack's friends and acquaintances through the animal clinic, Paul's family, Daniel, our friends from town that joined in Jasmine's quarterly dinners, and the teachers from the elementary school. Jack was standing at the front of the church. Jasmine had just walked down the aisle, looking gorgeous in her blue willowy dress and holding an arrangement of wildflowers. I could see Daniel looking at her and nodding, saying with his eyes what he wanted to say out loud. Another wedding in the near future?

As Sam and I stepped into our place at the back of the church ready to go down the aisle, I squeezed his arm. Sam would give me away today. I wanted to take it all in before we started walking. Here beside me was a man who was every bit a father to me. From the first day I arrived in Haywood, he had let me know he was here for me. I loved this man. I hoped for many years of deep friendship with him.

My forever love, Bug was sitting prim and proper beside Daniel. We had been on this adventure together from the start. I couldn't have made this move without her or endured all the bumps and curves up to this point today. I loved this furball with the honey-colored eyes that stared right at you understanding all your thoughts and words.

My adoptive grandparents, the people of Haywood Home, all came today to witness this bond between Jack and me. They had taught me more in a year than I had learned in my lifetime. I learned about struggle, hard work, the love of family, enduring hardships of weather, illness, death, and the wisdom to put everything into perspective and gratefulness to God for all that life threw at you. For it was in the hardships experienced that we truly learned to grow in grace and empathy with others. There were more lessons to learn and I couldn't wait to grow into a better person because of their wisdom and our deepening relationship.

Jack—I promised myself I would not cry and streak my face with mascara. I might have to break that promise. God, You have put the perfect person in my life to go through the ups and downs together. I didn't come out here looking for love, just a home. How can one person be so lucky to find both. *God, please help me be grateful for each day with this amazing man. Help me love him, care for him, and comfort him in all the days we have together.*

"I'm ready, Sam." We slowly walked down the aisle as I took in everything and everyone. My eyes found this amazing man, and I saw ahead of us a lifetime of love and devotion. I couldn't wait to begin this journey with him. When we reached the altar, Sam put my hands in Jack's and took his place next to him as best man.

Pastor Michael led us through the marriage vows and while I listened to all he said, I was also in a daze this was really happening. Jack's hands held mine and ever so often squeezed them in reassurance.

"Do you take this man . . ."

"I do."

Acknowledgments

So many people close to me have emboldened me on this journey I began a few years ago. I would be remiss not to first acknowledge my parents, Bob and Freda Harrison, who saw the beauty of sharing artistic gifts with others late into their lives; my brother, Bob, has been gifted with befriending others easily and sharing laughter so freely: my sister, Pat, early on has had an amazing gift for portraying beauty on paper. They instilled a love for creativity throughout my life. My precious children have been the source of joy and inspiration in writing my first novel. Jill and David are so talented in their own right, that they nudged me to find my creative side and see where that led. I was able to draw from both their families, ideas and thoughts that I used throughout the book. Thank you, family.

Dear friends have also influenced me through their example of not letting retirement be an end chapter, but a new one to explore dreams. My friends are so talented and selfless. They are wonderful examples of wisdom and generosity and love of God. Thank you, friends.

Two special people who have been our closest friends for over 40 years are Rick and Christine Leonardi. Rick is an accomplished writer and author with a wealth of knowledge he so willingly shared.

He helped plant the seed for writing my own story and has been totally supportive along the way. Christine and I connect on so many levels and I value her critique. She has been unfailingly generous with her praise. They have given me the encouragement I needed to see this venture through to the end. Thank you, Rick and Christine.

Bert Entwistle, an accomplished author and hunting/fishing buddy of Steve's gave me advice early on when I was first dabbling in this endeavor. He said, "Finish the story." And I did. Thank you, Bert.

When I first realized this pipedream was becoming a reality, I thought of my beautiful, artistic granddaughter. I wanted Arabella to design the cover of the book. Her gift, honestly derived from her great grandmother, great grandfather and great aunt, is amazing. She so willingly wanted to help me, even though she was super busy with everything high school. She still took time to do an awesome work of art. Thank you, Arabella.

I finished my manuscript and looked to my brother-in-law Don Kallaus for tips on what to do next. He started his own publishing company 13 years ago and through his passion for reading and writing, I knew he could point me in the right direction. The phone call that started out to glean information, ended up with him offering to edit and publish my book and put me over the moon! He took a novice piece of work and turned it into a real book. Thank you, Don.

This book never would have been started let alone finished with out the belief my husband, Steve, had in me. From the beginning he encouraged and pushed me to write. I have always enjoyed writing and gathered a lot of writing knowledge from a creative writing course I took one summer, but that was many years ago. Since then, my writing consisted of journaling. I had this story in my head for quite some time, but Steve convinced me to put it on paper. He read every word I wrote and gave me countless pieces of advice, from grammar corrections to more in-depth ideas for plot and characters. I could never have done this without him. Thank you, Steve.

A sweet friend, Sheila Dobbins, shared her expertise in editing as I continued to prepare my book for final print. Sheila has been so positive, supportive, and encouraging. A wonderful person to have in my corner. Thank you, Sheila.

Last, and most importantly, I want to acknowledge God. We're all given gifts and I do believe that by using those gifts we are thanking Him.

About the Author

Katherine Butler retired after 31 years of teaching elementary school in the public school system. Her greatest passion was teaching her young charges to read and helping them develop a love of books to last a lifetime. Since retirement she has become very involved in church activities, quilting, and reading. She and her husband, Steve, have two married children who have given them five very creative grandchildren who bring them great joy. Katherine and Steve live in Moore, South Carolina, with their little brown dog, Remi.